Born and raised in North Georgia to a nurse and a biologist who encouraged him in the arts, Mark S. England has been writing stories for as long as he could read. Mark had a fairly ordinary childhood; he was a boy scout and a stage actor before being diagnosed with bipolar disorder at age 18. After graduating from the University of South Carolina, Upstate, Mark was a classroom teacher for several years, but found that unfulfilling. Now, Mark works in public mental healthcare as a certified peer specialist. In addition to writing fiction, Mark enjoys playing music, bowling and spending time outdoors. Mark is passionate about his family, cats and the rights of the mentally ill.

This work is dedicated to my parents, who first encouraged me to create, and who always believed in me, even when I did not believe in myself.

Mark S. England

THE NIGHTINGALE SINGS

A Fable of the Poet

AUSTIN MACAULEY PUBLISHERS®
LONDON * CAMBRIDGE * NEW YORK * SHARJAH

Copyright © Mark S. England 2025

All rights reserved. No part of this publication may be reproduced, distributed, or transmitted in any form or by any means, including photocopying, recording, or other electronic or mechanical methods, without the prior written permission of the publisher, except in the case of brief quotations embodied in critical reviews and certain other non-commercial uses permitted by copyright law. For permission requests, write to the publisher.

Any person who commits any unauthorized act in relation to this publication may be liable to criminal prosecution and civil claims for damages.

This is a work of fiction. Names, characters, businesses, places, events, locales, and incidents are either the products of the author's imagination or used in a fictitious manner. Any resemblance to actual persons, living or dead, or actual events is purely coincidental.

Ordering Information
Quantity sales: Special discounts are available on quantity purchases by corporations, associations, and others. For details, contact the publisher at the address below.

Publisher's Cataloging-in-Publication data
England, Mark S.
The Nightingale Sings

ISBN 9798891555112 (Paperback)
ISBN 9798891555129 (Hardback)
ISBN 9798891555136 (ePub e-book)

Library of Congress Control Number: 2024920790

www.austinmacauley.com/us

First Published 2025
Austin Macauley Publishers LLC
40 Wall Street, 33rd Floor, Suite 3302
New York, NY 10005
USA

mail-usa@austinmacauley.com
+1 (646) 5125767

Table of Contents

Part One: Lesbos 617–609 BCE   11

Part Two: Ortygia 609–604 BCE   93

Part Three: Syracuse 604 BCE   169

Author's Note   244

Μοῦσα, σὺν ἐμῇ καρδίᾳ σύμμαχος γένοιο· ἀρχομένης τῆσδε βίβλου περὶ Ψαπφοῦς, τὴν λυρικὴν ποιήτριαν, σὺν σοφίᾳ καὶ χάριτι τὴν λόγον μου κοσμήσῃς

Part One
Lesbos 617–609 BCE

ἀρχὴ ἥμισυ παντός

Even at the tender age of nine, Sappho could not clearly remember a time when she was a virgin. On the other hand, she would always remember quite clearly the first time she picked up a lyre. And the days before that were bleak indeed.

By so-called natural law, her first husband was not her husband at all, but her uncle, her father Skamandronymous's younger brother Agathon. Skamandronymous was a merchant who owned a vineyard and held a seat on the high council of Mytilene—he had once been elected archon for a term of one year—and appearance was everything to him. He must have the perfect business, the perfect family, and Sappho knew almost from birth she must do nothing to besmirch that image.

The first time Agathon touched Sappho, she was exactly five years old. As it has been said, she was too young to have a memory of that encounter. And it was just as well, for it was a violation of an inexcusable sort. Not that any violation is excusable—especially committed against one so young—but Sappho might have been broken so much earlier had she been able to remember the event that stole her innocence forever.

Agathon lived with his brother and his brother's wife Kleis in a modest house by the sea in the city-state of Mytilene on the eastern shore of the Greek island of Lesbos. Agathon was a scoundrel by all accounts, but he was not a black sheep in the family. He worked hard in his brother's wine-importing business and was often sent to various ports on the Great Sea, sometimes as far as Italy or Egypt. Skamandronymous trusted Agathon and paid him well. And he often said if he were to die, Agathon should look after his wife and daughter.

Skamandronymous was not without heart; he certainly didn't know about the peculiar education Agathon was giving to Sappho. He loved Sappho deeply, perhaps even more than he loved his reputation, and that was why Sappho kept silent about her uncle. If Skamandronymous ever found out about certain things, he would surely kill his brother, and rightly be put to death. So do children protect the ones who should be protecting them.

It was on Sappho's fifth birthday, observed at the new moon of the fourth lunar cycle of the year, that Agathon first made his move. Skamandronymous and Kleis had planned a public celebration for their only daughter, and every member of the high council of Mytilene was invited. Sappho's parents as well as the house slaves were quite busy seeing to the preparations for the many guests, and so Agathon was put in charge of dressing the girl. A bleached linen peplos and a garland of laurel had been selected for her to wear, and Agathon helped her out of her house clothes.

Once Sappho was naked, her uncle exposed himself to her and put her tiny hand on the throbbing head of his erect penis. Thus was Sappho robbed of her childhood in one act which would certainly not be the last of its kind.

He consummated their bizarre relationship a month later.

But while this story starts on Sappho's birthday, it is not the events of her fifth birthday that concern us at this point, but rather of her ninth birthday, after she had been raped regularly, sometimes monthly, by Agathon for years. It was for her ninth birthday celebration that her father Skamandronymous hired a pair of musicians to play at Sappho's party. A lyrist and an *aulētēs* would provide the entertainment for the day, introducing the eminent entrepreneur's daughter intimately, if not for the first time, to proper Greek music.

Skamandronymous was an educated man. In the Athens of his birth, that meant he had studied music in addition to poetry, mathematics, military science, and history in his youth. Most of the scholars of the day were accomplished students of music and its mathematical constructs. Greek music was both an art and a science. It even had its place in the charting of the harmonious movements of the celestial bodies, the stars, and the planets, the study of which was perhaps the origin of the expression, *the music of the spheres.* All young Greek men of any breeding were taught such things as a matter of course in their upbringings. It was not something one questioned.

Fortunately, Sappho was not dressed for the celebration by Agathon this time, but by her governess, a slave from Thrace named Irini. Irini was forty-three years old and had studied poetry in the court of the governor of Crete as a younger woman before Skamandronymous had purchased her when Sappho was seven. Irini took care of Sappho's day-to-day needs and taught her the works of such greats as Hesiod and Homer. Sappho, being a girl, was not sent to school—a woman, like Irini, who could read at that time and place was rare—but she loved the poetry lessons given to her by this kindly woman, and looked forward to being read to by her as much as she dreaded the lecherous attentions of her uncle.

Sappho, for her part, was fascinated by the musicians her father had hired. The *aulētēs* was a flamboyant young man with curly blond hair and a sandy beard. The aulos he played was made of two lengths of river cane, one which provided the melody and the other which was a drone. At Sappho's request, he showed her the parts of the instrument that went in his mouth. The sound was produced by the vibrations of two double reeds that fitted within the musician's embouchure, and he inflated his cheeks to push air through the pipes even when he was inhaling with his lungs. This allowed the sound to continue uninterrupted as the *aulētēs* breathed almost normally. He offered the instrument to Sappho to try herself, but she found that no matter how hard she blew on the reeds, she could not produce even the slightest sound. The *aulētēs*, thoroughly amused by Sappho's first attempt at music, tousled her hair and resumed playing.

The lyrist's harp—or rather, lyre—was another thing entirely. It was constructed entirely of olive wood and was very large. Its seven strings were made of sheep gut, said the lyrist, and were specially tightened to produce a specific sequence of notes. Sappho held out her hands and begged the lyrist to allow her to try the lyre, but the musician frowned and shook her head. She was clearly quite proud of the instrument—it must have cost her a great deal of money—and was reluctant to risk Sappho's ruining it in her attempt to play. But Skamandronymous was watching and offered the lyrist twelve staters of electrum—an enormous sum—to allow Sappho to have a go.

The lyrist had Sappho sit on a stool covered in pillows and showed the girl how to hold the base of the lyre in her lap. Then she instructed Sappho in the proper position for her hands as she plucked the strings. It was important, said the lyrist, to use primarily the left hand for the melody notes, and reserve the right hand for producing combinations of notes, or chords. Sappho immediately picked up on what chords sounded good and which ones were cacophonous. By the time she finished experimenting with the lyre a few minutes later, she was completely enamored with the instrument, and only reluctantly returned it to the grateful and fretful hands of the lyrist.

The party lasted well into the night with food and wine and dancing to go along with the music. And when it was Sappho's bedtime and

Skamandronymous asked her what she wanted for a present, Sappho didn't hesitate.

"A lyre," she said.

Sappho's new lyre turned out to be a fine example of Greek craftsmanship. Its sounding board was a large tortoise shell. The yoke and arms were made of wood from the Greek pine tree, a very sturdy material commonly used in constructing sailing ships. To Sappho's great delight, it had eight gut strings—one more than the musician's at her birthday party. Each strand of gut was anchored by a wooden peg at the top of the lyre's yoke, which could be twisted between the fingers to tighten the corresponding string. Sappho immediately tuned the strings by ear to match the notes produced by the lyrist's instrument; her expertise was evident even then. And the eighth string she tuned one full step higher than the highest of the first seven, allowing her to play an entire octave.

By the second week after her ninth birthday, Sappho was making up short melodies, and playing traditional songs by ear. Unlike with the aulos, playing the lyre was intuitive for her. The instrument became an extension of Sappho's psyche, and nearly every sound she made was beautiful. Skamandronymous was proud of his daughter's skill with her new lyre, but even he could not have predicted where this apparent hobby would go.

Twenty days after her birthday, Sappho composed her first song.

Aphrodite, be my guide
Eros loved me
But he lied

His arrow struck me in the heart
And here I am all
Torn apart

It was clumsy and amateurish, but it spoke to her feelings concerning her uncle. And the words were not lost on Irini.

"What do you mean by that?" she asked Sappho after hearing the song.

"What do I mean by what?" the girl answered neutrally.

"What about Eros's arrow has you torn apart?" pressed Irini.

Sappho shrugged. "It's just a song," she said.

Irini wasn't convinced, but Skamandronymous was delighted.

"Sappho," he said, "you are beautiful, my little bird. You must write many more songs about love."

In fact, Skamandronymous was so pleased with his daughter's first attempt, he ordered Irini to teach her to read and write so that Sappho would be able to record her new song and any others she might compose in the future. It was an unusual and momentous decision, and Kleis supported it completely.

And so Sappho's second education began.

Irini started by teaching Sappho the twenty-four letters of the Greek alphabet. These phonetic characters had replaced the old Mycenaean Linear B script, which had gone out of use at the beginning of the so-called Dark Ages, which ended about a hundred years prior to Sappho's birth. Contemporary Greek script was unique among Aegean writing systems in that it made no use of pictographs or ideograms, and that vowels were represented by full characters rather than diacritical marks. In Lesbos at that time there was no paper, and papyrus was at a premium. All of Sappho's reading and writing lessons were done on flat tablets of hardened beeswax, engraved with a sharp wooden stylus. Erasures were made by scraping the wax surface with a heated knife, and when the lessons were completed the entire tablet could be melted and reformed for another day.

Sappho took to the lessons quickly. She memorized the alphabet in less than a quarter-hour; admittedly, it was far easier than learning Linear B, which employed nearly two hundred individual syllabic signs and ideograms. But it was clear Sappho possessed the predisposition to become a fluent reader of Aeolic Greek. By the end of the first day, Sappho had mastered simple words like *world*, *tree*, *sea* and, of course, *music*. Sappho was so full of questions that Irini had to force her to quit for dinner. Why were there no marks signifying the different tonal accents? And why was the difference between long vowels and short vowels not written? Irini could not know this, but these questions spoke to Sappho's deep connection to the new craft she was learning. Greek of this time period does often include these specific indicators of pronunciation in modern texts, but in Sappho's day, the concept of written accent marks was unheard of. Sappho was ages ahead of her time.

That night Sappho sat down to eat with her parents and her uncle. The meal was simple: roast lamb, flatbread, olives, grape leaves, and imported wine from Peloponnesus. Sappho was so nearly bursting with excitement over her first reading lesson that she was almost able to overlook her uncle's lascivious leer.

"Papa," she said, "I learned the alphabet today. And tomorrow Irini's going to teach me to write the words of my song!"

Skamandronymous smiled. "I am pleased," he said. "You'll be writing epic poetry by the end of the week."

"Yes," agreed Kleis. "But do save time to practice your lyre. After all, it was for the sake of your music that Irini is teaching you to write."

"Yes, Mama," said Sappho complacently. "I want to get very good at both."

"I wager you shall," said Agathon. "There's no one more beautiful than our Sappho." He gave Sappho a pointed stare. "Isn't that right, brother?"

Skamandronymous nodded and picked up a bite of lamb between two scraps of bread. "It's true," he said. "Sappho, you have a gift from the gods. Orpheus himself was not more greatly blessed."

"Skamandronymous," said Agathon as he sipped his wine, "I should like the privilege of putting Sappho to bed tonight, and telling her a story."

"But, Papa," interjected Sappho in alarm. "Irini always reads to me before bed."

"Sappho," admonished Skamandronymous, "your uncle loves you as your mother and I do. Agathon," he continued, "you are a part of this family and you may certainly tell Sappho a bedtime story."

Agathon glanced at Sappho, who wasn't looking at all well, and said, "I will care for her like she was my own daughter."

Agathon dressed Sappho for bed without molesting her, and Sappho thought for a moment she might be in the clear. Then Agathon sat down beside Sappho's bed and put his hand on her forehead, her cheek, and finally her shoulder. He was very gentle.

"What kind of story would you like to hear tonight?" he asked.

Sappho discovered she was trembling. "Tell me a story about a musician," she said.

"Very well," said Agathon. "I will tell you a story about Apollo, for he is a great musician, skilled with the lyre, just like you."

"All right," said Sappho, guarded.

"So," said Agathon, "you know Apollo is an archer as well as a lyrist, yes?"

"Yes," said Sappho, nodding.

"Well," continued Agathon, "Apollo was always so proud of his skill with a bow. After all, he is the god of archers. But there was another archer among the gods whose skill Apollo was quite envious of. Do you know who that was?"

"Artemis?" ventured Sappho.

"Good guess, but no," said Agathon. "Artemis is Apollo's sister and he feels no jealousy toward her. It so happens it was Eros. Do you know about him?"

"Yes," said Sappho woodenly. "I know about him."

"Well," said Agathon, "Apollo is an artist, and as such, he is one who appreciates beauty. The way a man can appreciate a beautiful woman. Do you understand?"

"Yes," said Sappho.

Agathon placed his hand on Sappho's chest and the girl tensed. "So, one day, as Apollo was playing his lyre, the god Eros approached him and said, 'Apollo plays like an amateur. Hardly worth listening to. The man Orpheus is infinitely more gifted.' To which the highly insulted Apollo replied, 'And you, little one—take care with that bow and arrows. I wonder that mighty Zeus allows a child such as you to run around with such dangerous weapons.' And Apollo laughed at Eros, and Eros burned with shame and anger.

"So," Agathon continued, "Eros plotted his revenge. He prepared two special arrows for his plan. He made one arrow with a head of lead, and another with a head of gold. Then he followed Apollo as he went to the river one day to play his lyre. And there was a water nymph nearby whose name was Daphne, bathing in the river.

"Now," said Agathon, "Daphne was the daughter of the river god, and she had refused her father's command that she marry. And there were plenty of men ready to win her hand, as Daphne was very beautiful. By the time of this story, Daphne's father had given up on her ever taking a husband. Now, Eros knew about all this, and he saw that Apollo was watching Daphne bathe in the river, and he took his gold-headed arrow and shot it into Apollo's heart. Then, in virtually the same movement, he shot his arrow of lead into Daphne's heart. Do you know what happened then?"

Sappho's own heart was pounding, but all she did was shake her head.

Agathon smiled. "Well," he said, "as you can imagine, Apollo fell completely in love with Daphne. But Eros's leaden arrow had killed any chance that Daphne would return Apollo's affection. And so Daphne ran swiftly away from Apollo as Apollo chased her through the forest. Eros, of course, was watching all this, and he gave Apollo fleetness of foot so that he quickly caught up with the water nymph. Daphne, seeing that she had no hope of escape, cried out to her father for help. And the river god had mercy on his daughter and turned her into a sweet bay tree. Thus did Daphne escape Apollo's advances, and so did Eros have his revenge."

"Did you like that story, Sappho?" Agathon asked.

"I've heard it before," said Sappho.

"So, you understand why Apollo wanted to marry Daphne?" said Agathon.

Is that what you're calling it? Sappho thought. But all she said was, "Yes."

"And, why was that?" Agathon pressed.

"Because she was beautiful," said Sappho.

"That's right," said Agathon. "Just like you."

Sappho, knowing what was coming, squeezed her eyes shut, as if being blind would protect her from Agathon's unwelcome touch. And the touch came. And Agathon was putting his hand under Sappho's nightgown, probing her private parts with his fingertips. And Sappho gasped when he slid his finger inside her, and that gasp only emboldened him. And he began to feel all over down there and she gasped again as he rubbed her most sensitive place with his middle finger.

And then something happened to Sappho. Something wondrous and terrible. It was as unwelcome as Agathon's touch, but it also made her giddy with pleasure, like the beginning of a sneeze. And Sappho at once hated it and wished it would happen again and again.

Sappho was accustomed to playing with neighbor children when she wasn't studying with Irini. There were four of them altogether, and only one was a boy. His name was Thymaion, younger than Sappho by four years, and his parents worried that playing with girls would make him soft. But Sappho was the daughter of a high council member, and so they allowed him to be playmates with Sappho and her friends. The other girls were unremarkable in heritage and family; perhaps their parents, too, hoped some of Sappho's good breeding would rub off on them.

The girls' names were Larysa, Zosime, and Nastka. Everyone in the neighborhood considered Larysa to be the prettiest of them but held their tongues so as not to anger Skamandronymous. One day, when Sappho was ten and had endured five years of her uncle Agathon's favors, she and the other girls decided to play house and make Thymaion the husband.

Thymaion was a good sport, and so went along with the game, though he would rather have been playing sports or hunting with the boys who lived on the other side of Mytilene. And so he waited to see which of the girls would play his wife for the afternoon.

The matter came down to a contest between Larysa and Sappho. Larysa vainly said she should be the wife, as she was better-looking. But Sappho objected, hinting at her father's power and influence. In truth, Sappho was hoping to catch Thymaion alone, for what purpose she was not at the time entirely certain.

Eventually, Larysa insisted that Sappho demonstrate her strength and prove why she should be the victor. Sappho instructed the other girls to overpower Thymaion and hold him down. Thymaion took this exercise all in stride and did not struggle when the girls grabbed him by the arms and pinned him to the ground. But then Sappho stood before the hapless boy and lifted up the hem of her peplos—she wasn't wearing a *perizōma*, or loincloth, as was common for children—fully displaying her womanhood to Thymaion, the devil may care who else was watching.

And there were others watching, to be sure. A fisherman named Hector and his crew were unloading their nets from their boat which was tied to the nearby quay, and he and his men saw everything. Hector shouted mightily and chased the three wrestling girls off of Thymaion, before picking up the stunned boy and telling him to run home.

Sappho, for her part, did not run or even try to cover herself. Instead, she stood boldly exposed before Hector and the others and offered, using a crude slang term, to service them *juicily.*

Hector strode up to Sappho angrily and grasped her by the arm.

"Saucy little bitch," he said, disgusted. "Who is your father?"

Sappho answered the fisherman proudly. "My father is Skamandronymous, a seller of fine wine and a member of the high council of Mytilene!"

Sex among children was not a crime in Mytilene at that time, but sexual assault was certainly frowned upon, particularly when the victim was younger than the perpetrator. Skamandronymous listened to Hector's account of what had transpired near the quay, then gave the honest fisherman a half stater of electrum and sent him on his way. Skamandronymous then refused to speak with his daughter at all for the rest of the evening, leaving a fretful Kleis to detail to Sappho why what she had done was wrong.

Kleis was at a loss to explain her daughter's behavior. As she told Sappho that night that boys' and girls' bodies were beautiful creations of the gods and not for idle game-making or bullying, she did not once question the girl about how she knew so much about sex at her age. This matter did not escape Irini's attention, however, and that night, after supper, she approached the sullen Sappho as she lay in her bed, waiting to be read to.

But poetry was not the fare for Sappho's entertainment that night. Irini sat down beside the girl and said softly, "You are familiar with the story of Leda and the swan? Yes?"

Sappho nodded angrily. "You've told me that story before, Irini," she said.

"Then you know," said Irini, still speaking softly, "that Zeus, in the guise of the swan, raped Leda while Leda's husband the king was asleep."

"Oh, sure," said Sappho, rolling her eyes.

Irini suddenly slapped Sappho full in the face with the palm of her hand. Sappho was too astonished to be indignant. She put her fingers to the cheek Irini had struck and said pitifully, "What was that for?"

"That was for tormenting that poor boy the way you did today," said Irini. They both knew she could be whipped for striking the child of her master in this fashion. Sappho stared at Irini with wide, curious, scared eyes.

Irini continued. "What you did to Thymaion was a kind of rape," said Irini. "You've heard that word before, I know. I've used it with you myself, but I've never told you what it means. Do you know what the word *rape* means, Sappho?"

"I don't know," said Sappho. She was attempting to sound superior, but it came out as a whimper.

"I think you do," said Irini. "And I want to know who taught you."

Sappho sat up in bed. "You can't talk that way to me!" she said self-righteously. "You're a slave. My father could sell you tomorrow and I wouldn't care!"

"I am your father's slave, yes," acknowledged Irini. "But I'm also your friend, Sappho. If there's something you need to tell me, I want you to know you can do it."

A tear of shame welled up in Sappho's eye and she brushed it away. "I have nothing to say to you, Irini," she said. "I want to go to sleep now."

Irini, suddenly weary, nodded in silence, stood up, and walked to Sappho's bedroom door. There she stood for a moment, staring at Sappho, before exiting the room and making her way to the slaves' quarters.

Later that night, she took an oath before Athena. The girl would be made safe. She would see to that.

Skamandronymous and Kleis never mentioned Thymaion to Sappho again. The day after Sappho and her friends assaulted him, his parents enrolled him in a school on the other side of the city. Thymaion would study the law and marry a virgin far away from Sappho's influence. The other men on the high council of Mytilene did not speak of the matter to Skamandronymous, but

Sappho's father could feel the judgment in their voices and their looks. Something would have to be done.

Sappho's father often walked to the quay to inspect the cargo on his ships as they returned from far-flung ports on the Great Sea, and a few weeks after Sappho's encounter with Thymaion, he was overseeing the unloading of two dozen very large amphorae of red wine which had been brought from Anatolia by his largest ship, *Seirēn*.

On this particular day, Sappho had accompanied her father to the quay at her request and was playing on the dock where *Seirēn* was moored. Leaving Sappho on the dock, Skamandronymous stepped onto the ship's main deck to watch as the crane lifted the heavy clay amphorae from the hold, to deposit them carefully on the planks of the quay. Simonides, *Seirēn* captain, was overseeing the maneuver.

Skamandronymous watched as the first of the amphorae was brought up from the hold by the ship's crew. Simonides supervised carefully as the crane's ropes were affixed to the amphora.

"It's a mighty good shipment this time, boss," said Simonides to his employer. "Very good quality, I think you'll find."

"You've tasted it, I take it?" Skamandronymous said.

"Of course," confirmed Simonides. "Try it yourself."

One of the sailors carefully removed the amphora's heavy lid and Simonides dipped a small portion of wine out of the amphora with a bronze cup. He offered the cup of wine to Skamandronymous. Skamandronymous sipped the wine, swished it around in his mouth as he tasted it, then spat it overboard.

"Strong and smoky," he said appraisingly. "With a hint of nuttiness. Almonds?"

Simonides laughed. "You've got a palate like no other, boss," he said. "I knew you'd like it."

"Thank you, Simonides," said Skamandronymous. "You can look forward to a bonus this month. Now, get the rest of the jars off the boat and over to the warehouse."

"Sure," said Simonides, and he gestured to the sailors operating the crane to lift the amphora off *Seirēn's* deck.

Skamandronymous stepped back onto the dock, took Sappho's hand, and said, "Come, let us go home and have lunch."

Sappho squeezed her father's hand with her own and looked up at him with love.

Without warning, there was a sudden splintering sound and a shout of "Look out!" from the sailors on *Seirēn's* deck. Skamandronymous spun around in time to be struck in the chest by the amphora of wine he had just inspected; the crane's boom had broken. Skamandronymous fell on his back on the dock, pulling Sappho with him, the wayward amphora landing on his right foot and ankle with a sickening crunch.

Skamandronymous cried out in surprise and pain. Wine spilled everywhere. Sappho was knocked to the planks. Dazed, she crawled over to her prostrate father as Simonides gave a panicked shout to his men. Four stout sailors rolled the enormous bulk of the fallen amphora off of their employer. It was plain to see Skamandronymous's foot was crushed. Sappho flung herself over her father's chest and Skamandronymous screamed again. Simonides gently lifted Sappho off her father, saying softly, "He's broken a rib or two, girl." Then he took Sappho in his arms and yelled, "Someone find a doctor!"

Simonides and two of his men managed to get Skamandronymous and Sappho back to the house, Simonides carrying Sappho as if she were a very small child. A runner had gone on ahead of them to notify Skamandronymous's personal physician Praxites and to inform Kleis as to what had happened on the quay. Kleis and the doctor were both waiting at the front door when the sailors arrived at the house with their employer and his daughter. Kleis had done a little picking up, and had the house slaves freshen the bed in her husband's bedroom—it was customary for married couples in that time and place to sleep in separate rooms. Simonides's men placed Skamandronymous carefully on the bed, and Praxites bent over Skamandronymous to examine him.

"Tell me where the pain is," Praxites said to Skamandronymous.

"It hurts to breathe," gasped Skamandronymous. "Right side of my chest. And my foot."

"The wine jar landed squarely on his foot," said Simonides. "And I think he's got a broken rib."

"That would account for the painful respiration," said Praxites. "Let's get his sandals off."

Skamandronymous's foot and ankle were so swollen they had to use a knife to cut off his sandal. The doctor probed the crushed extremity, causing his patient to suck in air sharply, which made him then gasp again at the pain in his chest.

Praxites frowned. "This injury is beyond my skill to repair," he said soberly. "I think amputation would be the prudent choice."

"Amputation?" said Kleis in shock.

"You're not taking my foot, doctor," said Skamandronymous between agonized breaths.

"Skamandronymous," said Praxites, "the bones in your foot and ankle are hopelessly crushed. You'd be lame for life and perhaps in incredible pain, even if it healed."

"Then, I'll be lame," said Skamandronymous. "There's no danger of blood poisoning, is there?"

Praxites frowned again. "The skin isn't broken," he said. "Just the bones."

"Then I'm keeping my foot," said Skamandronymous resolutely.

Praxites nodded slowly. "Very well," he said. "But I want you to remain in bed until the injuries heal. The rib or ribs will knit back together normally with time, and the bones in your foot as well, though not like they were before. Forty days, Skamandronymous."

"I can't be bedridden for forty days!" Skamandronymous protested. "I have work to do."

Kleis put a hand on Skamandronymous's damp forehead. "Agathon can do the work while you're resting," she said. "You should do as the doctor says."

Skamandronymous scowled. "Oh, all right," he said. "I won't win this argument anyway. And to tell the truth, it hurts something awful."

Later, after the doctor had gone and while Kleis was ministering to her husband, Irini found Sappho alone in the garden, holding her head in her hands and crying. With all the fuss in the house centered around Skamandronymous's injuries, everyone seemed to have forgotten that there had been a second victim of the day's traumatic incident. Irini hastened to Sappho's side, knelt beside the girl, and put her arms around her shoulders. "Sappho," Irini said softly.

Sappho quickly and desperately returned the embrace, burying her face in Irini's breast. "Irini," she wept, "Papa may never walk again, and it's all my fault." Sappho moaned bitterly.

Irini broke the embrace and put her hand on Sappho's chin, looking into the girl's eyes. "This was not your fault, Sappho," she said. "It was an accident. Nobody blames you, so don't you dare do it either."

Sappho wiped tears from her eyes with the back of her hand. "But if I hadn't wanted to go see the boat today," she said, "Papa might not have gone himself."

Irini nodded. "Perhaps," she said, "but the fates do what they will regardless of our decisions. If your father hadn't been injured today, he might have had a heart attack instead. It does not do to dwell on things we can't control, or to assign blame where none exists. Life happens on its own terms. We don't have to like it, but we do have to accept it. Do you understand, Sappho?"

"I guess," said Sappho bitterly.

"Now," said Irini, "I think we should not speak of this again. You need to distract yourself. Why don't you play your lyre for a while?"

Sappho hugged Irini again and sniffled. "I love you, Irini," she said.

Irini smiled, a tear in her own eye. "I know, Sappho," she said. "I love you too."

It was dark when Sappho awoke. It was still night, but she was quite alert. She attempted to turn her head toward the window so she could see the moon, but she found she could not move her neck. Curious, she went to lift her hand and found she could not accomplish this either. She willed her legs and arms to move, but they would not. She was completely paralyzed.

Very mild fear started to work its way into Sappho's heart, and she tried to call out to Irini. But Sappho could not speak. She was helpless to move, helpless to call anyone's attention to her predicament. She was alone.

Despite her troubling state of paralysis, Sappho was still more curious than scared, and she decided to wait and see what would happen. Presently, however, she became aware that she was not alone in her bedroom. There was someone else, an intruder of some sort, and she could see a shadowy figure crouching between her bed and the doorway.

Suddenly, Sappho's ears were assaulted by a loud buzzing sound, like a mad gadfly, and that sound morphed into that of an aulos being played. Sappho knew there was no *aulētēs* in her room, nor in any other part of the house. She was hearing the impossible.

After about two minutes, the sound died away, but the intruder remained where it was. Sappho was about to chalk up the experience to a bad dream when the intruder rose up and rushed at her as she lay helpless in her bed. Before she could gasp in surprise, the shadow entity was upon her and she knew she was awake. She could no longer see the entity, but she felt it lying on her chest, crushing the air out of her lungs. Then she felt it wrap its arms around her torso in a horrifying embrace.

Sappho was now completely terrified, certain she was about to die. She could not move, she could not scream. And the demon—for that was all it could be, she reasoned—began to kiss her throat.

Sappho had resigned herself to death in the face of this horror when the demon suddenly let her go. A soft moan was all that came out of her throat, and she found herself beginning to float a few finger widths off her mattress. She was about to count herself lucky that she had not been killed by the entity, when it suddenly grabbed her by the ankles and yanked her toward the foot of the bed, pulling her off the mattress. Sappho finally found her full voice and tried to scream. It sounded piercingly loud to her, but no one came to help.

At length, she fell asleep and did not dream.

It was several weeks before Sappho told anyone about her nighttime experience, and it happened seven more times in the interval. Sappho began to show signs of stress that her parents noticed. Kleis asked her if she was having trouble sleeping, noting the dark circles under her eyes. Sappho shrugged the question off, muttering something about bad dreams. Sappho, shamed though she was, had not visited her father in his bedroom since the first episode with the hugging demon, as she had begun to think of it, had taken place. Every visitation from the demon was slightly different from the previous one;

sometimes the music did not play, and sometimes she could not see the shadowy intruder before it attacked. But it always sat on her chest and squeezed her, and Sappho nearly always felt the floating sensation once the attack was over. Sappho began to despair.

While Sappho was puzzling over the constant assaults by the hugging demon, Kleis was beginning to show signs of melancholy. Sappho assumed it was about Skamandronymous's injury and convalescence. But Skamandronymous was nearly healed from his trauma and was in no more pain. He would soon be able to walk with a staff. Kleis awoke the morning her husband first got out of bed since his injury with a headache and a fever and decided to remain in her own bed. Skamandronymous was irritated.

"What do you mean by this, woman?" he demanded. "I'm finally able to walk, after a fashion, and you choose to sleep late?"

But after an hour or so, Kleis's fever had not broken, and Skamandronymous summoned Praxites for his advice.

Praxites examined Kleis, feeling her forehead and probing her abdomen while Skamandronymous and Sappho stood by, watching. After a moment, the doctor stood up straight and muttered softly to himself.

Skamandronymous cleared his throat. "What's wrong with her, doctor?" he asked impatiently.

"She's feverish," said Praxites. "And her spleen is enlarged. I recommend bed rest and fluids. Water, juice, wine. I think she will shake the fever off in a few days, but she must take it easy."

"But what about her spleen?" pressed Skamandronymous. "What does that mean?"

"I don't know," Praxites admitted. "But I doubt it's serious. Probably a reaction to the fever. No heavy labor for a week, Kleis," he said to his patient. "Let the slaves handle all the chores."

"Thank you, doctor," said Kleis weakly. "I think I need to rest now."

"That would be my recommendation," said the doctor. "I'll just excuse myself now."

With one parent finally out of bed and the other now bedridden, Sappho could no longer keep silent about the stress of her nighttime visitor. On the morning after her mother fell ill, she sought out Irini for her advice. Irini listened soberly to Sappho as the girl recounted her narrative about the mysterious hugging demon, and how it crouched in front of the door before launching its attack on her body with its terrifying embrace.

"I'm really scared, Irini," Sappho admitted. "It makes me not want to go to bed."

"You're certain this wasn't a dream?" Irini pressed. "You're certain you were awake when this happened?"

"Yes," said Sappho simply. "It only stops when I finally go to sleep. I'm awake the whole time."

Irini frowned. "I know this creature, then," she said. "It used to come to the son of the governor of Crete when I was his slave. It is called the *ephialtēs*."

The word *ephialtēs* has been widely translated by scholars as both *nightmare* and sometimes *incubus*, in both modern and classical Greek. This night demon has visited countless victims from all cultures around the world over the millennia. The experience is almost universally described as terrifying and sometimes affects whole villages of people at a time. The incubus visitations are usually associated with psychological distress in the sufferer, and Sappho certainly qualified.

"Is it going to kill me?" Sappho asked Irini.

"No," said Irini. "It can only scare you. But there are precautions we can take. We must place a dish of sand beside your bed. When the *ephialtēs* comes to you, it will stop to count the grains of sand and morning will come before it can attack you. And the *ephialtēs* cannot stand the sunlight."

"Will that really work?" asked a skeptical Sappho.

"Well," allowed Irini, "I don't know for certain. But it can't hurt to try."

It ended up that Irini's magic didn't work at all. The hugging demon came back to Sappho night after night without ceasing. But Sappho didn't let on and kept the dish of sand beside her bed. The demon made its appearance at least once a week, despite Sappho's prayers to the goddess Hebe that it should stay away. As she suffered her uncle in silence, she suffered the *ephialtēs* in silence. Eventually, she got used to its horrific attacks, and the circles under her eyes faded. Not even Irini suspected she was still afflicted.

Eventually, Skamandronymous was back to his old self. He walked with a staff and with a limp, but he was robust and energetic as ever. He suffered no post-traumatic memories or flashbacks related to the accident on the quay, and still went weekly to inspect his ships as they returned to port. The high council members seemed to have forgotten Sappho's behavior toward Thymaion, and no longer gave him judging stares. Kleis recovered from her mysterious fever in about a fortnight, though the doctor said her spleen was still enlarged. Things were returning to normal for Sappho—a new normal, anyway. Sappho learned to accept the reality of the hugging demon in her life. It was part of her routine now.

As it always does, time passed and Sappho continued to grow up. Shortly after she celebrated her twelfth birthday, her parents began to talk strategy about the man she would marry once she came of age. Skamandronymous was a wealthy man and had considerable influence in Mytilene, and was certain there would be a queue of men waiting to become his son-in-law. After some debate, a young man named Aphelos was selected as the front-runner. Aphelos was the son of Pheronaktos, another high council member and a lawyer of great repute. Pheronaktos had served twice as the archon of the high council in the last ten years, elected by general vote of the council members; oligarchy was the law of the land.

After Sappho's traditional party, Skamandronymous invited Pheronaktos, his wife Gygaia, and their son to dinner. Sappho joined them for the meal, though she did not know she was being shown off to a potential husband. If she had known, she would have been loath to celebrate. Trading one man's sexual exploitation for another's would not have been her idea of a happy event.

Following dinner, Skamandronymous asked Sappho to fetch her lyre and play one of her original songs for their guests. Sappho, not knowing this was an audition, readily agreed, for she thrived on sharing her talent with family and strangers alike, and had become a true virtuoso in the past three years. She tuned up the instrument and sang.

To my temple from Crete you came
To an apple orchard where
Good incense burns
With holy flame

Apple branch freezes in water cold
The flowers cast their shades
While from the leaves come
His wiles bold

Sappho played and sang all twelve verses of her song, which she had composed a few weeks earlier. Her writing and singing were also excellent now, and she had the confidence of a professional poet. Her father and mother were extremely pleased and Irini was now nearly bursting with pride every time Sappho sang for her. Pheronaktos and Gygaia were also suitably impressed and the eighteen-year-old Aphelos stared at Sappho in appreciation. She was too young to marry now, but in two or three years, he figured she would make a wonderfully entertaining wife.

Sappho left the dining room after the applause ended and went to her room to practice. Pheronaktos watched her go, then turned to Skamandronymous and said, "She is beautiful, my friend. She would make a fine wife for our son, no doubt. Are you prepared to pay the dowry?"

Skamandronymous smiled. "I believe we can come to a deal which is mutually satisfactory. And Aphelos would of course inherit my business upon my death."

"Of course," agreed Pheronaktos.

"Your daughter is a very gifted musician," Gygaia observed. "How long has she been a poet?"

"Three years," said Kleis. "She has written more than a dozen songs."

"I take it you have someone record them for her?" Pheronaktos said.

"Actually," said Skamandronymous complacently, "she does that herself."

"You've taught your daughter to read and write?" Gygaia said. "What a curiosity."

"It seemed appropriate," said Skamandronymous smugly, "given her talent. I trust it will not be a problem that she has a hobby?"

Pheronaktos glanced at his son, who took a sip of wine and said, "Not at all. It will make her a most fascinating bride."

Pheronaktos chuckled.

While the adults were getting on with dinner and plotting a future for her that she could scarcely imagine, Sappho sat on her bed, playing her lyre and making notes on one of her wax tablets. She was averaging a new song every twelve weeks. Some were about the gods, some about nature, but most were carefully crafted love songs. She had a literary niche without being much experienced in the pleasures Eros provided. In love, at this point, she was still merely a victim.

And that was how Agathon found her, sitting on her bed with her lyre and tablet. "Good evening, Sappho," he said huskily.

Sappho looked up at him with a nameless dread, and for the first time in her life, she talked back to him.

"Predictable as ever, uncle," she said. "You're so very tiresome." And she set aside her lyre and lay back on the bed, giving Agathon a sultry look.

Agathon smiled. "You're a bold one tonight," he said. "Bold and beautiful. Almost too old to be any fun. Almost, but not quite."

"Let's get this over with," said Sappho, "so that I can write some more before bed."

Agathon drew nearer and sat down on the bed beside Sappho. "Do you have any idea what you do to me?" he asked.

"Yes," said Sappho bitterly. "Now do to me what you came in here to do or go away."

"As you wish," smiled Agathon. And he bent to kiss her neck.

"Sappho!"

Agathon jumped up off the bed at hearing Irini's sudden exclamation. "Irini!" he said in a panic. "Sappho was just showing me a song."

"Yes," said Irini, "I see. Sappho, do you need anything?"

Sappho picked up her tablet and scribbled something on it with the wooden stylus. "Just take this for me, Irini." And she held out the tablet to Irini.

Irini crossed to the bed and accepted the proffered block of wax. "Anything else?" she asked.

"Just leave us," said Agathon. "And hold your slave's tongue with my brother or you'll wish you'd never left Crete."

"Yes, of course," nodded Irini. She moved to exit the room.

"Irini!" Sappho blurted suddenly.

Sappho's governess stopped in the doorway. "Yes?"

"Read that," said Sappho. "It's my latest song."

"Yes, of course," said Irini again. And she was gone.

Agathon waited until the sound of Irini's retreating footsteps on the tile floor had faded to nothing, and then turned to his niece. "Now, little one," he said greedily. "Where were we?"

Irini carried Sappho's tablet back to the slaves' quarters where she sat on her bunk to think. She had suspected something was terribly wrong with her master's daughter for years, but she couldn't put her finger on precisely what it was. Sappho was incredibly musically talented, but the subject matter of her songs was entirely too mature for a girl of twelve. Then there had been the episode with Thymaion all those years ago. Irini was worried.

And Irini had cause to be.

Her master in the court of the governor of Crete had not told Skamandronymous this when he sold her to him, but Irini had been more than a slave there. She had been a member of the governor's harem. She had been forced to pleasure the governor himself, as well as many of his friends and associates, for years. She had even borne a daughter when she was twenty-four. The baby had been stolen from her upon its birth, and Irini never saw her again. It was most likely the child had been drowned, but no one in the governor's circle told her for sure. She pined for the daughter she had never known, which probably, she reflected, explained her love for Sappho.

When Irini turned thirty years old, she was rejected as a plaything by the governor. It was just as well, she figured. She was used beyond attractiveness now. Used and damaged. She was ordered to read poetry to the governor nightly, like a Hellenic predecessor to Scheherazade, though there was no promise of marriage, or life when the duty was one day concluded. Fortunately, Skamandronymous was able to purchase her for his daughter before the governor could order her death.

Despite her worry about Sappho, Irini was relatively happy in Skamandronymous's house. Happier in fact, than she had been since she was brought to Crete as a prize of war. She remembered little about her home in Thrace, a village called Calon. Her father had been a worker of bronze, and she had had five older brothers and sisters. Her mother had been the one who taught her to read and to appreciate Greek poetry. When the Cretans came when she was eleven, she was quite the scholar, and her capturers hardly knew what to do with her. They took her back to their foreign island and made her a curiosity. Such was the life of a slave girl.

Irini did not cry as she remembered these things. Her tears for herself had dried up years ago. But she ached for Sappho. Her songs were so beautiful, precocious as they were. She glanced at the wax tablet in her hands and read the words Sappho had inscribed there. It was a poem glorifying Eros's bow. And at the bottom of the tablet were three hastily added words: *Help me, Irini.*

Irini stared at this plea for a moment before realization fully sank in, and when it did, the answer was so plainly obvious Irini wondered how it had escaped her before. It was Agathon. It had always been Agathon. Irini put a hand to her chest, as if to still her now palpitating heart. Sappho's curse was living right under her father's roof and had been for years. How long had this been going on for Sappho? How many months or years? And when would it stop?

But Irini knew it would never stop until Sappho was broken. Predators like Agathon were the same everywhere. They used until what they were using was all spent, like a well run dry, or a cow that ceased to give milk and had to be slaughtered.

One thing was certain. Irini had to do something; but what? She could not tell Skamandronymous. He would not listen to a slave, and Agathon would then have Irini sold and go on tormenting Sappho. She felt impotent to help, but she knew she must.

And so Irini scraped Sappho's scribbled plea off the tablet with a knife, then lay down to think what her next move would be.

Irini prepared breakfast one morning the following week, taking over the duty from one of the house slaves who said she was feeling a severe headache. Skamandronymous, Kleis, Agathon, and Sappho all complimented Irini on the goat cheese and fruit she served, in addition to the flatbread she had baked fresh an hour before. The bread was full of golden raisins dried from grapes from a vineyard on the other side of the island.

But the real treat was the juice that came with breakfast. It was made from red grapes and pomegranate seeds and was spiced with cinnamon and cloves from the far eastern reaches of the world. It was rich and flavorful and Skamandronymous and Agathon in particular enjoyed it thoroughly.

"Absolute ambrosia," declared Agathon as Irini poured him a third cupful of the stuff.

"I agree," said Skamandronymous. "I might have to reassign you, Irini. But Sappho would never forgive me."

"Serving you is my pleasure, master," said Irini politely. "I am glad you like it." Then she left the dining room.

"Sappho," said Skamandronymous, "it is time you were told something important. Do you know why I invited Pheronaktos and his family to dinner last week?"

"No, Papa," said Sappho carefully.

"Your mother and I would like Pheronaktos to be part of our family," Skamandronymous explained.

Realization dawned on Sappho in an instant. "You want me to marry his son?" she said, taken aback.

"Ridiculous!" said Agathon quickly. "She is far too young."

Sappho glared indignantly in Agathon's direction at the irony of this declaration.

"Actually," said Skamandronymous, "Sappho is right. She is to be betrothed to young Aphelos and married when she turns fifteen. Pheronaktos will share my fortune and Aphelos will inherit everything when I die."

Agathon glanced at his brother. "Sappho will remain in our household, though, yes?" he ventured.

"Yes," said Skamandronymous. "Aphelos will move in with us and live as our son. Everything has been decided."

Sappho looked away from Agathon. "I can still write my songs, though, Papa, can't I?" she said.

"Of course, Sappho," said her father. "Your talent is too precious to waste."

"That is good," opined Agathon. And he took a large gulp from his cup, the pomegranate juice mixture running into his beard.

Skamandronymous took up his staff that afternoon and limped to the front door, saying he was going to the harbor to inspect a shipment that should be arriving that day. Agathon, who sometimes joined his brother on such excursions, was feeling rather ill—his heart was racing, he said—and excused himself. Sappho, not wanting to be in the house with Agathon should his sickness be a ruse to get close to her—a ruse he had employed before—went with her father. She had been traumatized by her father's accident on the quay when she had accompanied him as a nine-year-old, to be sure. But she figured it was astronomically unlikely such a thing would happen again. At least not for a while.

Sappho followed her father onto the quay, where a boat called *Anankhei Kharybdin* was moored, loaded with its cargo of Maltese wine. Skamandronymous stood on the quay and watched the amphorae as they were taken off the ship, one by one. He took a lungful of the Aegean Sea's fresh salt air and put a hand on his daughter's shoulder.

"Sappho, my girl," he said, "this is all a man can ask for. A good family, a successful business. a sunny day with birds crying overhead. It was for happiness such as this that Prometheus first brought man the fire of the gods from Olympus. It is on days like this that I am most glad to be alive, and on which I believe I could, in fact, die content. Do you understand, Sappho?"

"I think so, Papa," said Sappho as she put her arm around her father's waist.

"Everything I have done since the day you were born," Skamandronymous continued, "has been done with your future in mind. In three more years, you will marry Aphelos, and he will own my business, but it will always be yours, Sappho. That is the legacy I leave to you."

Sappho suddenly found herself tearing up and she sniffed softly. "But, I don't want your legacy, Papa," she said softly. "I want you and Mama, both of you forever."

Skamandronymous smiled. "That is something the fates would never allow," he said gently. "One day my thread will be cut, and your mother's. And if we are worthy of the Elysian Fields, we will look down on you fondly for the rest of your life. But if Kharon's boat on the River Styx is our lot, it will all have been worth it to have given you all the good things you deserve. We love you more than life, Sappho. I hope you know that."

"I love you, too, Papa," said Sappho.

And they stood and watched the seagulls for a long time.

Agathon was still feeling poorly when Sappho and her father returned to the house from the harbor. Kleis had put him in his bed, and Irini was seeing to him, bringing him cups of fresh wine, while they waited for the doctor. Skamandronymous was worried—Agathon was almost never sick—and asked to be alone in the room with his brother so they could talk business.

Praxites arrived an hour later, and examined Agathon while Skamandronymous, Irini, and Sappho looked on; Skamandronymous and Irini with concern and Sappho utterly devoid of emotion.

"Interesting," observed Praxites. He lifted up Agathon's eyelid, then listened to his heart with his ear pressed against Agathon's chest. Agathon was trembling uncontrollably as the examination proceeded. "Does it hurt anywhere?" the doctor asked.

"My legs and arms ache," said Agathon as a line of spittle dripped from the corner of his mouth. "I feel terrible."

"Bring him some wine," Praxites said to Irini, and she nodded and hurried out of the room.

"What is wrong with him, doctor?" Skamandronymous asked.

"I'm not certain," Praxites admitted. "But his heartbeat is very slow and his pupils are dilated."

"Slow heartbeat?" Skamandronymous repeated. "But this morning his heart was beating too fast."

"Are you sure?" Praxites asked pointedly.

"Of course he's sure," said Agathon in irritation. "Please don't talk about me like I'm not in the room. I'm sick, not dead."

"Sorry, brother," said Skamandronymous, patting Agathon on the leg. "Come, doctor," he continued. "Let's allow Sappho to take care of her uncle and go talk in the atrium."

"Great!" huffed Agathon. "Now the details of my infirmity are to be kept from me. I'm not a child."

"Stop bellyaching," said Skamandronymous, and he and the doctor left the room.

Sappho stared at her uncle neutrally. Agathon beckoned to her. "Sappho," he said, "come here. I want to talk to you."

Sappho edged toward the bed.

"Closer, girl," Agathon insisted.

Sappho stood beside Agathon and he put a hand on her forearm. "Sappho," said Agathon, "I didn't want to worry your father, but you need to know this. I'm dying, Sappho. And there are some things I have to say."

"You don't have to say anything," said Sappho.

"Yes, I do," said Agathon firmly. "I have used you shamefully and I want you to know I'm—"

"I don't care!" said Sappho with sudden venom. "And I'm not going to say everything is all right so you can die with a clear conscience!"

"Sappho—"

Agathon fell silent as Irini entered with a cup of wine. Irini touched Sappho on the shoulder and Sappho stepped aside. Irini raised Agathon's head off the pillow so he could drink the wine, and wiped the mixture of wine and saliva that dribbled from Agathon's mouth.

"Thank you, Irini," said Agathon.

Sappho started for the door.

"Sappho!" said Agathon in a low, guttural voice.

"I hope you do die!" Sappho hissed. "And I hope it really hurts!" And with that, Sappho swept out of the room.

"That girl is so selfish," sighed Agathon to Irini.

"She'll come around," said Irini softly. "Have some more wine."

The next morning, Agathon was much worse. He was having difficulty breathing and his hands and feet were swollen. Praxites was called to see him immediately after breakfast. Praxites gave a cursory examination, then asked Skamandronymous, Kleis, and Sappho to join him in the atrium. The doctor looked grim.

"His pulse is thready, and he's going in and out of consciousness," he said. "Has he made water since he took to the bed?"

"No," said Kleis.

"That isn't good," said Praxites. "He's been drinking wine steadily, I take it?"

"Yes," said Skamandronymous. "What is the matter with him, doctor?"

"He's dying," said the doctor. "And there's absolutely nothing I can do. The good news is it's not contagious."

"What's wrong?" Skamandronymous repeated insistently.

Praxites took a deep breath. "I believe he's been poisoned," he said. "Probably with hemlock. And it is my opinion it was done deliberately."

"Poisoned?" echoed Skamandronymous. "How?"

Kleis went pale. "The wine," she said softly.

The doctor glanced at Skamandronymous then looked at the floor.

"Irini!" cried Skamandronymous as he rushed out of the atrium toward his brother's room, followed closely by his wife, his daughter, and the doctor.

They found Irini bending over Agathon with a cup of wine. Skamandronymous bellowed in anger, crossed the room on his ruined foot in a bound, and dashed the clay cup out of Irini's hand. The cup flew over the bed and shattered against the wall, spilling wine down the plaster in an angry, red streak. Skamandronymous seized Irini by the wrist with the hand that was not holding his staff. "You will not harm my brother!" he cried.

"Skamandronymous!" said the doctor. "Stop this! He's dead already. Or he will be in half an hour!"

Skamandronymous released Irini and knelt by the bed. "Agathon, brother," he said, weeping, "do not leave us like this."

Kleis rushed to her husband's side and placed her hands on his shoulders. Sappho watched from a safe distance. Agathon opened his eyes and looked about the room, then he grasped Skamandronymous by the hand and stared into his brother's eyes for a brief moment before foam poured out of his mouth, his eyes rolled back in his head and he went limp on the pillow, staring into space.

Skamandronymous wept for many minutes over Agathon's lifeless body. Sappho stared at Irini, but the slave governess would not meet her gaze. The doctor kept silent. Then Skamandronymous wiped his eyes and rose to his one good foot.

"Doctor Praxites," said Skamandronymous woodenly, "summon the provost marshal. I wish to make a criminal complaint. I swear by Zeus, you'll die for this, Irini."

Praxites nodded and wordlessly left the room. Sappho looked from Irini to her father then rushed into Irini's arms. "You cannot do this to her, Papa," she wailed. "I won't let you!"

"Sappho," said Kleis, aghast, "she murdered your uncle!"

"I have no defense," said Irini. "There can be no defense. No defense. I'm sorry, Sappho."

Sappho was still clinging to her friend when the provost marshal and his men arrived and had to be physically pried off Irini's waist so they could take the soon-to-be-condemned woman away.

The court proceedings the following week went as Irini wished. She made no defense and was quickly found guilty and condemned to death. Capital punishment in Lesbos and the larger Greek world at that time was carried out either by pushing the condemned off a high precipice, or by forcing them to ingest a massive dose of poison hemlock, as would be done many decades later to the Athenian philosopher Socrates. The archon usually left it up to a murder victim's family what method of execution would be employed, and in this case, Skamandronymous did not hesitate or even have to think before deciding Irini would die by hemlock poisoning.

Sappho was inconsolable. The injustice of the situation was more than she could bear, and only she and Irini knew what Irini's motive had been in giving Agathon the poisoned wine. But Irini kept silent, and Sappho was more than reluctant to tell her father his brother had been a rapist of children.

Criminal trials were hasty affairs in Lesbos, and punishments were administered swiftly. The archon ordered Irini to drink the deadly poison an hour after she had been sentenced. Irini had the right under Greek law, as did any convicted criminal, to suggest an alternative punishment, but she declined. Her only stipulation was that she be allowed to die in the presence of just one witness: Sappho. The archon overruled Skamandronymous in granting the request.

Irini was escorted by the provost marshal's men back to Skamandronymous's house and into her room in the slaves' quarters. And Sappho was led by her still protesting father to the door after her.

"You don't have to do this, Sappho," said Skamandronymous. "I'll speak to the archon again. She can't make you watch her die."

"I want to be with her," Sappho said simply. She was acutely aware of how disappointed her father was in her to hear her say this.

Skamandronymous held the door open for Sappho and Sappho silently walked inside. The room was lighted by a single oil lamp and Irini sat calmly on her tiny bed. One of the provost marshal's men placed a bronze bowl of dark liquid on the table beside Irini's bed, then exited the room, closing the door behind him.

After a moment of silence, Irini reached out her hand to Sappho. "Come, child. Sit with me,"

Sappho hesitated.

"Sit with me, Sappho," Irini repeated. "I'm not afraid. Neither should you be." Sappho crossed the room and sat beside her friend.

"I'm doing this for you, you know," said Irini softly. "If anyone but the two of us knew what your uncle did to you, it would destroy your father. And that wouldn't be good for you."

"I don't care," said Sappho. "It's not fair."

"Nothing in life is fair," said Irini patiently. "If things were fair, Agathon would never have hurt you and this whole affair wouldn't have been necessary. You didn't tell me how young you were when it started with him."

Tears of shame welled up in Sappho's eyes. Her uncle Agathon had ruined her short life and was entirely to blame, Sappho knew, but the shame was there nonetheless. "I don't remember when it started," she said. "I was too young. I guess he was always there, right from the beginning."

"May his soul drown in the River Styx," muttered Irini bitterly. "There must be a special place in Hades for men who harm children. I am confident I am going to a better place."

"Take me with you," Sappho said suddenly, throwing her arms around Irini.

"What?" Irini gasped.

"There's enough poison for both of us," said Sappho. "I don't want to live in a world where people are punished for being good."

Irini returned Sappho's embrace and ran her fingers through the girl's hair. "You're too little to know what you're asking," she said softly. "When you've lived a full life, like I have, you'll understand that some things are worth dying for and some are not. You're worth dying for, Sappho. Your old governess isn't."

"What am I going to do without you?" Sappho said, the tears running down strongly now.

"You're going to live, first off," said Irini sensibly. "And you're going to keep writing and singing your songs. You must promise me that."

"I'll write a song about you," said Sappho. "I'll definitely promise you that."

"That will be enough," Irini smiled in the flickering lamplight. "Now, I think it is time for me to go."

Irini released Sappho and turned to the bronze bowl on the table, filled with its noxious brew. She picked up the bowl. "I hope it doesn't taste too bad," she said. "I always disliked the taste of medicine." Irini put the cup to her lips and quickly drank down the draft. "Hmm," she mused. "Sweet, with a hint of pine needles."

Irini lay down on her bed for the last time. Sappho lay beside her and put her arm around Irini's waist. She never knew how long it took for the poison to have its deadly effect, but, too soon, the provost marshal's men came to remove the body, and the still weeping Sappho, from the room.

Irini was buried in an unmarked mass grave on the outskirts of Mytilene. Skamandronymous's family having come from Athens, Agathon was cremated according to the Athenian custom, and his ashes placed in a decorative urn which his brother set in a central location in the house's atrium. Sappho, to her eternal shame, did not keep her final promise to Irini. She never wrote a song about her, nor did she speak her name aloud much again. It wasn't a matter of not wanting to displease her father. Thinking about her old friend was simply too painful. She hoped Irini would eventually forgive her in the afterlife.

To Sappho's dismay, her episodes of sleep paralysis continued after Agathon and Irini were both disposed of. Agathon was no longer abusing her; it was true. But Skamandronymous spoke so highly of his brother at every opportunity, that even his death could not rid the girl of his presence. In addition, Kleis had fallen ill again, and Sappho was dreadfully worried she, too, would die and leave her even more alone than ever. The hugging demon came at least once a week, and Sappho now had no one to confide in about it. She still kept Irini's dish of sand beside her bed—not that it did any good—and she was glad her parents never questioned her about it. Sappho felt utterly abandoned.

Praxites was called once again to examine Sappho's mother, and again he had no answers; however, Kleis admitted her grandmother had suffered similarly when Kleis was a child. The fever was very low grade, and according to the doctor, not life-threatening. But her spleen was still enlarged and she was still feeling melancholy and general malaise. In addition, Kleis was now tired all the time and her skin was mildly jaundiced. Praxites was at a loss.

Six months after Agathon and Irini died, Sappho went to her mother, who was again bedridden, needing to talk but unable to find the words. Kleis had been resting in bed for a week at this point with the same set of symptoms, but now, in addition, her urine had turned strangely dark.

"Sappho, darling," said Kleis when she saw her daughter standing in the doorway of her bedroom. "Please, come in."

Sappho edged closer to her mother's bed and sat down on a stool beside her. "How're you feeling, Mama?" she said.

"About the same," Kleis admitted. "But never mind me. Something is troubling you. Tell me, what is it?"

Sappho told the truth in spite of herself. "I miss Irini," she said and started to cry.

Kleis waited until Sappho's tears had dried before she spoke. "Sappho," she said, "I know you and Irini were close, but she was an evil person. She betrayed your father's trust and poisoned his brother to death. You have to forget about her."

"What if I told you what she did, she did to protect me?" Sappho asked softly.

Kleis furrowed her brow. "What do you mean?"

And suddenly Sappho was sobbing again. And through her tears, she told her mother everything. She told her about Agathon's abuse, about her scribbled note to Irini for help, and about the meaning behind the words to her first song. Kleis listened calmly at first, but by the time Sappho was finished, Kleis was crying as well.

Mother and daughter held each other as they wept, Sappho for herself and for Irini, and Kleis because she felt she had failed as a parent. They cried for many minutes before they broke their embrace. It was Kleis who finally spoke first.

"Why didn't you tell us?" she asked.

"I was afraid," Sappho sniffed. "I was afraid Papa would kill him."

"And you mustn't tell your father now," said Kleis practically. "The news would kill *him*. It would kill him to know Irini died for doing what was his duty as your father. Sappho, I can't say how sorry I am. Your father and I have wronged you."

"But we still have to keep it a secret," said Sappho bitterly.

"Yes," said Kleis. "Nothing good can come of telling anyone now. I'm glad you told me, though."

For Sappho's thirteenth birthday celebration, Skamandronymous spent a great deal of money on food and wine. He hired musicians to play the aulos and the mantoura and even a tympanon. He did not, however, hire a lyrist this time. Skamandronymous was now so thoroughly enamored of his daughter's musical skill that he announced she herself should play the lyre at her party. Sappho swelled with pride and chose three of her songs to play and sing for the evening's entertainment.

Skamandronymous had an ulterior motive in this decision, however. He knew some members of the high council still looked down on Sappho for what had happened with the boy Thymaion. And if Skamandronymous could demonstrate Sappho to be a talented, serious artist, and an asset to the family of her betrothed, namely Aphelos, the judgment of those councilmen might abate.

Sappho sang:

You were a child
Once before
Come, sing, celebrate
And us
Adore

And later:

Virgins, keep your watch tonight
Your song of love
Makes the bride
A sight

Awake! And call the groom to me
The nightingale sings
And spreads her wings
So free

Then, finally:

The moon
Encircled by lovely stars
Hides her beauty
Shines
Upon Earth
None too soon

Skamandronymous lavished praise on Sappho when she had finished her songs. And all the guests applauded generously. Sappho blushed in spite of herself; this had been the first time she had played and sung for an audience this large. And she devoured the attention with gusto.

At one point, after the songs when the guests were full of Skamandronymous's good wine, Kleis approached Sappho in private.

"Irini would have been proud of you," Kleis said to her daughter.

"She should be here to share in this," said Sappho bitterly. "But I am not even able to say her name."

"She knows you love her," said Kleis dismissively. "Don't dwell on it, Sappho. Just enjoy your party."

One of Skamandronymous's guests, a councilman named Onomastos, had brought his daughter Thalia to Sappho's party. Onomastos and his family were from Athens, like Skamandronymous himself, and their families had known each other and had actually been rather close when he and Skamandronymous were boys. Onomastos complemented his old friend on his daughter's musical talent and encouraged Thalia to talk to Sappho later that night.

Thalia was a little younger than Sappho, by about six months, Sappho reckoned, and seemed a bit nervous to be in the presence of one of Mytilene's bright new celebrities. Sappho, who had not played with girls her age since the incident with Thymaion, gravitated naturally to Thalia. Onomastos's daughter was of pale complexion and had straw-colored hair, and was an early bloomer with regard to puberty. Sappho, who had been menstruating for over a year, was drawn to Thalia's singular beauty. At least, Sappho thought she was beautiful, and she told Thalia so.

Thalia smiled shyly. "Your music is far more beautiful than I am," she said.

"So, you say," said Sappho. "Would you like to be my friend?"

Thalia smiled again, less self-consciously this time.

And that was how it began.

Making friends with Thalia inspired Sappho to reach out again to her childhood companions Larysa, Zosime, and Nastka. The three girls had been reprimanded by their parents for their part in what happened to Thymaion, but they had not been forbidden to associate with Sappho. Sappho, for her part, was less interested in play than she was in appearing mature. Agathon's abuse had forced her to grow up too fast, and she found now she had little use for childish games. The week after Sappho's thirteenth birthday party, she was sitting in the agora with her friends, watching the young men come and go from the smithy, the market, and the courthouse. Unlike her inexperienced friends, Sappho was appraising them for more than just their physical attractiveness.

Nastka pointed. "I like that one," she said of a short, swarthy youth with black hair. "Isn't he cute?"

Zosime nodded. "He has nice muscles in his arms."

"Yes," agreed Sappho. "But can he perform?"

"What do you mean?" Zosime asked innocently.

"Never mind," said Sappho dismissively.

"Sappho doesn't have to worry about attracting a nice young man," said Larysa with authority. "She's already betrothed."

"That doesn't mean she can't enjoy looking," said Thalia on her new friend's behalf.

"My thought exactly," said Sappho archly. "It's never a crime to look."

"What's your intended like, Sappho?" Nastka asked.

"I really don't know," Sappho admitted truthfully.

"Is he handsome?" Larysa asked.

"I suppose," said Sappho, feigning boredom.

"I wonder what my wedding night will be like," sighed Zosime wistfully.

"I wonder if you'll ever have a wedding night at all," joked Nastka. All the girls but Sappho laughed.

"I'm serious," insisted Zosime. "What is it like?"

"What is what like?" Sappho said pointedly.

"You know," said Zosime coyly. "*It*."

"I imagine it could be very tiresome," Sappho yawned. "On the other hand, it could be divine."

"How would *you* know?" Larysa asked.

"Just a hunch," said Sappho.

"Have you *done it*, then?" Zosime asked, scandalized.

"Believe what you want," said Sappho. It came out like a boast.

"Well, Hera's knees," said Nastka gleefully. "I think she has!"

"Who was it, Sappho?" Zosime asked. "You can tell us."

"I'm not interested in your questions," said Sappho. "If you want to know what *that* is like, go get yourself a boy and find out."

"I'm in no hurry," said Nastka. "I would think it might hurt."

Sappho smirked.

"That's why you need a boy with *experience*," said Larysa. "Somebody who knows what he's doing."

"Don't you want to marry a virgin?" Zosime said, shocked.

"I don't," said Sappho suddenly. "And no sane man would want that either."

"Sappho!" said Zosime. "All men want to marry virgins!"

Nastka and Larysa nodded in agreement.

"You think so?" Sappho said archly. "I doubt it. *Seriously*, who would want a woman who has no idea what men desire?"

"You *have* done it, haven't you, Sappho?" Larysa said.

Sappho slapped her hands on her thighs and stood. "You bore me, Larysa," she said. "All of you do. Come, Thalia. Let's go to the harbor and watch my father's ships as they come in."

Thalia stood and followed Sappho away from the others.

A boat named *Doxa Poseidōnos* was unloading amphorae of wine when Sappho and Thalia got to the quay. Sappho sat down, semi-lotus, on the planks of the dock and she motioned for Thalia to join her.

Thalia sat. Sappho ignored her and watched the sailors in their filthy chitons as they worked the ship's crane. Many minutes passed this way until Thalia felt she had to speak.

"Sappho," she said, "I thought it was mean of them to accuse you of not being a virgin."

Sappho smirked. "Now, these are men, Thalia," she said. "Young and strong. The others are fools."

"Didn't you hear me, Sappho?" Thalia said in frustration. "I said—"

"I heard you," Sappho interrupted. "What they think doesn't bother me."

"But, what if they start a rumor about you?" Thalia pressed. "What if they tell the whole city you're not a virgin?"

"Then perhaps the truth will finally reach my father's ears," said Sappho.

Thalia furrowed her brow. "But wait. Are you saying you're really not a virgin?"

"Congratulations," said Sappho bitterly. "You get a crown of laurel for figuring it out."

Thalia was silent for a spell, then said softly, "Who was it?"

Sappho picked up a small stone and tossed it into the water. "It was my uncle," she said.

Thalia gaped. "Your uncle?" she said, horrified. "Why on earth would you lie with your uncle?"

"It wasn't my choice," Sappho said.

"You mean he forced you?" Thalia said. "What did your father do?"

"He doesn't know," said Sappho. "And I forbid you to tell him, or anyone else. Understand?"

"Of course," said Thalia softly. Then, presently, "What was it like?"

Sappho remembered the feeling she had when her uncle touched her, and she willed herself not to cry. "Sometimes it felt good," she said honestly. "But most of the time I hated it." She wiped a stray tear from her eye.

"But—" Thalia began.

"I don't want to talk about it," said Sappho quickly. "Not to you. Not to anyone. Not ever again."

Thalia regarded Sappho silently for a moment, then said, "All right, Sappho. Whatever you want."

Sappho composed herself. "Come to dinner at my house tonight. Your father won't mind."

"No," agreed Thalia, "he won't. But I should tell him just the same."

"Then, let's go," said Sappho. "I'm tired of these sailors."

Skamandronymous thoroughly approved of Sappho's new friend, mostly because he was close to her father, rather than for any particular virtue on the part of the girl herself. Thalia, he reasoned, would be a good influence on Sappho, and would steer her away from more lewd behavior like what had happened previously. Sappho's father knew the key to being accepted as blameless before the council once again depended on Sappho's appearing healthy and normal. And what could be more healthy and normal than a strong platonic relationship with a girl of good breeding?

Dinner that night was roast chicken and chickpeas with native vegetables and flatbread. And, of course, plenty of imported wine. Drinking alcohol was not reserved only for adults in Greek society at that time, and Sappho enjoyed her father's wine. And as long as she didn't overindulge, the wine kept flowing.

Skamandronymous looked at Thalia indulgently. "Your father and I were good friends in our youth," he said through a mouthful of bread. "I am pleased that you seem to be getting on well with Sappho. And I want you to know you are always welcome in my house."

"Thank you, sir," said Thalia with a glance at Sappho. "Sappho is my best friend." Kleis dabbed at her mouth with a linen serviette. "*Agapē*," she said to Skamandronymous, "I'm afraid I feel rather ill. Would you mind if I went to lie down for a while?"

Skamandronymous frowned. "Of course not," he said. "Shall I call for Praxites?"

"No," said Kleis, rising from the table. "I don't think it's as bad as that. Thalia, I'm sorry for retiring. It was wonderful having you over for dinner."

"Thank you," said Thalia.

They watched as Kleis left the room. Then Thalia said, "Was that about me?"

Skamandronymous opened his mouth, but Sappho cut him off. "No, Thalia," she said. "Mama has been sick. Sometimes she gets quite tired and depressed. The doctor can't figure it out."

"Praxites," said Skamandronymous importantly, "is a skilled physician. He'll discover what is wrong, mark my words."

"Yes, Papa," said Sappho.

A few minutes passed in silence. Then Sappho said, "I need new strings for my lyre. May I take Thalia to the market tomorrow?"

"Of course," said Skamandronymous.

"And," Sappho continued, "may I have a few staters to buy them with?"

Skamandronymous smiled. "You won't need that much for harp strings, Sappho," he said, reaching for his purse. "You always knew more about music than money." He withdrew a rough coin equal to one-sixth of a stater and gave it to Sappho. "That should be sufficient."

"Thank you, Papa," said Sappho.

Later, in the garden, Thalia sat on a rock, admiring the dianthus blossoms and waiting for Sappho. She was very happy with her new friend. Happy because Sappho was wise and beautiful, and because Sappho had confided in her about her uncle Agathon. Thalia had never known anyone quite like Sappho. She admired her and wondered what adventures the two might share in the future.

Thalia looked up. Sappho had entered the garden, carrying her lyre. She crossed in front of the dianthus and sat down beside Thalia.

"Music, Thalia?" Sappho inquired.

Thalia smiled. "I thought your lyre needed strings."

Sappho grinned. "My lyre always needs strings," she said conspiratorially. "They break all the time. And anyway, I didn't tell my father it needed strings tonight."

"You're a rebel, Sappho," said Thalia in appreciation. "Has anybody ever told you that?"

"Never," said Sappho complacently. And she began to tune the instrument.

"What are you going to play tonight?" Thalia asked with great curiosity.

"I'll show you," said Sappho as she plucked a scale. Sappho strummed all the strings from high to low, cleared her throat, and began to play a new piece from memory, the chords dark and slow.

I wish in truth
That I could die
I wept that she
Should say goodbye
She came around

She found her voice
Sappho, know
I have no choice

Farewell, I said
Remember me
Remember, too
Our love so free

Blossoms woven
In your hair
Grace your head
Your throat so fair

I breathed your scent
So pure, so clean
With you, I felt
Release so keen

In temple, shrine
We, always there
There was no dance
We did not share

Sappho plucked an arpeggio of notes with a flourish of her fingers, then laid her lyre aside and placed her hands in her lap.

"Sappho," said Thalia in admiration, "that was beautiful! Was it about anyone in particular?"

"Us, Thalia," said Sappho. "It was always about us."

Thalia was a true romantic. So carefree and lovely. Sappho ached with a longing she had never felt, and with each passing day, it grew more and more insistent. Now, every song was about her. Every cloud revealed her face. Every flower reminded Sappho of her unparalleled beauty. There was attraction in a fiercely sexual way, but Sappho knew that was only part of it. She wanted Thalia to be happy. She wanted it to be herself who was making Thalia happy. And she wanted Thalia to feel the way Sappho did.

But Sappho had to force herself to be in no hurry to pick this flower. As she had learned in Skamandronymous's garden, the plucked rose soon faded, never to bring joy and admiration again. Her strange friendship with this land-siren her father had brought into her life was too precious for Sappho to proceed quickly. Sappho lived in unceasing terror of ruining everything.

And so she waited.

Onomastos was as pleased by Sappho's friendship with Thalia as Skamandronymous was. He invited Sappho to dinner at his house as often as Thalia dined with Sappho and her parents. Those days, the two were never seen apart. And Sappho kept secret her love for Thalia. For love was all it could be, Sappho reasoned, that could feel so good and hurt so acutely as what she felt for Thalia did.

The other girls began to talk, though not about anything that could rightly be called scandalous. They figured Sappho for a traitor, as she had no time for them now she was spending every waking hour with *that Athenian girl*. It wasn't long before Thalia was invited by Sappho to spend the night. Onomastos gave his consent, and the two girls passed that night conspiring slyly beneath the covers, from Sappho's bedtime till dawn—neither one of them missing the sleep.

Over the next few months, Sappho was such a prolific writer of songs, even Kleis, who thought her daughter was a natural genius, was impressed. What she and Skamandronymous didn't know was that nearly all of Sappho's new poems were, in one way or another, written for Thalia. It didn't occur to either of Sappho's parents that they should be worried about their daughter's sexuality. Sexual orientation was much more fluid in Greek society then than now. Though, they might have been concerned if they knew Sappho was investing so much emotional capital in one relationship when she was already betrothed to the young Aphelos. What they did know was that Sappho was happier than she had been in years. Skamandronymous took this to mean Sappho was finding her place in the world at last. Kleis deduced she had finally broken free of the evil her uncle Agathon had perpetrated against her.

In reality, they were both partially correct, though neither suspected Sappho was also in love for the first time in her life. Sappho herself felt free in the way she imagined the seagulls felt, yet at the same time a prisoner to the fact that Thalia was completely unaware of Sappho's infatuation. In truth, though, Sappho would have laughed at her obsession being written off as mere infatuation. This was so much stronger, purer, and more real. Sappho knew she would eventually have to tell Thalia how she felt about her. That would truly set them both free when the two of them could profess their love for each other without secrecy.

Please, goddess Aphrodite, Sappho prayed nightly, *let this lot be mine.*

She was blissfully ignorant of the possibility that the wanting might somehow be better than the having.

When Sappho came to her senses, she was sitting bolt upright in bed, her nightgown drenched through with the sweat of pure panic. The hugging demon had come again. And it was much worse this time.

It began, as it often did, with the sound of the aulos being played discordantly. Then, Sappho saw the shadow intruder near the bedroom door. Sappho had almost grown accustomed to the *ephialtēs* attacks over the preceding years. They were still terrifying, but she usually trusted Irini's assurances that the demon would not physically harm her.

Usually.

Then, the demon came out of the shadows, leaped onto Sappho's chest, and whispered into her ear as it wrapped its arms tightly around her torso.

"Bend your basest desires to me, Sappho," it said gutturally. "I am your consort now."

Sappho tried to scream, to fight the *ephialtēs* off, but as always, she could neither move nor speak. Then, for the first time, the demon actually penetrated her. Sappho could not even gasp as it tore deep into her pelvis, cold as winter bronze. She silently prayed for death.

But death would not come.

Sappho was exhausted when she arrived in the dining room for breakfast the next morning. The hugging demon had almost stolen away all her joy at being in love with Thalia. Skamandronymous noticed Sappho's beaten countenance and commented on it.

"Sappho, my girl," he said, "you look dreadful. What's the matter?"

"I don't have enough sand beside my bed," Sappho muttered.

"I beg your pardon?" Skamandronymous said, confused.

"Never mind," said Sappho bitterly. She noticed the empty place at the table. "Where's Mama?"

Skamandronymous frowned. "She's feeling poorly again," he said.

"Oh," Sappho commented dully. "I hope she feels better soon."

Skamandronymous had a bite of goat cheese. "I'm sure she will," he said. "She just needs a little rest."

But Kleis was not feeling any better by noon. By then, the stress of the *ephialtēs* attack had mostly worn off for Sappho, and she went to her mother's room to check on her. She found Kleis lying on her back, half asleep.

"Mama?" Sappho ventured. "Are you all right?"

Kleis's eyelids fluttered briefly. "Sappho?" she murmured. "Is that you, dear?"

Sappho sat on a stool beside her mother's bed. "Yes, Mama, it's me. It's Sappho."

Kleis took Sappho by the wrist. "Don't ever stop singing, my little nightingale," she said. "Don't ever stop." Kleis released Sappho's wrist and rested her hand on her own chest. "I wish to speak with my husband, Sappho. Run get him for me?"

"Of course, Mama," Sappho answered, rising from the stool and feeling a flicker of dread. "I'll get him. Wait here, Mama. I'll get him."

Sappho cursed herself silently for her stupidity. Of course, her mother would wait there. What else was she going to do?

Sappho found her father in the garden, cutting the purple-blossomed stalks of an aconite plant. Skamandronymous loved his garden; cultivating and breeding flowers was a hobby he had always enjoyed, and now that he was in his mid-forties and moving into middle age, he spent more and more time at it. It was what he did, Sappho knew when something was bothering him. Sappho figured she knew what her father was worried about today, and hated to compound the problem, but she had promised her mother.

"Papa?" she said.

Skamandronymous turned to face Sappho and offered a tired smile. "Sappho," he said. "Have I ever told you how beautiful you are, my girl?"

"Only every day for as long as I can remember," Sappho said. "You're biased."

"Come here."

Sappho slowly approached her father. Skamandronymous reached out and tucked an aconite blossom behind Sappho's ear. "You are my greatest joy, Sappho," he said. "I could die penniless and count myself among the richest of men for having had you for a daughter."

Sappho's smile faded slightly as she thought suddenly of her uncle. *That wasn't his fault*, she thought.

Skamandronymous did not overlook the expression on Sappho's face. "Sappho, darling," he said, "what's troubling you?"

"Mama's asking for you," said Sappho, dodging the question.

"Ah, yes," said Skamandronymous. He bent and placed his pruning knife on the ground beside his watering urn and spade, then stood up again, gripping his staff. "Do you know what your mother said when you were born?"

It was a question her father had asked before, but Sappho played along and shook her head.

"She said," Skamandronymous mused, "'This child is going to outshine the graces.' That's what she said. I'll just go see your mother now." He placed a hand on Sappho's shoulder as he limped toward the doorway to the interior of the house. "Don't ever change, Sappho," he said. "You're far too lovely for that."

"Yes, Papa," Sappho murmured.

When Kleis had not improved by nightfall, Skamandronymous grew worried. Kleis's grandmother had died at the age of forty-six after having displayed similar symptoms. Reluctant as he was to give credence to his concerns, Skamandronymous decided to call for the doctor.

Praxites came an hour later and asked to be alone with Kleis. He stayed with her for what seemed to be a very long time before he emerged into the hallway where Sappho and her father were waiting.

Praxites frowned. "Her heartbeat is weak and arrhythmic," he said. "I do not know the cause." Praxites paused. "I should like to take her to an *asklēpieion* for healing by the gods." *Asklēpieia* were similar to hospitals, but instead of providing medicine, they treated the sick by praying for divine intervention.

"I don't like the thought of sending her away, doctor," said Skamandronymous uncomfortably. "We will pray for her here."

Praxites sighed. "It may not matter, in truth," he said, defeated. "She could recover, or not. It could go either way. Equal probability."

The doctor's words shoved an icicle of terror into Sappho's heart.

Kleis did not die that night, or the next. But each day she remained in bed, too weak to do much more than swallow some broth and wine. Sappho resigned herself to a deep depression. Not even her music could bring her pleasure. Her only escape from the certainty that her mother was deathly ill was the time she spent with Thalia. And even that was not a true respite, for now that Sappho was in anticipatory mourning, she didn't have the energy to do what she felt she must do soon, and that was confess her love to her friend.

And Thalia comported herself like a true friend indeed. She stayed by Sappho's side every waking moment, and often while they were asleep. She accompanied Sappho to the market, to the quay. She even sang Sappho's songs to her, as best she could without the lyre to accompany her. Thalia had a dreadful, flat voice, and every once in a while managed to coax a smile out of Sappho with her own pitchy renditions of her friend's music.

At Skamandronymous's insistence, Praxites stayed in the house most of the time during those days. The doctor could do nothing for Kleis, but his presence was comforting nonetheless.

On the fifth day, Praxites came to Skamandronymous and Sappho as they sat having lunch. The look on his face told them all they needed to know.

"I think you two had better go to her," he said haltingly. "I think she has not much time."

Sappho immediately jumped up from the table with a cry of, "Mama!" Skamandronymous wearily set down his serviette and got to his good foot, leaning on his staff. "Thank you, doctor," he said, and he followed Sappho to Kleis's room.

When Sappho got to her mother's room, followed by her father, she found Kleis half-conscious and breathing shallowly. Kleis's skin was a deep yellow and she was terribly thin due to only having consumed liquids for days. Sappho sat beside her mother and put a hand on hers as Skamandronymous stood in the doorway, his face very pale.

"Mama?" ventured Sappho. "It's Sappho. Can you hear me?"

Kleis's eyes rolled around for a moment before they focused firmly on Sappho's face. Kleis smiled. "Sappho," she said. "I knew you'd come. Have you been singing, *agapē*?"

A stray tear ran down Sappho's cheek. "Yes, Mama," she lied. "Every day."

Kleis grasped Sappho's extended arm. "No tears, *agapē*," she said as firmly as she could. "No tears for me. You have a wonderful life ahead of you. Live it, Sappho." Kleis drew in a shallow breath. "Live it."

Kleis's fingers released Sappho's arm, and her hand went limp on the bed. Skamandronymous rushed to his wife's side and kneeled, letting go of his staff. He put a hand on Kleis's and the other on Sappho's shoulder. Praxites sighed as he stood in the doorway. Skamandronymous broke down, sobbing over Kleis, still holding onto his daughter.

Sappho wiped away the tears with forced stoicism. She silently promised herself she would never cry again.

Sappho again broke her promise. As soon as the women from the temple came to take Kleis's body away, Sappho ran to the garden, threw herself upon the ground, and vomited into the rose bushes. Her mother was dead, her confidant, her admirer. Now there was only one person in the world who knew the truth about Agathon. Sappho retched and retched until only bile came up, then cried as she never had before.

Presently, Sappho sensed she was no longer alone. She wiped her mouth with the back of her hand, knowing her face was a mess, and turned to face whoever was watching her.

It was Thalia. Beautiful, faithful Thalia. She stood in the interior doorway, watching Sappho with concern. Sappho wanted to smile. She wanted to go to her friend and kiss her, but instead, she collapsed again in tears. Thalia watched patiently until Sappho's sobs abated, her chest heaving, then went to Sappho's side and knelt where Sappho was sprawled ungracefully in the grass.

"Sappho," Thalia said gently. "They told me what happened."

Unable to speak, Sappho nodded, a sour taste in her mouth, bile burning her throat. She sat up and clung to Thalia, holding her close for many minutes.

Thalia stroked Sappho's hair. "I know nothing I say can make it better, Sappho," she said. "But I'm still your friend. I'm here if you need me."

Sappho finally found her voice. "I do need you, Thalia," she said. "I do need you. I'll always need you."

They sat in the grass of the garden, holding each other for a long, long time.

Kleis was cremated in the Athenian fashion, and her ashes were placed in an urn, which Skamandronymous set beside Agathon's. Sappho became despondent and withdrawn in the days following her mother's death. She did not play her lyre and walked about the house in silence. Thalia came every day, and while her presence soothed Sappho's soul, she could not raise Sappho's spirits. Sappho's depression was focused on one single fact—that her remaining parent believed her uncle to have been blameless. Sappho began to grow bitter and resentful.

Skamandronymous responded differently to Kleis's passing. He threw himself into his business, burying himself in work. He did not talk to his daughter about their mutual loss, leaving Thalia to comfort her alone. Every day, he limped off to the quay, whether there was a ship arriving or not, just to get out of the house. Kleis had been a necessary part of his existence, and the hole she had left behind was deep and cavernous.

Three weeks after Kleis died, Thalia invited Sappho to spend the night at her house. Sappho, needing a distraction, accepted. "There's just one condition," said Thalia.

"Oh?" Sappho queried.

"Bring your lyre."

Thalia's father Onomastos was delighted to have Sappho over for a visit. "Sappho," he said when she entered the house with his daughter, "I was so very sorry to hear about your mother. How is your father getting on?"

"Why don't you ask him?" Sappho answered rudely.

Onomastos ignored Sappho's disrespectful tone. "Well," he said, "do tell him the council wishes you both well."

"Thank you," said Sappho without much enthusiasm.

Onomastos smiled softly. "Let us know if there's anything you need, won't you?" he said. "Now, you two run off and have fun."

Sappho and Thalia went to Thalia's room. Thalia sat on her bed as Sappho looked on from the bedroom door. "Come," said Thalia warmly. "Sit with me."

Sappho set her lyre on the floor and moved toward the bed.

"No, silly," said Thalia patiently. "With your lyre."

Sappho picked up the instrument and sat down on Thalia's bed. She stared at her friend.

"Now, play something," said Thalia.

"Thalia," said Sappho softly, "I don't think—"

"Sappho," insisted Thalia, "play something."

Sappho took a deep breath, about to say something harsh, when she saw the emotion in Thalia's eyes. Her eyes were bright green with flecks of gold and brown, and their expression was encouraging and plaintive. Sappho knew what she had to do.

She placed the lyre in the playing position on her lap, strummed a few experimental chords, and then began to pluck out the melody to one of her earlier songs. The chords were simple, childish—or, rather child-*like*—and Sappho didn't even have to think as the music flowed from her expert fingertips. When the song was over, she played a skillful segue into another tune, this one more recent and more complicated. The notes rose and fell, slowly at first, then increasing in tempo as Sappho moved into an instrumental piece she had composed to be danced to. Thalia watched silently and listened, the same lovely smile on her face that she always wore when Sappho played. Now that Kleis and Irini were gone, Thalia was the one person on earth most appreciative of Sappho's music. Sappho played for Thalia, only for Thalia. Every note was hers.

Sappho finished the dancing piece, then slowly lowered her hands from the lyre's strings, pausing to brush a lock of hair self-consciously out of her eyes, and placed them in her lap.

Thalia stared into Sappho's brown eyes with her startling green ones and nodded. "Now," she said, "how did that feel?"

Sappho realized she was trembling slightly. "It felt good," she said. "I had forgotten."

"Your mother wouldn't want you to stop playing," said Thalia, "not now, not ever, not for her or anything else. Do you believe that?"

"Yes," said Sappho. "I believe that."

"You're the most beautiful person I know," said Thalia. "Promise me you'll never quit your music again."

"I promise," said Sappho tremulously. She was close enough to Thalia to feel her breath on her cheek.

"Promise me—"

And Sappho stopped Thalia's words with her parted lips. It was a real kiss, a true kiss, and Thalia returned it with passion and fullness. The kiss waxed and waned in intensity and Sappho could taste the pomegranate seeds on Thalia's sweet tongue as it swirled and probed around her own. Sappho wrapped her arms around Thalia and Thalia put her hands to Sappho's cheeks. Sappho was fairly drunk with desire, and her right hand slipped off Thalia's left shoulder and instinctively reached for the softness of Thalia's still-developing breast. Sappho could feel the want building in herself, in her heart, her breasts, her pelvis. It was an exquisite feeling that she had never experienced with her uncle. This was real, this was right, this was—

Thalia suddenly pulled away and Sappho, continuing to lean forward, nearly dropped into Thalia's lap. She looked up into her beloved's face and saw Thalia's expression of love and pain and uncertainty. Sappho blinked in confusion.

"I...I shouldn't have done that," Thalia stammered. "Oh, what you must think of me, Sappho."

"What must I think of you?" Sappho gasped. "I think the *kosmos* of you, Thalia. You are the love of my life!"

Thalia returned Sappho's passionate stare with a look of dismay. "But, Sappho," she said, "it can't possibly be like that. I couldn't possibly—"

"Why?" Sappho demanded, feeling both anger and despair building. "Why can't it be like that? Aren't you listening to me?"

"Yes," said Thalia in sorrow. "I hear everything you're saying, but. By Zeus, I'm afraid I've made a horrible mistake."

"Love is not a mistake, Thalia," said Sappho in desperation. "I know you love me. Tell me I'm right. You're a liar if you deny it."

"I don't deny it," said Thalia, growing more and more upset. "But not in the way you imagine. It just isn't right, Sappho."

"How did you *think* I was going to imagine it?" Sappho demanded furiously. "For months, you've been my best friend. For months, I've written love songs for you. For months, you've led me on with absolutely no shame at all, and now I'm just *imagining* things? You little *temptress*!"

Sappho enraged, grabbed her lyre roughly by the yoke and stood. Thalia reached up after her. "Where are you going?"

"I'm going home!" Sappho shouted. "And don't follow me. Don't you ever come near me again!"

"Sappho—"

"I know the way out."

And then she was gone, leaving Thalia crushed, alone, confused and ashamed. Sappho never spoke to her again.

Sappho went straight home. She entered the atrium and set her lyre on the tile floor, covering her face with her hands and shaking with anger and despair. How could she feel so strongly for Thalia, when Thalia felt nothing for her? *That isn't right*, Sappho thought. *Thalia said she loved me.* But how could she do this to Sappho if she loved her? Thalia had strung her along, kissed her, and offered words of love, then rejected her out of hand. It was cruel. It was evil. It was—

Sappho lowered her hands from her face and the first thing she saw was Agathon's urn. Rage suddenly erupted within her and she rushed across the atrium, grasped the urn in both hands, and dashed it to the floor where it shattered, spilling the remains of her uncle all over the tiles. Suddenly furious at her mother for leaving her, Sappho took up Kleis's urn as well. She was about to smash it on the floor when the shame of what she was doing hit her like a wave.

Sappho lowered the urn to the floor, sat down, and wept. She wept for Irini, for her mother, for Thalia, and for herself. She had thought, after Agathon's death, that life would be easy and pleasant. But Sappho had never been as miserable as she was at this moment. She wanted to die, but she was too afraid of not existing to do anything about it. Sappho sprawled out on the floor and continued to cry bitterly.

And that was how her father found her when he got home half an hour later.

Skamandronymous was furious. His brother's ashes had been desecrated and his daughter was in hysterics. Someone would have to be held to account for disrupting his household in this way. It was several minutes before he could get Sappho to stop crying, and when she finally ceased wailing, she put her arms around her father's legs. Skamandronymous lowered himself to the floor, leaning on his staff, and held Sappho close.

They held each other like that for a moment, Skamandronymous stroking Sappho's hair, then Skamandronymous asked softly, "Who did it, Sappho?"

Sappho did not hesitate. "Atykhos," she said.

Atykhos was a sixteen-year-old house slave from North Africa. No one knew his birth name, but his Greek name meant *unlucky*. And Atykhos was most unfortunate indeed that Sappho had accused him of destroying Agathon's urn and apparently attempting to destroy Kleis's.

Sappho bore Atykhos no ill will. She had chosen his name at random. Sappho had considered telling her father the truth about his brother right then and there. But she remembered her mother's admonition that Skamandronymous must never know what Agathon had done to Sappho. So Sappho held her tongue.

Atykhos's punishment was twofold. He would be whipped in public in the agora the next day, and he would be sold immediately. Like Irini, he made no defense, knowing he could not contradict the daughter of his master. But he looked right into Sappho's eyes as each lash of the whip fell, and Sappho felt his gaze for the accusation it was. Sappho stared back inscrutably. After all, he was only a slave. Then Sappho remembered Irini had just been a slave and broke eye contact with Atykhos and looked at her feet.

With Atykhos sold away, there was no one to clean the bathrooms, and Skamandronymous had to make some reassignments until he could purchase another boy. Sappho found this annoying. After her break with Thalia, she became obsessed with her physical appearance, and bathed daily, even though the doctors said this was dangerous. She changed the style of her hair, wearing it in braids that fell around her ears. She asked her father's permission to wear some of her mother's jewelry, and Skamandronymous consented. Sappho chose a pair of silver earrings—she would have her ears pierced immediately—and a copper ring set with a large pearl.

Skamandronymous could not help but notice Sappho's new attention to her own beauty coincided with her ceasing to associate with Thalia, but he did not think to conclude the two trends were related. He simply assumed Sappho and Thalia had had a falling out, and that Sappho was merely growing up. Both were true, of course, but Sappho had been so deeply burned by Thalia's rejection that she had decided to attempt to attract the first new admirer, male or female, who came along. It was a few days after her fourteenth birthday that this strategy finally paid off.

The young man's name was Palabos. He was seventeen and an apprentice to the local metal-smith. He was not particularly witty or handsome, but he had a charming smile and rather large biceps which Sappho couldn't help but appreciate. Most importantly, his eyes were most assuredly not green.

Palabos, being a day laborer, was not invited to Sappho's birthday party. But he came by the house later that week to drop off some bronze cuff bracelets Skamandronymous had ordered for Sappho's birthday present. Sappho herself opened the door when he arrived, and she gave him an appraising look. *Not bad*, she thought. And she immediately resolved to seduce him.

"Hi," said Palabos after a moment. "Um, I'm looking for Skamandronymous. Is he home?"

"He's at the harbor," said Sappho, leering at Palabos as she leaned on the doorpost. "Can I help you?"

"I, um, have a delivery for him," said the young man, indicating the small wooden box he was carrying. "Are you…"

"I'm his daughter," Sappho said, taking the box. "My name is Sappho."

"Sappho," echoed Palabos. "That's a pretty name."

And that's a pretty pathetic line, Sappho thought. But all she said was, "Would you like to come in?"

"Um, yeah, sure," said Palabos.

He certainly was not a linguistic genius. Sappho stood aside and ushered him inside.

"Would you like some wine?" Sappho offered. "My father sells wine."

"I don't think I should—"

"Oh, don't be so dull," Sappho admonished. She took Palabos by the hand and led him into the garden.

Palabos sat down on a rock. Sappho gave him a sultry smile. "Wait here," she said. "I'll get the wine."

Sappho's heart was pounding as she went to the cupboard. Was she going too fast? She wasn't certain. She had waited months before making her move on Thalia. But, of course, she was in love with Thalia and was afraid to rush things. She was most certainly not in love with Palabos. He was a means to an end. Sappho was lonelier than ever without Thalia, and a lover—in the shallowest sense of the word—would be welcome company. As it would be phrased millennia later in another land, she needed someone on the rebound. It mattered little who.

Sappho found two bronze cups and a pitcher of wine, poured Palabos and herself each a measure, then closed the cupboard and made her way back to the garden.

Palabos was still sitting on the rock and looked up expectantly as Sappho entered the garden. "Sappho," he said, "I really don't have much time right now. I need to get back to the—"

"Live a little," said Sappho as she handed Palabos a cup of wine. She sat down beside him. "Now, what's your name?"

"Um, Palabos," said the hapless—*possibly witless*, Sappho thought—apprentice smith.

Sappho looked at Palabos's arms with approval. "Tell me, Palabos," she said, "are you daring?"

"Daring?" echoed Palabos.

"Yes, daring," said Sappho. She threw her head back and downed her entire cup of wine in three swallows, knowing Palabos was staring at her. "Are you daring, Palabos? I am. Drink your wine."

Palabos put his cup to his lips and sipped. Sappho laughed almost cruelly.

"Definitely not daring," said Sappho. "What a pity. We will have to do something about that. Finish your cup."

"It's rather early in the day," Palabos stammered. "I'm not sure I should—"

"Here," said Sappho, taking Palabos's cup and draining it herself. "There," she said. Sappho leaned close to Palabos, knowing her hair must be brushing maddeningly against his shoulder. With cold calculation, she kissed him very lightly on the lips, breathing the wine into his nostrils, then pulled back. "Now, go," she said. "And if you want to see me again, I might allow it. If you're nice. If you want to. You can find the door, can't you? I'm suddenly feeling flushed."

Palabos stood and tripped on his sandals on the way out of the garden.

Yep, Sappho thought. *He'll do.*

Sappho waited forty-eight hours before she made her next move—though waiting was driving her mad with anticipation. She did not love Palabos. Not the least bit. That she was sure of. But the thought of exploiting him was most exciting. Sappho went to the smithy at lunchtime, when her father had gone to the harbor to do nothing in particular. The metal-smith was a strapping man in his late twenties named Alexandros, and he stopped hammering the piece of iron he was working on when he noticed Sappho entering from the street.

"Good day, missy," he said, wiping his brow. "You're Skamandronymous's daughter, right? The musician?"

Sappho affected her warmest smile. "Yes, sir," she said. "I was wondering if I could speak to your apprentice."

"No problem," said Alexandros. He set down his hammer and tongs. "Palabos!" he shouted over his shoulder. "You've got a visitor!"

After a moment, Palabos emerged from the rear of the shop. He blinked in confusion, or perhaps anticipation when he saw Sappho. "Sappho!" he said, sounding nervous. "What're you doing here?"

Sappho smiled coyly. "I wanted to thank you for the bracelets," she said, holding up her wrists and displaying the cuffs. "Didn't my father tell you they were for me?"

"Um, no," said Palabos. "And you're welcome," he added after a pause.

Sappho gave Palabos an inviting stare. "I was wondering," she said. "Would you like to have lunch with me?"

"Well, I," Palabos began, falling silent, flustered.

Alexandros laughed. "Go eat with the pretty girl, Palabos," he said. "You can have half an hour."

"Okay, sure," said Palabos, relieved. Sappho was quite aware that neither he nor his master knew she was betrothed. Palabos wiped his hands on a rag and approached Sappho.

Netted him like a fish, Sappho thought.

Sappho took Palabos to the market, where there was a kiosk where food was sold. Palabos ordered lamb and flatbread for two, the precursor to the modern *gyros*, and paid for both. Sappho was fairly certain Palabos would insist upon paying—so certain, in fact, that she had brought no money with her. They took their food to the center of the agora and sat down on the courthouse steps across from the altar to Artemis. From there, they could watch the citizens of the city-state go about their business while they ate.

Palabos chewed his primitive sandwich slowly and appreciatively. It was seasoned with black pepper, onions, olive oil, and sliced cucumbers. Sappho watched him eat, knowing he had no inkling as to her real motives. She bit into her food, intentionally allowing some of the olive oil to drip down her chin.

Palabos smiled and reached out his hand. "You've spilled. You've dropped." He was quite unsure of himself.

"Yes?" Sappho said sweetly.

"You've got some… on your face," Palabos finished.

"Oh!" Sappho laughed. "Can you take care of it for me?"

"I guess so," responded Palabos. He reached out his hand again and wiped the olive oil off Sappho's chin. "There."

"Thank you," said Sappho.

"Yeah, sure," answered Palabos.

"You're a real gentleman," Sappho observed.

"Um, thanks," said Palabos.

"Most girls appreciate a true gentleman," Sappho said.

"I guess," said Palabos again.

Sappho looked him in the eye. "I'm not like most girls," she said seriously.

"What does that mean?" Palabos asked without stammering.

"You know what I mean," Sappho said.

"Are you saying that—"

"Finish your lunch," Sappho interrupted.

They ate in silence for a moment. When Palabos had swallowed the last of his lamb and bread and was about to lick the oil off his index finger, Sappho gently, but firmly, took him by the wrist. Staring directly into his eyes, she took his finger into her mouth and slowly, very slowly, withdrew it without breaking eye contact. Palabos sighed an exhalation that told Sappho, had he been standing, he would have gone weak in the knees.

Finally finding his voice, Palabos said, "Sappho, would you like to—"

Sappho interrupted him again. "Take me home, Palabos," she said.

"Um, are you…" said Palabos, confused and, Sappho hoped, thoroughly aroused. "Well, okay," he finished finally.

They rose from the steps and left the agora, Sappho noticing a fat man with an iron-gray beard standing beside the altar to Artemis and watching them intently. The man frowned and then motioned to two young boys who were standing nearby, holding a kid on a rope. The boys led the kid up to the altar and forced it to the ground. The fat man drew a knife and quickly slashed the kid's throat. The two boys hoisted the kid up by its hind legs, allowing the blood to drain out of its dying body. Then they placed the carcass on the altar, upon which a pyre had been built. Taking a torch, the fat man lit the pyre. The carcass began to burn.

The fat man stared after Sappho and Palabos. "Artemis, have mercy," he muttered, then turned his attention to the pyre.

Palabos walked Sappho back to her front door, where Sappho turned around to face him at the threshold.

"So," she said, "what do you think of me?"

"I, um," Palabos began, then paused, then said, "I think you're very nice."

A real charmer, this one, Sappho thought. But all she said was, "Thank you."

Then, without warning, she kissed him. It was as deep as her kiss with Thalia but with none of the emotion. It was a slow, teasing kiss, and Sappho let it linger so that Palabos got the full effect.

Sappho pulled away. Palabos looked stricken. Then he blurted out, "I want you to know my intentions are entirely honorable." It was the most sophisticated thing he'd yet said to her.

Sappho smiled. "But what if mine aren't?"

"Oh, Sappho," Palabos said, cringing.

Sappho put her index finger to Palabos's lips. She was really enjoying this. "Don't say anything," she said softly. "Now, go away. I promise you'll see me again soon."

Palabos nodded slowly and—could it be possible?—sadly. He opened his mouth as if to speak, but after a moment he seemed to think better of it. He closed his jaw, then turned from Sappho in the doorway and walked off, his shoulders slumped.

Sappho could not have been more pleased. Everything was proceeding just as she'd designed.

Despite her plans going well, Sappho found herself unable to rid herself of her melancholy. Thalia had injured her deeply, but was that really Thalia's fault? Sappho had initially blamed her former friend for everything. But she kept entertaining the maddeningly intrusive thought that she had been unfair to Thalia. Thalia admitted she loved Sappho. But there were three kinds of love— *agapē, eros,* and *philia.* Sappho had felt—still agonizingly felt—all three for Thalia. Apparently, however, for Thalia, there was no *eros* for Sappho.

But it had seemed so real.

Why had Thalia rejected her? Could it be that Sappho was unlovable? Sappho dismissed that idea quickly. Thalia loved Sappho. Sappho's parents loved her. Irini had loved her. Sappho supposed, in *eros*, even Agathon—

No. Agathon had been a monster. Whatever he had felt for Sappho, it had not been love. Sappho had suffered for years under his ministrations and she was glad he was dead. As much as she missed Irini, Sappho was grateful that her old governess had poisoned the bastard. There had been no love of any kind there.

But Thalia…

Thalia had seemed perfect. She loved Sappho intensely for who she was, exactly the way she was. Sappho had written more than half a dozen songs for her friend, and Thalia had not objected then. How could Thalia have been so cruel as to accept the gift of those songs only to throw the emotions behind them back in Sappho's face? Then it occurred to Sappho that Thalia may have missed what Sappho had been hinting about all those months that they were friends. Could she really have been that blind? Sappho didn't know, but she kept coming back to the inescapable conclusion that Thalia had, intentionally or not, accepted Sappho's affection until it became inconvenient. In the end, it had been Thalia's choice to reject Sappho, and Sappho blamed her entirely for that.

Sappho continued to bathe, dress well, and make herself desirable-looking. The face she presented to the outside world was one of calm, yet energetic, confidence. Her father was as proud of her as ever, and Aphelos, who visited from time to time—sometimes with his parents and sometimes alone—expressed admiration for his intended and her beauty. If only he knew Sappho was in love with someone else, and actively pursuing yet another…Sappho's despair ran deep, but it did not show.

As for Sappho's other friends, they—particularly Larysa—were pleased that Sappho had broken things off with Thalia. Sappho was *their* friend first, after all. To their way of thinking, Thalia had been nothing more than a foreign pretender. Sappho, for her part, returned to the other three girls and was immediately welcomed. Sappho was their wise and worldly mentor. They remained scandalized that Sappho was not a virgin, but their curiosity was stronger than any judgmental sentiments they harbored toward her. Sappho felt entirely within her element.

The girls spent their time those days at the harbor, at Sappho's insistence. She told them that's where they would find the most attractive men, but in truth, Sappho just wanted to steer clear of the agora. Sappho had been quite aware of her and Palabos's being watched by the gray-bearded priest of Artemis the day they had had lunch together and decided it would certainly not do to risk his telling Larysa and the others about Sappho's new paramour. Likewise, she did not want to run into Palabos himself while she was with her friends. Those relationships were best kept separate, by Sappho's reckoning.

The day after Sappho kissed Palabos on her front step, Sappho was sitting with Larysa, Nastka, and Zosime on the quay, watching the sailors. Sappho's three friends chatted animatedly with each other about boys while Sappho took in the scenery in silence. Zosime was particularly enamored with the young captain of a ship—not one of Sappho's father's—called *Gorgō*. He was well-proportioned and tall with reddish hair and beard, and his chiton was stained with sweat. Sappho judged him to be about thirty and thought he was handsome enough. Not that Sappho was concerned with men. Not really.

"Ah," Zosime mused, "it must be wonderful to be loved by a man."

"Seems like that's all you're ever interested in," observed Nastka.

"As if you're any different," chided Larysa. "You talk of nothing else."

"Men are all identical," Sappho interjected suddenly. "They all want the exact same thing and it's very tiresome. And," she added, "they're so very easy to manipulate."

"Tell us about your man, Sappho," Zosime begged. "The one who…you know."

The other girls stared at their friend in anticipation.

"There's nothing to tell," said Sappho. "Like I said, tiresome."

"But you must have felt *some* way about it," said Larysa. "Come on, Sappho. Share with us. We don't judge you."

Sappho sighed. She was not going to avoid talking about it. "What you have to understand is," she began, "all men are horny bastards."

This was not an anachronism. One of the classical Greek slang words for *penis* was *keras*, literally *horn*, as of a goat or a cow. The Greeks were most likely the inventors of the precursor to the modern English expression.

"Really?" Zosime said. "All of them?"

"Well," said Sappho, "maybe not all of them. But I'm betting most. Seriously, men are driven primarily by sex." The others sat up attentively upon hearing the word *sex* spoken so casually by their friend. "Sex," Sappho continued, "is the most powerful force in the world. It literally started the Trojan Wars. Haven't you been told the story of Helen of Troy? Prince Paris was willing to die and risk his entire kingdom just to get her into bed. Yeah, men are so predictable."

"Tell us more, Sappho," encouraged Nastka. "Tell us everything."

"Well, for starters," said Sappho, "men are very proud of their equipment. Size matters a lot to them." She thought of her uncle's own package, and how he was constantly boasting to her about it, and frowned. "They place far more emphasis on size than on anything else."

"Does it really matter how big they are?" Larysa wondered. "I figured they were all the same size."

"I honestly don't know," admitted Sappho. "I'm really not as experienced as you seem to think I am. I know enough, though. Enough to tell you men *think* it matters."

"I hope they're not *too* big," said Zosime. "It sounds uncomfortable."

"It is, at first," confirmed Sappho. "But you get used to it. It gets easier."

"How does it feel?" Larysa asked. "Once it gets easier, that is?"

"It's impossible to describe," said Sappho. "If you're not ready, it feels very coarse. But if he takes his time, it can feel different."

"How different?" Nastka pressed her.

Sappho thought about the feeling her uncle had given her when she was nine, the feeling she loved and hated in the same instant, and again frowned. "Just different. There's nothing to compare it to."

"But is it good?" Zosime said.

"Yeah," said Sappho. "It's pretty good. But I'm telling you, if you don't want it, it doesn't matter how good it feels. If you don't want it, it's awful. Simply awful. And that's all there is to it."

"So," ventured Nastka, "who was your man?"

Sappho felt a sudden surge of hate for Agathon, which she quickly swallowed.

"That's not important," she said. "What matters is that it wasn't my idea."

There was silence for a moment, then Larysa said, "Are you saying you were raped, Sappho?"

Sappho averted her gaze. "Pretty much," she said.

Another awkward silence.

"Sappho—" Zosime began.

"I'm tired of talking about this," Sappho interrupted. "I'm going home."

And she left the others sitting on the quay.

One week later—Sappho was determined not to rush things, not because she wanted a wholesome relationship with Palabos, but because she realized she wanted to draw things out, tormenting him—Sappho showed up at the smithy. Alexandros saw her coming and when she reached him at his anvil, he smiled warmly.

"Well, hello there, Sappho," he said. "Are you here for business or pleasure?" Sappho gave him her most winning smile.

"I'm here to see Palabos," she said.

"I suspected as much," Alexandros said. "Palabos!" he called over his shoulder. "Your girlfriend's here!"

Sappho quickly glanced around to see if anyone had heard Alexandros call her Palabos's girlfriend. All the people in the agora seemed to be attending to their own affairs. Palabos emerged from the room behind the anvil. Sappho could see the excitement in his eyes when her gaze met his. She had him right where she wanted him.

"Sappho," said Palabos. "I thought you had forgotten me."

"Never," said Sappho coyly. "I've just been busy. My father often needs my help with things. He's lame, you know."

"Oh, yeah," acknowledged Palabos. "So, what brings you here?"

"I have something for you," said Sappho. "But you have to come to my house to get it."

Palabos glanced at Alexandros, who raised his hands and said, "Far be it from me to stand in the way of young love. Take an hour, Palabos. But just one hour, please."

"Um, thanks," said Palabos.

Sappho took him by the arm and led him away from the agora.

As soon as they arrived at her father's house, Sappho took Palabos straight to her bedroom. It was the right moment to step things up, she had decided. She sat down on her bed and motioned for Palabos to join her. She stared into his eyes. "It's time," she said.

"Time for what?" Palabos said.

"Time for this," said Sappho, and she kissed him. She kissed him aggressively, almost violently, and he rose to the occasion. After a moment, she whispered, "Touch me, Palabos."

Palabos obliged, putting his hand on her breast. Sappho felt the excitement building. She had never been with a man on her own terms, and she found herself wanting him as much as he seemed to want her. After a long moment, she pulled away and said, "Here." She rose from the bed and slipped off her sandals. Palabos watched her intently. Sappho took a deep breath. Was she sure about this?

Of course, she was.

Sappho lifted the hem of her peplos, then took it all the way off and dropped it on the floor. Next, she took off her *strophion*, a band of cloth Greek women wore to bind their breasts, and her *perizōma*. She hadn't been naked in a man's presence since before Agathon died, and she found it both disturbing and exhilarating. Palabos stared. Sappho sat back on the bed. "Take off your clothes and join me, Palabos," she said huskily.

Palabos obliged quickly and with enthusiasm. In fact, once he was naked, Sappho could see he was most enthusiastic indeed.

Sappho lay back on her mattress, legs akimbo. "Go down on me, Palabos," she said.

"Do what?" Palabos whispered.

"Kiss me, you fool," said Sappho. "Down there."

"Oh," said Palabos, and he followed her instructions.

After it was over and Palabos had gone back to the smithy, Sappho reflected that sex with him, while exciting at first, had been a letdown. He clearly had no experience; Agathon at least had that—though Sappho despaired at comparing Palabos to Agathon. He had absolutely no skill at pleasuring a woman the way Sappho had wanted to be pleasured. He was clumsy and disappointing.

Furthermore, Sappho did not have a recurrence of the strange, wonderful, terrible sensation her uncle had given her all those years ago. Sappho wondered if that had been a fluke. Surely it could be made to happen again, but probably not with Palabos.

It wasn't fair, Sappho told herself after the encounter. She had spent days seducing Palabos. And she had, after swearing her to secrecy, gotten one of the older female slaves to tell her how to avoid pregnancy. To this end, she had consumed a great deal of fennel prior to her encounter with the apprentice smith. Sappho had been assured this would work. And then, after all that planning, Palabos had had his way with her, and she was unsatisfied.

It simply is not fair, Sappho thought again. How could it be that the only time she felt that much pleasure was when she was being subjected to sexual assault and incest? Sappho wondered if she would ever be happy again. After three days of thinking about her situation, she determined the only thing to do was to bed Palabos again.

On the third day, Sappho went through the motions of luring Palabos from work so she could take him a second time to her bedroom. This time, however, Alexandros was markedly less enthusiastic about having his apprentice skip work for an hour.

"Don't make this a habit, Palabos," he said.

Sappho quickly escorted Palabos to her father's house, and then to her room. She got out of her sandals, peplos, and undergarments and motioned for Palabos to do the same.

"Aren't you going to kiss me first?" Palabos asked.

"Strip," Sappho commanded.

Palabos obeyed. His member was stiff and twitching with anticipation.

"Good," Sappho said. "Now, lie back on the bed."

Palabos was breathing heavily as he followed Sappho's orders. Sappho pounced on him and took him into her mouth the way her uncle had shown her—it is worth noting the women of Lesbos were rumored to have actually invented this particular maneuver. Palabos sighed, "Sappho…"

Sappho played him like a flute until she judged him to be on the verge of ejaculation, then backed off him.

"What're you doing?" Palabos asked helplessly.

"Shut up," Sappho growled. She straddled his pelvis and guided him into her. His warm hardness excited her greatly.

"Sappho!"

Sappho had a moment of confusion before she realized Palabos had not been the one who had spoken her name. Palabos groaned and slid out of her. Sappho felt disappointment fill her loins and she glanced over her left shoulder. Aphelos was standing in the doorway to Sappho's bedroom, a look of shock on his face. "Aphelos!" cried Sappho, more upset over the interruption of her pleasure than at having been caught by her intended in the very act of infidelity. "What in Zeus's name do you think you're doing?"

Aphelos scoffed in disgust. "What am *I* doing, Sappho? How dare you ask me that!"

"It's not what you think!" Sappho said in a panic. "He forced me!"

"With you on top of him?" Aphelos said. "It certainly doesn't look like force to me!"

"Aphelos," said Sappho, "you mustn't tell my father."

"He's going to want to know why I've suddenly decided not to marry you," said Aphelos.

"But you have to marry me," said Sappho. "Our parents have made a bargain!"

"To Hades with their bargain!" barked Aphelos. "My wife being the biggest whore in Lesbos was *not* part of the bargain!" He turned to leave.

Sappho jumped off the bed and faced her intended. "Where are you going?"

"I'm going back to the dining room to talk with our fathers," he said with great restraint. "The three of us just got here to discuss business. Now, I think you should put your clothes back on and join us, don't you?"

Aphelos left the room. Sappho glanced at Palabos. His erection had faded. He moaned in frustration and embarrassment. "You're engaged?" He stammered to Sappho.

"Betrothed," said Sappho bitterly. "It's not the same thing. Get dressed. I'll take you out the back way."

In the end, Aphelos did not tell Sappho's father, or anyone else, why he was breaking off the arrangement. He simply said he had changed his mind. Pheronaktos was disappointed, but quietly accepted his son's decision. Skamandronymous was furious.

"What did you do?" he asked Sappho pointedly.

"I told him his father was an ass," Sappho answered.

"What on earth for?" Skamandronymous fumed. "You don't even know Pheronaktos!"

"Well, I don't like him!" said Sappho.

"Sappho," Skamandronymous said in frustration, "this isn't like you. In fact, I haven't recognized you since you stopped playing with Thalia."

"It's my business, Papa," said Sappho dismissively. "And that's that."

"Not in my house, it isn't," said Skamandronymous angrily. "I insist you tell me what's going on!"

"You couldn't possibly understand," said Sappho. "All you care about is marrying me off. You've never cared about me!"

"That's not true!" said Skamandronymous defensively.

"Oh, yes it is," hissed Sappho. "Otherwise you never would've let him—" Sappho cut herself off, tears stinging her eyes. She wanted her mother. She wanted Irini. She wanted Thalia.

Skamandronymous took his daughter by the shoulders. "Never would have let who do what, Sappho?"

Sappho stamped her foot and screamed in her father's face. "You never would've let your perverted brother destroy my childhood!" She spun on her heel and rushed toward her bedroom.

Skamandronymous caught her halfway and turned her violently to face him. "What did you say?" he bellowed.

"I said," cried Sappho, "your brother had his way with me countless times for as long as I can remember! Your perfect, beautiful daughter was Agathon's plaything for years! And you did *nothing* to stop him, Papa! The signs were all there and you did nothing!" She tore her arm out of her father's grip and ducked into her room.

Skamandronymous followed her, stopping in the doorway as Sappho flung herself upon her bed. "It's a lie!" he shouted. "I don't believe you! You're lying to me!"

"It's not a lie!" Sappho cried. "Irini knew! Why do you think she killed him? Irini knew! Why didn't you?"

Skamandronymous's shoulders slumped as he realized he believed her. "Sappho," he said. "Sappho, I—"

"Get! Out!" Sappho screamed, and she buried her face in her pillow and wept.

Skamandronymous stared at Sappho—his lovely, talented, damaged Sappho—then, defeated and deflated, turned and left her alone in her misery.

Skamandronymous took Sappho's revelation regarding Agathon quite hard. Instead of comforting his daughter, he withdrew into a depression. In the time when Sappho needed him most, he was absent.

Sappho buried herself in her music. She played both new and old songs unceasingly. In the absence of her mother, Irini, or Thalia, her lyre became her best friend.

Sappho sang:

O my maidenhood
Where have you gone?
Why have you left me
Here so alone?

Said my maidenhood
Gone have I been
Nor shall I visit you
Ever again

Skamandronymous heard this last one and muttered so that Sappho could hear, "Mourning the loss of her virginity when it left her for playing the trollop." He shook his head and limped out of the room.

Sappho fumed. How could her father, the only man she loved, blame her for what Agathon had done? Sappho could only conclude that Skamandronymous's desire to have a perfect family outweighed his love for his daughter. Was he afraid Sappho would tell the council about Agathon? Sappho wasn't sure, but she did know he need not worry about that. What Agathon did was his own fault, but Sappho still felt enduring shame about it. She certainly would not tell anyone else.

Of course, Sappho had promised her mother she wouldn't tell Skamandronymous either.

Following her revelation to her father regarding Agathon, Sappho's birthday celebrations were perfunctory affairs, lacking guests and lacking in general frivolity. Sappho didn't care. Her aim was to get out of her father's house at her earliest convenience. Aphelos, to his credit and as has been said, never told anyone about Sappho's fling with Palabos, but that didn't improve her marital prospects. Having been rejected by the son of a major figure in Mytilene government made her suspect, if not an outright pariah. By the time Sappho was seventeen, she had determined the only way to liberate herself was to take a lover, and a wealthy one at that.

And so she came to Kekonimenos, a trader in refined silver and gold who was well respected in Lesbos society. He was thirty-four years old—twice Sappho's age—and quite well-to-do. He lived near the agora in a very large house and regularly offered generous gifts in sacrifice to Artemis on the city altar.

Kekonimenos was married, true, but that didn't matter to Sappho. Lots of men took mistresses. Sometimes they fathered bastards with them. But they were always generous to them, or so Sappho had observed. Kekonimenos's wife Maira had borne her husband three sons, Boros, Kastor, and Meurios. They were between five and ten years old and, like their father, quite handsome.

Sappho met Kekonimenos for the first time in a fairly prosaic way. She had gone to the market one afternoon to purchase strings for her lyre. Kekonimenos was there to sell a gold brooch to the proprietor, and not looking where he was going, accidentally stepped on Sappho's foot. Kekonimenos behaved as a gentleman should, with multiple apologies, and he offered to pay for Sappho's lyre strings. Sappho, seeing the piece of jewelry in his hand, realized he was well off and a worthy target.

She gave Kekonimenos her most winning smile. "I would not think to trouble you for a couple of pieces of gold, sir. But if you would do me the honor of walking me home, I would consider us even."

Kekonimenos, to Sappho's delight, did escort her home. And as they walked together, Sappho peppered him with questions. Where did he live? What did he do? Was he married? Had he ever traveled beyond Lesbos? Kekonimenos answered her questions happily, and Sappho laid on the charm. By the time they got to Skamandronymous's house, Sappho had appraised Kekonimenos as an intelligent, sensitive man far superior to Palabos, and she was certain Kekonimenos would accept her favors. She turned around to face him on the doorstep, as she had with Palabos three years earlier and smiled.

"Do I get to kiss you now?" she said.

"You have to ask?" Kekonimenos answered.

He was a good kisser.

And so Sappho became Kekonimenos's mistress. She was quite bold, often meeting him at his house in the middle of the day. Skamandronymous barely took notice that Sappho was out of the house nearly every afternoon, or that she seemed to be happy for the first time in years. He had grown disinterested in his daughter and concentrated on his other obligations.

And Sappho was happy. Even the hugging demon had ceased its nighttime visitations. Things were finally going her way.

Her first time in bed with her new lover was amazing. Like Agathon, Kekonimenos was gentle, but he was also experienced in a way Sappho figured Agathon was not. After being her uncle's plaything for most of her childhood, she had concluded he had never had what could rightly be called a successful relationship, liaison, or even an encounter, with an adult woman. Sappho had been his way of accessing pleasure for whatever reason unavailable to him from women his own age.

Midway through their lovemaking, the intensity of the experience with Kekonimenos began to build as if Sappho were swiftly climbing a steep ladder of sexual stimulation. It is relevant to note the Greek word for *ladder* is actually *klimax*. Sappho found herself gasping for air, shocked at the feelings Kekonimenos was giving her. For the first time since she was nine, she felt that curious burst of sensation like that which her uncle had given her. Only this time it was completely welcome. There was no sense of violation. The feeling started in her pelvis and exploded throughout her body, right to her fingertips, and she cried out in the ecstasy of it. Kekonimenos actually kept thrusting for another two minutes and the powerful feeling came again. By the time Kekonimenos was finished, Sappho was both thoroughly physically exhausted and sublimely fulfilled.

After a few minutes of lying there, listening to each other breathe, Kekonimenos turned to Sappho and caressed her cheek. "How was that?" he said.

Sappho was still stunned, but she had retained enough of her mental faculties to give a clever response. "You have to ask?" she said, her jaws agape. "What is it called?"

Kekonimenos smiled gently. "Orgasm," he said.

Sappho met Kekonimenos for lovemaking at least three times a week. She was not in love yet, but she could be. She wanted to be.

Six weeks into their affair, as they were lying in bed together one-day *post coitum*, Kekonimenos put his hand on Sappho's and smiled.

"Sappho, *agapē*," he said, "do you have any idea what you do to me?"

Sappho frowned, remembering her uncle asking her the same question, years ago. "Why don't you tell me?" she said.

"I think I'm in love," said Kekonimenos. "What do you think of that?"

Sappho's heart leaped in her chest. It was the first time since Thalia that she had come this close to what she wanted most—a committed monogamous relationship based on respect and trust.

And, of course, love.

"You love me?" Sappho ventured carefully.

Kekonimenos kissed Sappho's fingers. "I do," he said. "Listen, I want to be with you forever. I'm going to divorce my wife and marry you. I want to make you mine. Will you marry me, Sappho?"

Here it is, at last, Sappho thought. "Yes!" she said, abandoning all her caution. "Oh, yes, of course I will!"

And he made love to her again.

Sappho was glowing with happiness when she got home that afternoon. She would finally have what Thalia had been unable to give her. She would be married to a kind, sensitive, witty man. It would be a marriage not arranged by parents but born of love. And she did love Kekonimenos. Or, at least, she told herself she did. At any rate, how could she not love the man who had just professed his undying love for her?

Perhaps her certainty that Kekonimenos loved her was genuine. Perhaps it was what she chose to tell herself she believed. Either way, when she missed her period the following month, she barely gave it a thought. Kekonimenos would take care of her.

That was all that mattered.

It was frustrating to Sappho, however, that she could not tell her father about this happy turn of events, a situation entirely attributable to the fact her fiancé was, at the moment, still married to the mother of his children. Even Skamandronymous, who still cared that Sappho should marry a suitable man, would have raised an eyebrow at word of her engagement under such circumstances.

But Sappho was genuinely happy. She was happy for the first time since she was five years old and, of course, she could not remember that. It no longer mattered what her uncle had done to her. She had a real man now, a good man. A man who loved her for who she was, and who made her feel good about herself. Sappho celebrated her good fortune in song and felt she could dance with joy.

So danced the girls of Crete
Nimble on their feet
Softly round the shrine
On blossoms, grass divine

Sappho was already planning her wedding. As was customary, the event would last three days. On the first day, there would be a feast at Skamandronymous's house. Everyone who had a connection to the family would be invited, and Sappho herself would offer a sacrifice to Artemis. The second day would see the marriage ceremony itself. Sappho would be ritually bathed before the event to signify her purity—Sappho did recognize the irony of this. And on the third day, the guests would deliver gifts.

There would, of course, be music, wine and dancing. Sappho might even play her lyre herself. After all, a wedding was for highlighting the bride's beauty and virtue—why not her talent as well? To say Sappho was excited would have been a gross understatement.

Three months into Sappho's affair with Kekonimenos, it was no longer possible to deny that she was expecting his child. Sappho had not menstruated in that time and she was experiencing periodic morning sickness. She was not overly concerned. Kekonimenos loved her and he would also love their child. But the necessity of getting married as soon as possible had presented itself.

So, one afternoon, after her customary romp with Kekonimenos, she addressed their plans. "When can we get married, *agapē*?" she asked.

"Soon," said Kekonimenos. "These things take time."

"I hope not too much time," said Sappho. "How long does it take to get a divorce, anyway?"

"A few months, I would think," said Kekonimenos.

"You mean you don't know?" Sappho wondered. "I would have thought you'd have researched it by now."

"Patience," Kekonimenos admonished. "Let's not get in a hurry."

"Patience?" Sappho echoed, feeling sudden, prickling doubt. "You promised you'd marry me."

"And I will," insisted Kekonimenos. "I just need more time."

"How much time?" Sappho insisted. "How long are you going to make me wait?"

"I don't know," Kekonimenos snapped. "Stop nagging me, Sappho. Why all this rush to get married, anyway?"

"Because I'm pregnant," Sappho blurted, and she looked away, feeling like crying.

Kekonimenos took her chin in his hand and turned her face toward him. "Whose child is it?" he asked pointedly.

Sappho sat up in bed. "How can you even ask me that?" she said, appalled. "I have never been unfaithful to you!"

"So you say," said Kekonimenos. "How do I know it's true?"

"How dare you talk to me that way!" Sappho exclaimed. "*Agapē,* you know me!"

"Do I?" Kekonimenos said. "I'm not sure. Not sure at all."

"You would turn me away when I'm carrying your child?" Sappho said bitterly.

"Even the possibility that the baby is yours dictates that you should care for it."

Kekonimenos sat up in bed. "Sappho," he said mildly, "get out of my house. Get dressed and go home. Now."

Tears of frustration and shame welled up in Sappho's eyes. She willed them away. "How can you be so cruel?" she said. "I thought you loved me!"

"I thought I did too," said Kekonimenos distantly. "Now, I believe I asked you to leave."

Sappho nodded slowly, a knot tightening in her stomach. "Very well," she said. "I'll go. But I'm keeping our child. And when it is born, I hope it looks exactly like you, so that everyone will know the truth of its parentage."

Sappho got out of bed, jerked on her clothing and sandals, and left Kekonimenos in his bedroom.

Sappho made it all the way back home before the floodgates of her eyes burst open. Now she sat on her own bed and wept. She felt used. She felt dirty. Everything she once believed about men had again been proven true. Kekonimenos had never loved her, never intended to marry her and give her a home. He had been after an easy roll in the hay, and that's exactly what Sappho had been duped into giving him. Now she would be a single mother with a bastard child, not even regarded by the father of that child. Sappho was cursed, it seemed to her. And now she had to do one of the most difficult things in her life.

She had to tell her father.

Sappho had absolutely no idea how Skamandronymous would react to the news she was pregnant. He would not be happy, of course, but whether he would actively punish her or simply ignore her further was up in the air as far as Sappho was concerned. Either way, life for Sappho would not be pleasant. But there was nothing she could do to keep him from discovering the truth. Pregnancy was not something that, ultimately, could be concealed. It would become obvious in time.

Sappho fully expected her father to be ashamed of her. But would he recognize his grandchild? Sappho did not know. She had always thought of her father as kind and gentle. But she had, in part, blamed him for Agathon's crimes toward her. And Skamandronymous himself had blamed Sappho for the same. Sappho loved Skamandronymous deeply and always had, but she dreaded going to him about her predicament; however, upon deeper reflection, Sappho estimated things would be much worse for her if Skamandronymous discovered the truth through the inevitable course of nature, as opposed to by Sappho proactively telling it to him before it became obvious to the world.

And on top of everything, Sappho mourned the loss of Kekonimenos, her first true lover. As cruel as he had been to her at the end, she missed him terribly. He had made her feel good without taking anything from her, at least in the beginning. She ached for this loss as much as anything else.

Sappho sang:

The moon
And the seven daughters
Settle
On the horizon
Swift turns the hour
And I lie in bed alone

Sappho reckoned she had been pregnant for no more than ten weeks. She wanted to strangle the slave who had told her eating fennel would prevent this. But perhaps no birth control method was perfect, she supposed. At any rate, she would begin to show soon, and at that point, everyone would know what kind of woman she was.

And what kind of woman was she? Try as she might, Sappho could not view her situation from an angle that showed what had happened to her was her own fault. Agathon had molested her. Thalia had rejected her. She had loved—she told herself—Kekonimenos in good faith and he had rejected her as well. Her father would not speak to her. Sappho decided again she was indeed cursed, but more than that she felt betrayed. No one in her life ever stayed. Everyone left even Irini. *But that's not fair to her*, Sappho thought. Irini had died protecting Sappho. It seemed to her that Irini had loved her the most.

I don't deserve this, Sappho told herself.

And she certainly didn't. But it would be some time before she entertained the notion that her own point of view might be part of the problem.

It was a week after Kekonimenos had spurned her that Sappho screwed up the courage to tell her father about her delicate condition. She dismissed the kitchen slaves from cooking that night so that she could prepare her father's supper herself. Sappho had never been what could rightly be called a talented cook, but she knew the basics and hoped Skamandronymous would appreciate the gesture. Sappho puzzled over the lamb and chickpeas. She overbaked the flatbread. She had better luck slicing cucumbers and pitting olives. And she opened a jar of spiced Athenian wine as a special treat for her father. She did everything she could think of to please him before hitting him with her news.

And Skamandronymous rose to the occasion. He ate and drank with enthusiasm, and Sappho had his full attention for the first time in years. *I should have tried this before*, Sappho thought. *The old cliche about the way to a man's heart being through his stomach must be true.* Sappho actually felt a glimmer of hope that her father would react favorably to her coming declaration.

She waited until Skamandronymous was eating dessert—a passably good honey pie—before she spoke. "Papa," she ventured, "did you enjoy your supper?"

Skamandronymous looked at his daughter—if not with love—with appreciation. "I did," he said. "Your cooking is getting better."

Sappho smiled. "I'm glad you like it," she said.

"I may have been wrong about you, Sappho," her father continued. "You might make a good wife after all. Not that you should do slaves' work. But a good wife knows she must strive to please her husband."

"Yes," Sappho agreed distantly.

"Sappho," said Skamandronymous, "I have been thinking. You must marry, and you must marry soon. I know a man on the high council who has recently been widowed. He has two small children and he needs help raising them. I have spoken with him about you, and he is receptive to the idea of a bargain. He has agreed to marry you without payment of dowry, on the condition that you are a virgin." Skamandronymous frowned. "I don't think it's necessary to tell him about… certain things. But he is a good and honorable man, Sappho. I have told him we have an agreement. Do you understand?"

Sappho nodded silently.

"Well, that wasn't very enthusiastic," said Skamandronymous, cross. "I would think you'd jump at the prospect of a good marriage at your age. Especially considering your natural liabilities."

"Papa," said Sappho softly, "I can't marry your friend."

"Why on earth not?" Skamandronymous asked.

"Because I'm pregnant," Sappho said simply.

Skamandronymous stared at her for a full minute before he responded. "Who is the father?" he asked quietly.

"Kekonimenos," said Sappho.

"The jewelry dealer?" Skamandronymous said.

"Yes," Sappho confirmed.

"How did this happen?" Skamandronymous asked.

"I should think that would be obvious," Sappho said bitterly.

"Don't take that tone with me," said Skamandronymous darkly. "I believe Kekonimenos is already married."

"Yes," Sappho confirmed. "With three sons."

"Go to your room," said Skamandronymous after a pause.

"Papa," said Sappho, "I'm not a child."

"Go to your room!" Skamandronymous shouted, pounding his fist on the table. "Now."

Sappho nodded slowly. "Very well," she said.

Sappho rose from the table and left her father fuming over his honey pie.

Sappho sat on her bed, staring at her lyre. Her father had taken her news better than she had feared. Still, though, he had not taken it well. She wondered what he would do once he'd had the opportunity to think about the situation for a while. Would he acknowledge his coming grandchild? Would he confront Kekonimenos? Sappho had no idea.

Sappho picked up her lyre and began to play one of her sadder songs. The music was soothing, and as she played, Sappho felt herself growing calm again. Everything was going to work out, she told herself. Irini had believed in her. Her mother had believed in her. Thalia had believed in her. Distracted, Sappho accidentally strummed a flat chord and frowned, annoyed, at the thought of those who had abandoned her.

But she played on.

By this point in her life, she had composed fifty or sixty songs. Most were about love. Some were purely instrumental. Others were poems. Some were long. Some were only a few lines. She played through them all now, her heartbreaking that there was no one left in her life who cared to listen. Sappho was alone.

Sappho played. Music was her solace. The chords were her confidants. Music didn't judge her, didn't reject or disappoint her. Her songs understood her in a way no man or woman could. Music had made her an object of beauty. And she needed it particularly now that she had become an object of shame. She had promised the ones she loved she would not abandon her songs, her craft, and she silently swore again that she would not.

Sappho refused to capitulate to life, even if life had other plans.

A few hours later, when Sappho's hands ached from playing, she sat upright on her bed at the sound of voices coming from the atrium—her father's and another man's. Sappho could not make out the words, but the conversation sounded heated. She rose from her bed and slipped quietly out of her room and down the hall to the atrium. She stopped short of the entrance and listened.

"I tell you, Skamandronymous," said the other man, "the girl is with child out of wedlock, and from an adulterous union, no less. This pregnancy is an affront to the goddess of chastity."

"I am not concerned about the goddess of chastity," said Skamandronymous. "You cannot ask what you are asking of me."

"You must listen to me!" came the voice. "The child must not be allowed to live."

"That will not happen, I say!" said Skamandronymous.

"You have no choice!" said the other voice. "Sappho has to die, too, to fully appease the goddess."

Sappho had heard enough. She stepped into the atrium and into the view of her father and the other man. She recognized him immediately. It was the priest of Artemis who kept the altar in the agora. He smiled at her darkly.

"You're saying my father should kill me?" she said. "How dare you!"

"Sappho," Skamandronymous said calmly, "stay out of this."

"I will not!" said Sappho. "This concerns me as much as it does you!"

"You are a disgrace to your father's house," said the priest. "You are beyond redemption."

"Perhaps," said Sappho. "But that is not for you to decide. I will stand before Artemis myself and be judged by her. Not you."

"No," said Skamandronymous softly. "I will not put them to death."

"But, Skamandronymous," protested the priest, "the goddess—"

"I will offer a choice kid in sacrifice to the goddess," said Skamandronymous. "Artemis will either accept it or not."

The priest scowled. "This is a dangerous choice, Skamandronymous," he said. "You risk her wrath upon your household."

"My household is in shambles," said Skamandronymous. "My wife and brother are dead. My daughter has betrayed me."

"You cannot choose to—" began the priest.

"But I will disown her," said Skamandronymous. "Tomorrow she will leave this house, never to return."

"Papa?" Sappho said, not believing her ears.

"Don't ever call me that again," said Skamandronymous. "You are a stranger to me now."

"Good, Skamandronymous," said the priest with a bow. "Heaven's grace be upon you. I take my leave." And he ducked out of the atrium.

Sappho gaped at her father.

"Close your mouth, girl," said Skamandronymous harshly. "Go back to your room and stay out of my sight."

Sappho nodded and retreated from her father's presence. Skamandronymous limped toward his garden.

Two hours later, Sappho heard a knock at her bedroom door as she lay silently on her mattress. She was not crying. She had no tears left. She was still stunned at her father's declaration and had been wondering what would become of her, should she have to live on the street.

Sappho looked up from her pillow. Thalia was standing in the doorway. Sappho blinked, unbelieving, then stared when her mind confirmed what her eyes were telling it. Thalia stared back for a moment before she spoke.

"Sappho," she said, "your father told me what happened. I wanted you to know that I'm sorry."

Sappho said nothing.

"I wanted you to know," Thalia continued, "that I'm still your friend. If you want, you can come live with my parents and me. They're willing to take you in."

Sappho did not respond.

"Sappho," said Thalia, "I love you. Come live with me."

Too late, Sappho thought. She turned over in bed, her back to the door.

She did not see Thalia wait, watching her, for a full five minutes before she left. She did not see Thalia at all ever again.

Part Two
Ortygia 609–604 BCE

ἐκ λόγου γὰρ
ἄλλος ἐκβαίνει λόγος

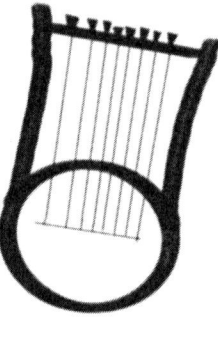

Sappho's father allowed her to pack one traveling bag, along with her lyre, before he took her to the harbor the following morning. Simonides and his ship, *Seirēn*, were there. Skamandronymous had not told Sappho where she was going or what would become of her. He had, in fact, said very little to her since waking her up from a fitful slumber an hour earlier.

Sappho blinked in the sunlight. Simonides approached from the ship, walking up the quay toward his employer and his daughter. "Good day, boss," he said. "Nothing to deliver today. In fact, we're preparing to depart."

"Yes, I know," said Skamandronymous. "And I want you to take her with you." He indicated Sappho, who was quite aware her father hadn't spoken her name.

"Take her?" Simonides echoed. "Take her where?"

"What is your most distant port?" Skamandronymous asked.

"As distant as distant gets, boss," answered Simonides. "We are going as far as Sicily this time."

"Then take her to Sicily and be done with her," said Skamandronymous.

"Certainly," said Simonides cautiously. "But I have to wonder why you'd put a pretty young thing like her on a boat full of sex-starved sailors. You have a great deal of faith in your fellow man, sir."

"I have faith in you, captain," said Skamandronymous. "And I have faith in the persuasive nature of refined gold."

He offered Simonides a small, heavy leather bag. Simonides opened the bag and his eyes widened. "How much is there?" he stammered.

"Twenty or so ingots," Skamandronymous replied. "About eleven minae altogether in weight, I should think. A gift from the girl's... friend."

"This is mine?" Simonides said.

"If you can guarantee her safety until you reach port," said Skamandronymous evenly.

Simonides nodded. "I believe I can say we are in agreement," he said.

"Good," said Skamandronymous. "If you will excuse us a moment."

Simonides bowed respectfully. "Of course."

Skamandronymous pulled Sappho aside. "Sappho," he said, "I want you to know I love you. I will always love you. That has not changed. It will never change. But what you have done is at odds with the sort of man I am. Do you understand?"

"You mean I am a danger to your reputation," said Sappho.

"You can no longer stay in Mytilene," insisted Skamandronymous, ignoring her. "I'm doing this for you as much as I am for me. You'll have a fresh start in a new country. No one will know your past. No one will know anything you don't tell them." Skamandronymous brushed an imaginary tear from his eye before continuing. "I'm sorry for calling you a stranger to me. You will always be my daughter. I hope, one day, this will all make sense to you."

Sappho nodded sullenly. "Oh, I understand, Papa," she said.

"Now go," said Skamandronymous. He gave Sappho a quick kiss on the forehead, then turned and limped away.

Sappho picked up her bag and her lyre and turned to Simonides, who was standing a few yards away, where *Seirēn* was docked. He smiled and beckoned to her. Sappho walked toward him.

"We must get you on board, miss," said Simonides to Sappho. "We're sailing in about an hour."

"All right," said Sappho woodenly.

Simonides led her up the gangplank and onto *Seirēn's* deck, past twelve staring, sweaty sailors. Sappho did her best to ignore them all. Aft of the mast, there was a cabin, and Simonides ushered Sappho inside.

Sappho found herself in a smallish room, lighted with a bronze oil lamp. There was also a hammock, a chamber pot, and a small table and stool.

"This is my cabin," said Simonides. "It's yours, for the duration."

"Where will you sleep?" Sappho asked.

"On deck with the men," said Simonides. "And before you object, it will be a lot safer for you that way. Most of them don't see a woman for weeks at a time."

"Thank you," said Sappho.

"I must say," said Simonides, "that's a nice lyre you've got there."

"Do you play, captain?" Sappho asked.

"Me?" Simonides laughed. "Not hardly. What kind of music do you play?"

"I mostly play my own songs," said Sappho modestly.

"A musician and a poet," said Simonides. "I'm impressed. What are your songs about?"

"I've written a variety of pieces so far," said Sappho. "But I specialize in short songs to the greater glory of Aphrodite."

"Love songs, eh?" Simonides said with a wry smile. "You'd definitely better not spend much time on deck. You'll give the men ideas."

"In my experience," said Sappho, "men have ideas independent of a woman's actions."

"Perhaps you're right," allowed Simonides. "Anyway, let me know if you need anything miss…"

"Sappho," she said. "My name is Sappho."

"Great Zeus's toenails!" said Simonides. "You're the boss's daughter! I thought I recognized you. Haven't seen you in at least three years. Why are you leaving Lesbos?"

"My father feels my behavior is incompatible with his social standing," said Sappho. "I'm not precisely what you'd call a well-mannered daughter."

"Well," said Simonides in embarrassment, "I don't mean to get in your business. I need to see to the ship. I'll be back once we're underway."

"All right," said Sappho neutrally, and she sat in the hammock.

Simonides glanced at Sappho for an instant before ducking out the door to the main deck.

Sappho found herself exceedingly lonely over the next few days. She missed her mother and Irini. She missed Thalia. She even missed her father and Kekonimenos, as much as they had misused her. Sappho needed a friend.

Simonides turned out to be very attentive. He checked on Sappho several times each day and spoke gently to her each time. He made sure she had plenty to eat and drink, and Sappho suspected he treated her much better than even his own men. Not that he was a cruel captain; he rarely raised his voice in anger to the other sailors. Simonides simply seemed to care deeply that Sappho was comfortable.

To pass the time on the voyage, Sappho played her lyre almost constantly. It had been a while since she wrote a song, and *Seirēn* had no papyrus or wax tablets for recording new poems, so Sappho concentrated on pieces she had already written. Most days, she played until her fingers were sore. And she had to replace broken strings many times.

On the ninth day at sea, Simonides came to Sappho around midday. Sappho was playing her lyre, as usual, but she lowered her hands when the captain entered the cabin.

"I'm sorry," said Simonides. "You didn't have to stop."

"I don't mind," said Sappho agreeably. "I have to take lots of breaks. I get tired."

"How long have you been playing?" Simonides asked.

"I'm not really sure," said Sappho. "A couple of hours, maybe."

"No," said Simonides kindly. "I didn't mean today. I meant in your lifetime."

"Oh," said Sappho. "About eight years."

"I think you're rather good," said Simonides.

"Thank you," said Sappho. "Would you like to sit down?"

"Uh, sure," said Simonides. He sat down on the stool.

"I meant with me," said Sappho. "In the hammock."

Simonides gave Sappho a questioning look, but he rose from the stool and sat down beside Sappho in the hammock, which sagged heavily under their combined weight. Sappho placed her lyre on the floor. Then she placed a hand on Simonides's thigh. Something inside her told her what she was about to do was foolish, but her crushing loneliness was overwhelming her.

"How long has it been for you, captain?" she asked.

"How long?" Simonides said.

"Since you were with a woman," Sappho clarified.

"I don't think—" Simonides began.

"Good," Sappho interrupted. "Don't think."

And she kissed him. Simonides rose to the occasion and kissed her back. The kiss lasted many moments before Simonides pulled back. Sappho put her hand on the back of his head and pulled him to her again. Simonides resisted.

"I don't think this is a good idea, is what I was trying to say," he said, smirking.

"It's all right," said Sappho, irritated. "I'm already pregnant."

"That's not the point," said Simonides, putting his hand on hers and lowering it to her lap. "Your father paid me well to keep you safe from the men on this boat. That includes me."

Simonides rose from the hammock. Sappho scowled. "Don't you find me attractive?" she asked bitterly.

"I do," affirmed Simonides. "But you represent trouble I don't need."

Sappho fumed. "But what about what I need?" she asked.

"What you need," said Simonides, "I cannot give." He moved toward the door. "Do keep playing," he said. "You have a gift. I hope you find what you're looking for."

And he left her alone in the cabin. Sappho pounded her fists on her thighs in frustration. *Am I losing my touch?* she wondered to herself. It struck her that what she had actually lost was Simonides's friendship. And with that realization, she felt more alone than ever.

After *Seirēn* had passed twelve weeks at sea, Sappho reckoned she was on the brink of madness. She had never been cooped up in such surroundings in her life, and she despaired at ever seeing the moon and the stars again. She loved her father, but now she was beginning to wonder why. How could he have been so cruel as to send her away in this manner? Simonides had been perfectly cordial with her since she had made her pass at him, and she returned his cordiality with courteous disdain. She hoped Sicily would be more inviting.

On the afternoon of the ninety-second day, the captain came to her in the cabin. She looked up at him with only mild curiosity. "Yes?"

"We're arriving in port at Ortygia in a few hours," said Simonides. "I was wondering if I could ask a favor of you."

"Ortygia?" Sappho echoed without interest.

"It's an island off the east coast of Sicily which serves as the center of the capital city of Syracuse," Simonides explained. "It's where you get off."

"I see," said Sappho. "What favor?"

"Well," said Simonides as he scratched his scruffy beard, "the men have asked if you would be willing to play one of your songs for them."

"Really?" Sappho said. "What for?"

"They've been listening to you practice for weeks now," Simonides said. "And they're curious. They've been asking a great many questions about you, actually."

Sappho nodded. "All right," she said. "Now?"

"If that's convenient," said Simonides.

"Oh, yes," said Sappho. She rose, picked up her lyre, and followed Simonides on deck.

The sailors stood on the deck, staring at her. Sappho glanced around. "I'll need someplace to sit," she said to Simonides.

"Yes, of course," said Simonides quickly, and he dragged over a three-legged stool. "Will this do?"

"I suppose," answered Sappho. She sat, tuned her lyre, and began to play. She played through one instrumental stanza before singing:

Sea nymphs
Bring my brother home
Guard him, grant him
Every wish

So shall end
His stray from home
As friends dance and
Foes mourn

Let him honor his
Sister still at home
Who beat the troubles
That made her weep

Sappho sang three more verses, then finished the piece with a flourish of chords and lowered her hands from the strings. The sailors were silent for almost a minute, and Sappho vaguely wondered if she had offended them. She had chosen that particular song because it referenced the Nereids, the sea nymphs all sailors would be familiar with. But then the men began to applaud. They clapped softly at first, but then the flood of their appreciation burst forth and some of them even cheered. Sappho blushed for the second time in her life.

"Far sweeter music than I knew a lyre could produce," said Simonides appreciatively. "More melodious than purest gold."

"I shall have to remember that comparison, captain," said Sappho, embarrassed. "I might incorporate it into a song some time."

"I'd be honored," said Simonides.

"Seriously, captain," said Sappho to Simonides, "what did you really think of it?"

"I thought it was divine," said Simonides.

"I think it needs a little work," said Sappho.

"Artists!" sighed Simonides. "Always their own harshest critics."

"It's true," Sappho admitted.

There was an uncomfortable silence, then Simonides took charge. "All right, you dogs," he said to the sailors, "every man to his station! I want to be in port in three hours!"

The men groaned and got to work. Simonides turned to Sappho. "You should get back indoors. I appreciate your giving them a song, but right now you're a distraction."

"Of course," said Sappho. And she returned to the captain's cabin.

Simonides was an experienced mariner, though he lacked even the simplest of navigational instruments. The astrolabe would not be invented for centuries to come, the sextant centuries later, and ships had to stay within sight of shore much of the time or risk getting hopelessly lost on the Great Sea. But Simonides had made the trip to Sicily many times and his estimation of their arrival time was sound. They reached the harbor at Ortygia a little less than three hours later. He came to tell Sappho this once the ship had moored, but she had already guessed that they had arrived by the shouting she could hear on deck. Sappho had packed her belongings and made herself ready to disembark by the time Simonides came for her, and she followed him off *Seirēn's* deck and onto the planks of the quay.

Sappho looked around. She could see hundreds of people, men, women, and children of every extraction, milling about, caring nothing for this smallish wine boat that had just docked, or for her foreign-looking passenger. Sappho was overwhelmed.

Simonides hovered nearby. "What are you going to do, miss?" he asked.

Sappho hadn't a clue. "What would you suggest?" she said.

"Your best bet for lodging is closer to the center of town," said Simonides. "You can get a ride with one of the merchants taking goods into the city. Or you can walk."

"A ride sounds good," said Sappho. "I have no idea where I'm going."

"Do you have any money?" Simonides asked gently.

"I have a few staters, I think," said Sappho halfheartedly.

Simonides brought out the bag of gold Skamandronymous had given him on the Mytilene quay. He offered Sappho three ingots of the precious metal. "Here, take these."

"Oh, no," said Sappho, flustered. "I couldn't. My father gave that to you for my safe passage."

"And he overpaid me greatly, too," said Simonides. "I insist. You need them more than I."

"Thank you," said Sappho gratefully. And she accepted the gold. "How much is it?"

"Not much," Simonides admitted. "About a mina and a half, I guess. But it's worth far more than your staters, I can assure you."

"I'm obliged," said Sappho.

Simonides pointed to some buildings beyond the quay. "Over there, behind the warehouses, is a tavern," he said. "Don't go inside if you value your safety. It's full of whores and thieves. But you can find a merchant wagon outside that should suit your purposes. I wish I had the leisure to show you more of the city, but I have duties to attend to for your father."

"I understand," said Sappho. "Thank you, captain."

"You're welcome, Miss Sappho," said Simonides. "I hope I see you again."

"So do I," said Sappho candidly.

Simonides nodded, bowed, and then quickly turned and returned to the ship, already shouting orders to his men. Sappho stood staring at the ships for a moment, then picked up her lyre and started walking slowly in the direction Simonides had indicated. Once she was among the warehouses, Sappho felt as if she had been totally consumed by the darkest part of the city. She left the warehouses behind and looked around for the tavern Simonides had mentioned. It was easy enough to find and Sappho approached it slowly.

The tavern's doorway had no door, and there was a great deal of commotion coming from within. Sappho stood in the doorway and watched the patrons. She had never seen such a shady collection of people in her life. It was obvious to her that Simonides had been quite correct about whores and thieves, and while Sappho knew she should keep her distance, some small part of her wanted to join in their revelry. She started to take a step inside when a voice startled her from behind.

"Just what do you think you're doing?"

Sappho jumped in surprise. She turned to face the man who had spoken. He was dressed like a day laborer and his hair and beard were unkempt. He was certainly below Sappho's station, she thought; but then she realized, in Ortygia, she had no station.

"I was just—"

"Just about to get yourself in a whole mess of trouble," the man interrupted.

"That place ain't fit for a proper lady."

"How do you know I'm a proper lady?" Sappho asked.

"Your clothes is clean," said the man. "And your jewelry is nice. You're not from around here, are you?"

"Is it that obvious?" Sappho said.

"Yep," said the man. "Now, get away from here." He turned away and started to walk off.

"Wait!" Sappho said.

The man turned around. "Yeah?"

"Are you going into the city?" Sappho asked.

"What's it to you?" the man said.

"I need to find someplace to stay," said Sappho. "Someplace nicer than this. Do you have an ass or a wagon or anything?"

"I hope so," said the man. "I'm taking some stuff to market."

"Can I get a ride with you?" Sappho asked.

"You got any money?" the man asked.

"Some," said Sappho.

The man grinned. "Yeah?" he said. "Show it to me."

Sappho withdrew one of Simonides's gold ingots. "I have this," she said. "Is it enough?"

"Let me see that," said the man.

Sappho gave the ingot to the man and he tested its weight then bit it. Then he grinned. "This'll do," he said. "Follow me."

The man led Sappho away from the tavern and to a wagon loaded with half a dozen small clay amphorae. Two donkeys were hitched to the wagon.

"Pardon me for asking, sir," said Sappho, "but are you a wine dealer?"

"Olive oil," said the man. "Why do you ask?"

"My father is a wine dealer," said Sappho.

"Good for him," said the oil merchant. "Now get on the wagon. I ain't got all day."

Sappho complied and the merchant drove the wagon away from the harbor.

The ride to the center of town took about half an hour, and Sappho was glad she had decided not to walk. If she had thought the harbor was unfriendly, it was nothing to what she was seeing now—hundreds of people going about their business, not stopping to greet each other as they did in Mytilene. Everyone seemed focused entirely on themselves and not at all on each other. It was utterly foreign to Sappho. Did anyone ever say so much as *good day* here? It appeared not.

The wagon stopped in front of a street shop with a canvas awning. The oil merchant got down from the wagon and motioned for Sappho to do the same. Sappho stood beside the wagon, holding her lyre and her traveling bag, without the slightest idea what she was going to do next.

The oil merchant started haggling with the shop owner as two strong-looking young men began to unload the amphorae of oil. Sappho watched awkwardly before finally raising her voice, "Excuse me?"

The oil merchant stopped haggling and glanced at her. "What?" he said.

"Where do I go from here?" Sappho asked.

The oil merchant shrugged. "Not my concern," he said. "Find yourself an inn. Good luck." And he returned to haggling with the shop owner.

Sappho looked up and down the street. There were many shops offering all manner of goods. It seemed to be the center of Ortygia's business district, and that one could purchase anything here. Sappho heard the sudden squawk of a bird and focused her eyes on a beggar sitting in the dust on the opposite side of the street. A gray parrot sat on his shoulder. "Alms for a blind man?" the parrot croaked. "Alms, please?"

Fascinated, Sappho started across the street—and was nearly run over by a speeding chariot pulled by two magnificent black horses. Sappho jumped backward out of the way and landed on her backside in the dust of the street. The chariot driver cursed over his shoulder at her as he drove around a corner. "Clear the damned street, woman, by Hermes!" he shouted. "You'll get yourself killed!"

Sappho sat up, dazed, and then quickly checked her lyre for damage. Finding it sound, she got to her feet, glanced carefully up and down the street, and crossed once she determined it was safe. She approached the beggar. He was dressed in a filthy gray chiton and his feet were bare. The parrot on his shoulder bobbed its head and focused on Sappho with its beady little eyes.

"Alms for a blind man?" it said. "Alms, please?"

"Good day," Sappho said to the blind beggar. "You have a very talented bird, sir."

"He's a damned nuisance, my lady," said the beggar. "I taught him to speak for me, but now he won't shut up."

"Well," said Sappho, "I think he's wonderful."

"Where are you from, lady?" the beggar asked. "I don't recognize your accent. Crete? Hellas?"

"Lesbos," said Sappho. "I'm from Lesbos."

"Lesbos?" the beggar echoed. "Never heard of it. Must be far away."

"It is," said Sappho wistfully. "I actually just got here."

"I hate to ask you," said the beggar, "seeing as how you just arrived, but do you have any money?"

"I have a little," said Sappho, "but I need to keep at least some of it. I don't know where I'm going to spend the night. And I just paid half a mina of gold to get a ride here from the harbor."

The beggar spat in the dust. "Half a mina?" he said, disgusted. "You've got even less sense than this parrot here. You could have gotten a ride for less than half a stater."

"I didn't know," said Sappho. "My father always handled the money."

"How much gold do you have left?" the beggar asked.

"About a mina, I think," said Sappho. "I don't know for certain."

"It's dangerous for a nice young lady like you to walk about the city with that much gold on her," said the beggar shrewdly. "Best to break it up. I have a hundred staters of white gold in my bag here, the profits of a week's worth of donations. Give me the rest of your gold, and they're yours."

Sappho hesitated. She was naturally cynical, but something told her to trust this man. "All right," she said, and she handed over the two remaining gold ingots.

The beggar gave her his bag. Sappho glanced at its contents. The pieces of money could only loosely be called coins. Metal currency in those days consisted of roughly disc-shaped lumps of electrum, a prized natural alloy of gold and silver commonly found in riverbeds, known colloquially as *white gold* or sometimes just *gold*. Pure gold was known as *refined* gold. Pure gold and silver minted coins were about a century in the future, and the practice of embossing money with images even further. The lumps were stamped or incised with punches or grooves to show they were pure electrum all the way through but were otherwise unmarked.

Sappho nodded. "Thank you, sir," she said gratefully.

"You're welcome, my lady," said the blind beggar. "Now, go someplace else. This part of the street is mine."

"I don't suppose you know where I can find an inn?" Sappho said hopefully.

The beggar pointed down the street. "That way," he said. "Good day."

"Good day," said the parrot, bobbing its head. Then it uttered an oath Sappho was not familiar with and squawked loudly.

Sappho walked down the street in the direction the beggar had indicated. It was late afternoon and the light was beginning to fade. She knew she would have to find a place to spend the night soon. She walked for nearly half an hour, and she was tired and hungry. Finally, she came to a large building on the outskirts of the business district. It looked like an inn. Finally, feeling some hope, Sappho stepped cautiously inside.

The inn's main room was only half full but alive with activity, and Sappho was encouraged to see that its patrons appeared more respectable than those of the tavern near the harbor. About a dozen people, both men and women, sat at tables, eating and drinking and engaging in lively conversation. A fire burned cheerily in a fireplace opposite the front door. Sappho stepped up to a smallish bar where a woman in her mid-forties stood, cleaning a clay bowl with a rag. "Good evening," Sappho said politely.

"Good evening, yourself," said the woman. "You're not from around here."

"No," confirmed Sappho. "I just arrived from Lesbos."

"Lesbos, eh?" the woman said. "You're a real traveler, aren't you?"

"Apparently," Sappho agreed.

"Look at this!" said the woman, raising her voice. "We've got a customer from the other side of the world! Our most distant one yet!"

The inn's patrons laughed merrily then returned to their conversations.

"I don't suppose that comes with a discount?" Sappho said.

"Nope," said the woman. "I guess you're wanting a place to stay."

"Yes," said Sappho. "I have money."

"Do you, now?" the woman said, amused. "How much?"

"About a hundred ten staters of gold, I think," said Sappho.

"Hopping Hera on a pony!" exclaimed the woman. "Our richest customer yet, too. Let me see them."

Sappho opened the beggar's coin bag and showed its contents to the woman. The woman reached into the bag and took out a handful of the rough, striated electrum globules. She stared at them for a moment then sighed. "You don't know much about money, do you, missy?" she said.

"What do you mean?" Sappho asked, taken aback.

"These coins are one-twelfth staters each," said the woman. "You've got a lot less here than you thought, girl. Where did you get this?"

"A blind beggar in the marketplace gave it to me," said Sappho unhappily. "I gave him a mina of refined gold for them."

The woman sighed again. "Well, I hate to tell you this," she said, "but you've been had. This blind beggar, he had a gray bird on his shoulder?"

"Yes," confirmed Sappho. "A parrot. And it talked."

"That would be old Leotykhides," said the woman. "He's a real scoundrel. And he's not really blind, you foolish girl."

"I didn't know," said Sappho, crestfallen. "Shouldn't we tell the authorities?"

"No point," said the woman. "He's probably halfway to the mainland by now. I'm assuming you still need a place to stay?"

"Yes," said Sappho.

"Well," said the woman, "it's getting dark, and your money won't go as far as you thought. How would you like a job?"

"A job?" Sappho echoed.

"That's what I said," confirmed the woman. "It's been a real strain running this place alone since Hades was kind enough to take my husband last year. What are you good at?"

"I can sing," said Sappho. "And play the lyre."

"I'm talking about real work, girl," said the woman in exasperation. "Can you cook? Clean? Tend the fire and the lamps?"

"Yes," said Sappho uncertainly.

"Now, that sounded enthusiastic," said the woman, rolling her eyes. "All right, I'll give you a try. But if you turn out to be a lazy girl, you'll be out on your ass in the street before you knew what hit you."

"I understand," said Sappho, feeling a burst of hope.

The woman looked at Sappho appraisingly. "It is just you, right?" she said. "You don't have a boyfriend or a baby to get in the way, do you?"

Sappho hesitated a bit too long at the question.

"Out with it, girl," said the woman sternly.

"No boyfriend or anything like that," said Sappho. "But I am with child."

"Are you, now?" the woman said. "Well, I'm a fair-minded woman. When are you due?"

"I'm not entirely certain," admitted Sappho. "Fourteen, fifteen weeks, maybe."

"And when the baby comes," said the woman, "you won't let it get in the way?"

"No, ma'am," said Sappho sincerely.

"Very well," said the woman. "I guess we'd best find you a room, then."

"Thank you," said Sappho gratefully, "I'm sorry, your name is…"

"Alkestis," said the woman simply. "Call me Alkestis."

"And I'm Sappho," Sappho said.

"Pleased t'meetcha," said Alkestis.

Sappho's new employer turned out to be exceedingly kind, if a little rough around the edges. Alkestis quickly learned Sappho was not as experienced in domestic matters as she would have hoped. Still, it was easier than running the inn on her own.

The inn was called The Battered Muse, and Alkestis was certainly battered. Over the next few weeks, she told Sappho about her hellish marriage to a man named Euagoras, a drunkard and a lout. The inn was legally his when he was alive, an inheritance from his father, who had first opened the place. Euagoras had used Alkestis ill and worked her like a dog for thirty years. He had been particularly angry at her for her failure to produce him a child and had died of an excruciatingly painful bowel ailment after three decades of meanness. The local authorities were suspicious at first; it was no secret that Euagoras had beaten his wife incessantly. And there was an investigation into his death. It appeared Alkestis might be charged with murder until the doctors cut her late husband open and discovered his appendix had exploded, flooding his body with poisonous gangrene. Of course, medicine of that era knew nothing of the causes of infection, and the word *appendicitis* was millennia away from being coined. But it seemed clear to all concerned that Euagoras had died of natural causes. His abdominal cavity was a mess.

Sappho kept quiet about her own experience with familial abuse. She didn't want Alkestis to blame her as her father had done. But Sappho hoped, at some point, to be able to share her story with her employer. After all, she hadn't pried into why Sappho was expecting, but not married. It appeared as if Alkestis might be as fair-minded as she said.

Although Alkestis had initially talked down to Sappho about her musical skills, she quickly learned they were something she could capitalize on. Sappho played her lyre most of the time when she wasn't busy helping run the inn, and a few of the patrons overheard her practicing in her room. Eventually, one of them, a regular named Naukles, asked if Sappho would be willing to play for them all. Sappho agreed, so one day, seven weeks into her employment, she entered the common room with her lyre.

"Now, that's a fine-looking instrument, Sappho," said Naukles appreciatively.

"Much more impressive than your own, I'd be willing to bet," Alkestis grumbled under her breath. Then, louder, "Shame on you, Naukles, for badgering the poor girl. Can't you see you're embarrassing her?"

Sappho smiled at this first hint of true friendship she had seen in years, sat at one of the empty tables, tuned her lyre and began to sing.

Aphrodite on your throne
Zeus's daughter bless me
Please do not leave me alone
Or in love distress me

If you ever heard me pray
Come to me and listen
From your father's house today
As with gold you glisten!

Sparrows drew your chariot forth
Over lawn and garden
Beating wings o'er fallow earth
Bringing heaven's pardon

Then you came with blessed face
Goddess smile undying
Asked what darkens Sappho's days
Asked me why I'm crying

Sappho, who's your cherished dove?
Sappho, who belongs you?
Whom shall I convince to love?
Sappho, child, who wrongs you?

If she runs away from you
She will surely chase you
Though she rejects love from you
She cannot debase you

Come to me, I pray, my love
Free me from my wanting

You will be my ally, love
My desires daunting

If *Seirēn's* crew had been impressed by Sappho's talent, their appreciation was nothing to what greeted her now. This strange young sylph from Lesbos was now Ortygia's new star. After years of playing in relative obscurity, Sappho had found an audience equal to her skill. Alkestis thanked the gods for her good fortune. Sappho and her music were going to turn The Battered Muse into a shrine.

Over the next three months, Sappho learned a multitude of domestic skills and became a real asset to Alkestis in running the inn. Sappho played her lyre for the patrons at least once a week, and by the time her baby was due people were coming from all corners of the city just to hear her sing.

Although she started out as Sappho's boss, Alkestis quickly became her friend. Alkestis found that she was fiercely protective of Sappho, and would not hesitate to cut off any patron's beer if they attempted to harass her. Now that people were coming to The Battered Muse from places beyond the local neighborhood, she had to do that all too often. The strangers who came to the inn were bolder in that respect, but all quickly learned to leave Sappho alone. They could look, but not touch.

As for Sappho herself, she felt free for the first time in years. Alkestis was a demanding employer, but she treated Sappho equitably. She never asked Sappho to do anything she herself would be unwilling to do, and she gave Sappho an ear whenever she needed to talk.

One day, about a week and a half before Sappho's baby came, she and Alkestis were sitting at a table in the inn's common room after the bar had closed and the overnight guests had gone to bed. They were talking lightly about Sappho's music and drinking beer imported from Egypt. Sappho, who had grown up drinking her father's fine wines, found the beer bitter, but the alcohol was satisfying and so she put up with the taste.

After about an hour of small talk, Alkestis set her cup down and said, "Tell me about the baby's father."

Sappho frowned. "His name is Kekonimenos," she said. "He's rich and he's married."

"Ye gods," Alkestis interjected. "You had an affair with a married man? I thought you were smarter than that, Sappho."

Sappho sighed. "I am," she said. "But love and intellect are often at odds."

Alkestis topped off her cup from the pitcher on the table. "That's certainly true," she said. "I suppose he said he would marry you?"

Sappho blinked, surprised. "How did you know?" she asked.

"Men are all the same," said Alkestis, taking a swig of beer. "They'll say anything for a piece of tail."

Sappho smiled at Alkestis's slang. "Well," she said, "he said a lot of things. In the end, he discarded me the moment I became a liability."

"Typical," Alkestis muttered. "I suppose he swept in and seduced you, targeted you from afar?"

"Actually," said Sappho, "I initiated the relationship."

"More the fool, you," said Alkestis. "Why'd you do it?"

"The man I was betrothed to backed out of the deal," Sappho explained. "I needed another way out of my father's house."

"Apparently, you found it," Alkestis observed. "Why'd your intended back out?"

Sappho decided to trust Alkestis. It felt perfectly natural. "He caught me with another man," she said.

Alkestis gulped her beer. "Good heavens, Sappho," she said. "Are you good at anything besides music and getting into trouble?"

"Not really," Sappho admitted.

"So," said Alkestis, "how old were you when you started getting into that kind of trouble?"

Sappho frowned. "I'm not really sure," she said.

"You don't remember your first time?" Alkestis said incredulously.

"No," said Sappho.

"Were you drunk?" Alkestis asked.

"No," said Sappho. "I've never been drunk. I was too young."

Alkestis nodded in understanding. "Who was it?"

"It was my father's brother," Sappho said softly.

"Damn him," muttered Alkestis. "Did your father find out?"

Sappho nodded. "He blamed me," she said. "Threw me out of the house, and so here I am."

"Took his brother's side, did he?" Alkestis said.

"What did your uncle say?"

"Nothing," said Sappho. "He died before my father found out." She could not tell Alkestis about Irini. After years without speaking her name, Sappho found the word impossible to pronounce.

Alkestis leaned back from the table. "Well," she said, "pardon me for saying so, but it sounds like your father did you a favor sending you here. Personally, I'd love to strangle him for you."

Sappho frowned again and sipped her beer. "It's not his fault," she said.

"Bullshit," said Alkestis. "Every bit of it is his fault. Well, you're free of his judgment now. I hope you know that."

"I do," Sappho nodded. "Thank you for being my friend."

"You're welcome," said Alkestis. She raised her cup. "To friends."

Sappho smiled and raised her cup as well. "To friends," she agreed.

They both drank.

The baby was born in the middle of the morning eleven days later. Sappho was serving a late breakfast to some of the overnight guests of the inn when her water broke all over the clay floor of the common room. She doubled over in pain as the first contraction hit, dropping three cups full of grape juice, which spilled all over one of the guests.

"Watch it, you clumsy tart!" exclaimed the man whose chiton had been ruined.

"Alkestis!" cried Sappho, ignoring him. "I need you!"

Alkestis, who had heard the cups fall on the floor, was already by Sappho's side. "It's coming?" she said.

Sappho nodded and then gasped as the second contraction hit her. "It's coming *right now!*" she said.

"Here now!" said the irate guest. "What about my clothes?"

"What about them?" Alkestis snapped.

"That girl owes me a new chiton," said the guest.

"Can't you see this is an emergency?" Alkestis said.

"To Hades with your emergency," said the guest. "I demand compensation!"

"Forget about your bill, then," said Alkestis harshly. "That's your compensation. Now, get out of my inn."

"But—" the irate guest began.

"I said get out!" Alkestis repeated. "And don't come back!"

The man looked down at the juice stain, then met Alkestis's glare and thought better of whatever he had been about to say and left without a word.

The other patrons gathered around Sappho and Alkestis, concerned. Most of them were locals and regulars and knew Sappho personally. Alkestis lowered Sappho to the floor.

"Shouldn't we do this in one of the bedrooms?" Sappho asked between stabs of pain.

"No time," said Alkestis, peering under the hem of Sappho's peplos. "The baby's crowning."

Sappho had no idea what *crowning* meant, but it sounded serious.

"Don't we need a midwife?" Sappho said, panicking.

"Don't worry," said Alkestis calmly. "I've done this before. Now, push!"

Sappho gritted her teeth and followed Alkestis's instructions for the next hour and fifteen minutes. The pain was unbelievable. Nothing could have prepared her for it. It hurt to push, but she could not stop herself. She was on the verge of asking Alkestis to put her out of her misery when the pain suddenly stopped and she heard the baby's cry. Sappho looked up. Alkestis was smiling.

"That must have been some kind of miracle," Alkestis said, holding the baby in a linen towel. "I've never seen one come that fast. Congratulations, Sappho. It's a girl."

"It's a girl?" Sappho gasped. "Can I hold her?"

"Let's get you to your bed first," said Alkestis. "Then, yes. Any thoughts as to a name?"

"Yes," said Sappho. "Her name is Kleis."

Sappho sang:

My mother said
When she was a girl

Those girls with raven locks
Should wear a violet ribbon in their hair

My mother said
When she was a girl
Those girls with fiery locks
Should wear a crown of blossoms in their hair

Your mother says
Dear Kleis, my girl
For your fair auburn locks
There can be no decoration at all

Young Kleis was a fussy baby and kept Sappho quite busy attending to her. Had Alkestis not become Sappho's friend, she might have thrown Sappho out on her ass on the street as she had threatened to do the day she hired her. In reality, however, Alkestis had grown quite attached to Sappho and, rather quickly, to Kleis. Alkestis had never been a mother. She was quite happy now to be an aunt.

When Sappho wasn't busy helping run the inn or playing her lyre for the guests, she would often spend time in the common room, allowing Kleis to nurse and socializing with the regulars. Breastfeeding in public was not much of an issue in Greek society at that time, and Sappho was not embarrassed. Alkestis allowed Sappho some slack to care for the baby and even took frequent turns tending to her herself.

Sappho's song about Kleis's hair—she was born with a great brown shock of it—was the first of many she wrote for her daughter. In truth, Sappho wrote a lot of songs in those days; inspiration seemed to be all around. Ortygians continued to flock to The Battered Muse for Sappho's music and Alkestis was turning the largest profits in years.

But besides the money, Alkestis was glad to have a friend at last. When Euagoras was alive, she had not been allowed to make friends of her own. There were *his* friends and *their* friends, but not *her* friends. Sappho showed Alkestis the value of having another woman to talk to and confide in, and in this respect, Sappho had made Alkestis the wealthiest she had ever been.

The fact that Sappho had confided in her as well, revealing the socially damning details of her past, was not lost on Alkestis either. Sappho had not told her this, but Alkestis suspected Sappho had always been lonely. And aside from Thalia's doomed friendship, she was correct. And even Thalia had not known everything about Sappho. Sappho never told her of the hugging demon, for example. Alkestis reckoned they both were starved for a healthy friendship. This made their bond all the more fulfilling.

But as healthy as Sappho's friendship with Alkestis was, her inbred knack for finding the unhealthy eventually asserted itself. There was, among The Battered Muse's regulars, a very minor public servant named Diotrephes. He was twenty-four years old and rather handsome in a boyish, carefree way. He worked for the governor of Syracuse in some capacity, but he never talked in detail about that. He was actually quite modest, and that was the attribute that first attracted Sappho to him.

Diotrephes usually came to the inn every day for lunch, and of course, to hear Sappho play. He didn't eat to excess and Sappho was delighted to discover that he drank neither wine nor beer. She did not look down on those who drank alcohol at all—far from it. But Diotrephes's abstention made him unique among The Battered Muse's patrons, and this also made him very attractive, to Sappho's way of thinking.

After a few weeks of serving Diotrephes lunch, Sappho decided to introduce herself. And, true to her style, she employed a ruse. Sappho placed the lamb and chickpeas Diotrephes had ordered in front of him, then affecting dizziness, sat heavily in the chair beside him. She rested her serving tray and her elbow on the table then, a little dramatically, covered her brow with her palm.

Diotrephes looked at Sappho with concern. "Are you all right, miss?" he asked.

"Oh yes," Sappho sighed heavily. "At least, I will be in a few moments. I get so tired these days. I recently had a daughter, you see, and I never fully recovered from a difficult delivery. And now I have the duties of a mother on top of everything. Yes, very tired." And Sappho sighed again.

Diotrephes smiled kindly. "Maybe you should take a break."

"I would," said Sappho wearily, "but I have so much to do."

"Well," said Diotrephes, laying down the piece of bread he was eating, "I happen to know your employer quite well, actually. And I can say with certainty she wouldn't want you to suffer. Take a break, I insist. And if Alkestis says anything, I'll tell her I made you sit with me."

Sappho brightened carefully. This was going well. "You'd do that for me?" she said, placing a calculated hand on Diotrephes's arm.

Diotrephes did not react to her touching him. "Absolutely," he said. "A young woman should not have to work like a slave, even in the lower classes."

Sappho bristled inside at being called a member of the lower classes. Her father would have had words with anyone who dared suggest such a thing when she was younger. But she carefully concealed her irritation. "Thank you, sir," she said in a grateful tone.

"Would you care for some bread?" Diotrephes offered.

"Oh, I'm fine," said Sappho. "Alkestis feeds me well enough."

"Some wine, then," suggested Diotrephes. "I don't drink, but I have it on authority it's good here."

"That would be lovely," said Sappho. "Thank you. My name is Sappho."

"I know," Diotrephes chuckled. "Everyone here knows who you are." He waved Alkestis over from the bar. Alkestis approached the table, ignoring Sappho. "A cup of wine for young Sappho, here, please," he said. "She's...entertaining me."

"Right," said Alkestis neutrally, and she went to fetch Sappho's drink.

"You're not originally from Ortygia," said Diotrephes, smiling. "You're from the eastern islands. Let me guess. Lesbos?"

"Very good," said Sappho, impressed. "How did you know that?"

"It's your accent," Diotrephes explained. "I can tell by the way you drop your rough breathings at the beginnings of certain words. And you pronounce your long vowels differently. Do you know what a vowel is?"

So patronizing, Sappho thought, and before she could stop herself she said defensively, "Of course I do. I've been able to read and write since I was nine."

"So, women are taught to read in Lesbos?" Diotrephes said. "How fascinating!"

"Not all women," said Sappho, feeling a little pride. "Just me. My parents wanted me to be able to write down my songs. It's for posterity's sake."

Alkestis returned and placed a cup of wine in front of Sappho. Sappho looked up. "Thank you," she said.

Alkestis only nodded in reply and moved off.

"I didn't mean to offend you," said Diotrephes agreeably. "*Posterity* is rather a sophisticated word for a barmaid. You're not what you're pretending to be, are you?"

This was taking a turn Sappho hadn't counted on. Diotrephes seemed to be able to see right through her. Her gut was telling her to back off, but she felt committed now. "My father is a respected merchant and an important figure in the government of the city-state of Mytilene," she said. "I was brought up quite comfortably."

"And he sent you away because you got pregnant," concluded Diotrephes. "Now everything makes sense. Why else would a cultured, talented young woman be working in a dive like this? I am right, aren't I?"

"If this place is such a dive," said Sappho hotly, "why do you come here every day?"

Diotrephes winked at her. "I like the atmosphere," he said, and he ate a chickpea. "Would you like to be my escort sometime? There are parts of Ortygia you should see. The library, for one."

"A library?" Sappho gasped, forgetting herself. "Ortygia has a library?" She had never dreamed of seeing such a thing.

"Well, after a fashion," Diotrephes admitted. "A few hundred scrolls of papyrus from around the world, among other things. But it should impress an intellectual girl like you."

Sappho was completely disarmed. "When can we go?" she said eagerly.

Diotrephes smiled. "How about tomorrow after lunch?"

Sappho whirled toward the bar. "Alkestis, can I—"

"Yes!" said Alkestis loudly. "For Zeus's sake, yes. Did you think I wasn't listening?"

Alkestis offered to look after Kleis for Sappho the next day before Sappho had the opportunity to ask. Diotrephes came to the inn at midday as usual and Sappho served him his meal. She did not hang around his table this time. Alkestis was being so understanding about the trip to the library that Sappho didn't want to push her luck. Diotrephes stared at Sappho all the while he was eating his lunch, smiling at her in his enigmatic way. Sappho had not been this excited since she first tried the lyre at her ninth birthday celebration.

Finally, Diotrephes finished eating. He rose and approached Sappho where she stood beside the bar. "Shall we?" he said.

"Most definitely," said Sappho.

Diotrephes led Sappho out into the street. "I hope you don't mind walking," he said. "I've never been good with horses and my station doesn't merit a chariot."

Sappho felt she could fly. "Walking is fine," she said.

Diotrephes led Sappho through the city and into the marketplace where Sappho had been dropped off by the oil merchant on her first day in Ortygia. Sappho was paying little attention to her surroundings, but then she heard a familiar voice.

"Alms for a blind man?" the voice squawked. "Alms, please?"

Sappho quickly turned toward the beggar and his gray parrot sitting on the side of the street. Diotrephes noticed and asked, "What is it?"

Sappho pointed. "That beggar over there cheated me out of a mina of refined gold when I first came to Ortygia."

"Did he?" Diotrephes said, his eyes narrowing. "Do you know his name?"

"Leotykhides," said Sappho. "And Alkestis says he only pretends to be blind."

"Well, we'll soon sort this out," said Diotrephes firmly. And he took Sappho by the hand and boldly approached the beggar. "Good day to you, man," he said, smiling. "Leotykhides, isn't it?"

"Who wants to know?" Leotykhides asked.

"My name is Diotrephes. I'm a representative of the governor," Diotrephes said. "And you have ill-used a friend of mine, I believe."

"I don't think so, my lord," said Leotykhides respectfully. "I am but a humble, blind beggar."

Diotrephes nodded, then drew the bronze dagger he carried on his belt and thrust it at Leotykhides's face. The beggar instinctively flinched and dodged the blow he could clearly see coming.

Diotrephes smiled. "I'm glad we cleared that up," he said. "This is Sappho, a friend of mine and a local artist. You took a mina of gold from her a few months ago and exchanged it for…what?" he asked Sappho.

"A pile of worthless coins," Sappho said.

"I, I don't know what you mean," stammered Leotykhides.

"Oh, I think you know exactly what I mean," said Diotrephes calmly. "How much money do you have in your bag there? Never mind. Let's see." He leaned over and snatched up Leotykhides's bag of coins. He looked through the bag. "Well, this is disappointing," he said. "There are only about four staters here. I guess I'll have to take it out of your hide."

Leotykhides put up his hands in terror. "Please, lord!" he wailed. "Don't hurt me! Take the money! Only leave me in peace!"

"Keep your money," said Diotrephes, still smiling. "We don't want it. But if I ever see you on this street again, I'll have you arrested for fraud. Do you understand?"

Leotykhides got to his feet, clutching his bag of coins. "Yes, my lord," he said, bowing deeply. "Right away. I'm gone. Leaving now, never to return. Ah, my life is hard!" The parrot swore at Diotrephes as its master dashed away and into the crowd.

"There," said Diotrephes to Sappho. "I hope that satisfied you."

"Completely," said Sappho. "But I almost feel sorry for him."

"He's a gutter rat," said Diotrephes. "Even a slave is above his station. Come, let's continue."

The library was the most marvelous thing Sappho had ever seen. It was the size of the atrium in her father's house and the walls were covered in scrolls. In the middle of the room was a pedestal upon which rested a large, ancient-looking fired clay tablet covered in wedge-shaped markings.

"What is this?" Sappho asked, fascinated.

"That is something very special," said Diotrephes. "It's a tablet from beyond the Euphrates, telling an ancient story from that part of the world."

"You mean this is writing?" Sappho said in wonder. She peered carefully at the markings. "Can you read it?"

Diotrephes laughed politely. "No one in Ortygia can," he said. "Not even the librarian. But the trader who brought it here from Egypt said it is the tale of King Gelgames and his quest for heaven's bull."

"What does that even mean?" Sappho asked.

"I've no idea," Diotrephes admitted. "But it is a treasure nonetheless. I often come here just to look at it."

"I want to learn to read this," said Sappho.

"Good luck," said Diotrephes. "You'd have to travel much farther from your home than Ortygia to find someone to teach you."

"Someday, then, maybe," Sappho mused, disappointed. She turned her attention to the scrolls. "May I handle these?" She asked her companion.

"Of course," said Diotrephes agreeably.

Sappho took one of the scrolls from the wall. She unrolled it and read it.

ΟΙΚΟΣ ΜΕΝ ΠΡΩΤΙΣΤΑ, ΓΥΝΗ Δ' ΕΠΕΙΤΑ ΒΟΕΣ ΤΕ ΑΡΟΤΗΡΕΣ, ΘΕΡΑΠΩΝ Δ' ΕΠΙΜΗΛΙΟΣ, ΗΔΕ Δ' ΑΝΑΓΚΗ. ΟΙΚΟΣ ΓΑΡ ΚΕΝΕΟΣ ΠΟΛΛΟΙΣ ΕΠΙΤΙΜΙΟΝ ΕΡΓΟΝ.

"I recognize this," said Sappho. "It's from *Works and Days* by Hesiod."

Diotrephes smiled. "You're well-read," he observed. "Though, I would have expected you to pronounce it *Esiod*, as someone coming from Lesbos."

"I don't drop *all* my rough breathings," said Sappho primly. "Anyway, I had a governess who taught me poetry when I was a child. She was from Crete—well, Thrace, originally." Sappho frowned. It was the first time she had spoken of Irini since she came to Ortygia. As painful as the memory was, it felt good to talk about it with Diotrephes. Sappho replaced the scroll in its place on the wall. "I could come here every day and not get bored," she said.

"I'm pleased you like it," said Diotrephes. "It is but a small example of what the city has to offer."

"It makes me think of my own songs, and recording them," said Sappho. "I wrote them out on wax tablets when I was in Mytilene, but I'd like something a bit more permanent now."

"I'm having visions of a great library in the distant future where people can admire your poetry on clay tablets," said Diotrephes, amused.

"That's not what I mean," said Sappho. "I hate to impose, but do you think you could find me some papyrus and ink? My father would be grateful."

"I won't do it for your father, Sappho," said Diotrephes. "But I'll do it for you."

"Thank you," said Sappho earnestly.

"You're welcome," said Diotrephes. "Do you like Homer?"

"I adore Homer," said Sappho.

"Then look at this," said Diotrephes, pulling another scroll from the wall.

Sappho took the scroll from Diotrephes and read it. It was the invocation to the muse from the *Odyssey*.

She would have to return often.

When Sappho turned in that night after feeding Kleis, she could hardly sleep for thinking about Diotrephes. He was unlike anyone she had ever known. He was kind, gentle, and a real intellectual. And he knew exactly how Sappho's mind worked; the trip to the library proved this. For the first time since Kekonimenos, she could not deny the truth. Sappho was in love.

But she was determined not to ruin this. She was going to take things extremely slowly. She had rushed things with Thalia and with Kekonimenos and had gotten her heart broken both times. This time, Sappho pledged to herself, she was going to do things right. Diotrephes would be the one she had searched for her entire life, she was certain. This required delicate handling. She would not make the same mistakes again.

It was a testament to how much Sappho trusted Alkestis that she felt comfortable sharing her feelings regarding Diotrephes with her. Three days after the trip to the library, Sappho was sitting with her employer in the common room after the patrons had gone to bed. Sappho breastfed a contented Kleis as they talked.

"What do you know about Diotrephes?" Sappho asked Alkestis.

"He's a political hack," said Alkestis. "He works for the governor."

"That's not what I mean," said Sappho. "I want to know about *him*."

Alkestis smirked. "He's well-educated," she said. "And an honorable man."

"I think he's marvelous," said Sappho.

Alkestis gave Sappho an appraising stare. "Do you, now?" she said.

"What does that mean?" Sappho said, irritated. "Do you know something I should know?"

"I know nothing you shouldn't find out for yourself," said Alkestis, and she took a sip of beer.

"Don't play games with me, Alkestis," said Sappho severely.

"I'm not," said Alkestis. "I just think there are some things a woman should learn on her own."

Sappho shifted the baby in her arms. "I thought you were my friend," she said.

"I am your friend," Alkestis insisted. "But if I told you the details of every life lesson before you experienced them yourself, you'd never learn anything."

"I suppose," said Sappho sullenly.

"Now, don't you get that way with me, missy," Alkestis said sharply. "Don't forget how much you needed me when we first met."

"You needed me too, Alkestis," Sappho observed.

Alkestis chuckled. "That's certainly true," she said. "Now, let's change the subject."

So, Sappho continued to serve Diotrephes his lunch and to talk with him about poetry. Sappho remained as reserved as possible toward him, intentionally not flirting, though it was difficult to mask her enthusiasm when he spoke about her songs. Diotrephes seemed quite likely to be the person who appreciated Sappho's music the most, and Sappho reveled in his admiration. She hadn't had such an ardent enthusiast for her poetry since Thalia had made her promise not to stop singing. This, too, told Sappho Diotrephes was definitely the one.

Sappho was jolly and carefree in those days, blithe to the point that she sometimes neglected Kleis. Alkestis noticed this and made a point of bringing it to Sappho's attention. Sappho was irritated.

"Don't you want me to be happy, Alkestis?" she said.

"Of course I do," said Alkestis. "But you're a mother. You have responsibilities."

"Kleis doesn't go hungry," said Sappho defensively. "Have I ever forgotten to feed her?"

"No," Alkestis allowed. "But there's more to raising a child than feeding it. She needs your attention, Sappho. She needs your love."

Sappho bristled at this. "You think I don't love her?"

"Calm down, girl," said Alkestis wearily. "That's not what I said. I'm just saying Kleis deserves to be happy as much as you do."

Sappho frowned. "I'm sorry, Alkestis," she said. "And you're right. Kleis needs me. But she needs her Auntie Alkestis too. You love her as much as I do, yes?"

"It's true," Alkestis sighed. "She's like a daughter to me. And she needs us both. Just promise me you'll spend more time with her. Otherwise, she might grow up confused as to which one of us is her parent."

"I promise," said Sappho. "I love you, Alkestis. You're my best friend."

"I love you too," said Alkestis. "Don't you ever forget that."

A regular named Panaitios spoke up from across the room. "Another beer here," he said. "Or have you forgotten you have customers?"

"I'll get it," said Sappho, grabbing the pitcher of Egyptian beer. She carried it to Panaitios's table and refilled his cup.

"Many thanks," said Panaitios. As Sappho turned from him, he swatted her on the backside.

Sappho whirled to face Panaitios. "That will cost you your next drink, sir," she said.

"Lighten up, Sappho," said Panaitios. "It is a barmaid's job to be entertaining."

Suddenly, Diotrephes was standing beside Sappho. "Is this gentleman bothering you?" he asked, smiling.

Sappho frowned. "Not at all," she said.

"I'm not convinced," said Diotrephes, hanging onto his smile. "You, sir. Panaitios, isn't it?"

"Yeah," said Panaitios. "What's it to you?"

"I think you owe Sappho an apology," said Diotrephes.

"Come on," sputtered Panaitios. "I was just having a little fun with the girl."

"Sappho is not a girl," said Diotrephes. "She's a lady." His hand dropped to the hilt of his dagger. "Apologize. Now."

Panaitios's gaze met Diotrephes's, then moved down to the dagger on Diotrephes's belt. Panaitios got to his feet, reached into his purse, and dropped a one-sixth-stater coin on the table. "Keep the change," he said to Sappho, then exited the inn.

Sappho turned to Diotrephes. "Thank you," she said.

Diotrephes nodded as Alkestis joined them at Panaitios's empty table. "My pleasure," he said. "That man will not be welcome here again."

"I don't know how I'm going to keep him away," said Alkestis. "He's been coming here for years."

"I will enforce the ban," said Diotrephes firmly. "No one lays a hand on young Sappho, here."

"I don't want to ban him," said Sappho.

"Sappho," said Diotrephes, "you could theoretically press a charge for assault. That cannot be tolerated. What if he does it again?"

"He won't," said Sappho. "Not as long as you're here to protect me."

Diotrephes glanced from Sappho to Alkestis. Alkestis nodded. "Very well," said Diotrephes. "But he and I will have words if he ever behaves like anything but a gentleman from now on. Sappho, sit with me. Let's talk about poetry."

Panaitios stayed away from The Battered Muse for several days after that, not even speaking to Sappho except to place his order when he returned. Diotrephes, for his part, *was* the perfect gentleman, and Sappho was still taking things quite slow. She enjoyed talking with him when her duties allowed, and they made several more trips to the library, to the agora, and once to the governor's menagerie.

Sappho ached to tell Diotrephes she loved him, and for him to tell her he felt the same. But remembering her experiences with Thalia and Kekonimenos, she forced herself to remain silent. She wanted real love. True love. A monogamous affair for life with someone who treated her the way she wanted to be treated. The way she deserved. It was her deepest and most passionate wish and always had been. She was *not* going to spoil this.

Then, one day, when Kleis was three months old, Diotrephes invited Sappho to go stargazing with him that night at the harbor. Sappho, who had not been to the harbor since she arrived in Ortygia, gladly accepted. She had never seen the city at night, and she imagined it might be rather dangerous, with thieves and murderers going about, but with Diotrephes as her escort, she did not feel afraid.

They set out shortly after sunset, once the inn's common room had closed. As was their custom, they went on foot. There was very little activity on the street. In those days, people went to bed when it grew dark. Diotrephes carried neither lamp nor torch, preferring instead to find his way by moonlight. Sappho marveled at his easygoing confidence. She knew no one else who would be so comfortable walking the streets of Ortygia after dark.

They reached their destination after almost an hour of walking. The harbor lay before them in the moon's silver light, which reflected from the glassy surface of the calm water. The waves did little to disturb the image of a great mirror extending out into the inky horizon, where it met the black firmament of the night sky. Sappho laughed as she ran down to the beach, kicked off her sandals, and splashed into the shallows.

Diotrephes stood back and watched Sappho play happily in the surf. He could not know what this excursion meant to her. He appreciated Sappho and wanted to stimulate her mind and senses. She was the most beautiful person he knew.

Eventually, Sappho came back to her friend. "Happy?" he asked.

"Oh, yes!" said a joyful Sappho. "Come, Diotrephes, join me on the sand." Diotrephes bent over and took off his sandals. "We can lie just above the water and watch the stars," he said.

Diotrephes lay down in the sand, his feet to the waves, and watched Sappho dance in front of him. Sappho splashed and played before her friend. Her heart was near to bursting for love of him. Finally, she ceased her frolic and turned to face Diotrephes. Was it time? She thought so.

Slowly and deliberately, Sappho wriggled out of her peplos and pulled it over her head, tossing the empty garment on the sand. Her undergarments quickly followed. Naked before Diotrephes, except for her jewelry, she carefully approached him where he lay and knelt beside him.

Diotrephes wore his customary, slightly amused smile. "What is this?" he asked. His nonchalance was maddening, Sappho thought, and it doubled the desire inside her. She hadn't felt this kind of wanton, carefree abandon since the early days with Thalia, so long ago now, it seemed.

"I'm yours, Diotrephes," she said. "Take me now, here, under the stars. I pledge myself to you."

But when she bent to kiss him, he put his hand on her shoulder. "Sappho," he said, "we can't do this."

"Oh, but we can," said Sappho. "I love you. I want to give the whole of my being to you."

"And I love you, Sappho," said Diotrephes. "But I can't do this."

The words felt like Eros's fabled leaden arrow in her heart. "What are you talking about?" she asked. "It isn't difficult. I've done it many times before. I don't care if you have no experience. I'll show you how it's done."

"That's not what I mean," said Diotrephes in dismay. "I literally can't though believe me, I've tried. I'm not the man you think I am."

"You're all the man I need," said Sappho, and she put her hand under his chiton. She quickly found his manhood under his *perizoma*, soft and disappointingly flaccid. But something was missing. Sappho stared at Diotrephes, confused. "What?" she stammered.

"Now I guess you know for sure," said Diotrephes. "I'm sorry, Sappho. I thought you already knew."

"Knew?" Sappho said in despair. But in her heart, she understood. "You're a eunuch?"

"Yes," said Diotrephes. "I am the chamberlain of the governor's harem. Everybody at the inn knows. I thought you did too."

Sappho withdrew her hand and put it to her forehead. "Everyone knows?" she said. "*Everyone?* Even Alkestis?"

"Even Alkestis," affirmed Diotrephes.

"So, what have you been courting me for?" Sappho wailed. "Why have you been pursuing me for months if you knew you couldn't follow through?"

"You are still beautiful to me, Sappho," said Diotrephes. "Your mind and your body are beautiful, even if I cannot love you in that way. I wanted your friendship, Sappho. I wanted to appeal to your intellect as a kindred spirit. I wanted to be your platonic admirer. I see, now, that I have misled you. And for that, I am sorry."

Sappho was dizzy with anger. This could not be happening *again*. What was *wrong* with her? Was she indeed cursed? "You're sorry?" she shouted. "You're sorry? You strung me along with poetry and flattery and now that things have come to their natural, inevitable conclusion, you're *sorry?* How could you *do* this to me if you loved me? How?" Sappho felt the tears sting her eyes and she hated each one of them.

"I only ever wanted to enjoy your beauty, Sappho," said Diotrephes. "We can still be friends, can't we?"

Sappho stood, wiping the tears from her face with sandy fingers. "I don't want your friendship," she said meanly. "Go to the crows. I hate you."

Diotrephes looked stricken. "Will you at least allow me to walk you back to the inn?"

"Seeing as you are my only protection in this city," said Sappho, "I don't suppose I have a choice." She retrieved her clothes and sullenly put them back on. "Let's go back now," she said. "I want to go to bed."

Diotrephes escorted a silent Sappho back to The Battered Muse, where Alkestis was waiting in the common room, holding Kleis and talking to her softly. Diotrephes bid Sappho a good night, but Sappho did not acknowledge him. Alkestis caught Diotrephes's eye and nodded, then the spurned eunuch withdrew from the doorway and disappeared into the night.

Sappho sat beside Alkestis and gave her friend a dirty look. "How could you not tell me?" she asked.

"It wasn't my secret to tell," said Alkestis.

"He didn't tell me either," said Sappho. "I found out. In the worst way possible."

Alkestis gave a tired smile. "Felt him up, did you?" she asked.

"It's not funny, Alkestis," said Sappho.

"Do you see me laughing?" Alkestis said sharply.

Sappho looked at the floor. "No," she said softly. "You wouldn't laugh at me. Would you?"

"No, I would not," said Alkestis. "I may not shield you from the lessons you need to learn, but as I said the other day, I love you, Sappho."

Sappho met Alkestis's gaze and saw the kindness in her eyes. "And if you love me, Alkestis," she said, "you wouldn't be ashamed to show it, would you?"

"Of course not," said Alkestis. "I show it all the time."

"I'm glad," said Sappho. "Our love is right. Our love is perfect. No matter what the rest of the world might say." And she reached up and placed her hand on Alkestis's cheek.

Alkestis's response was immediate. Without disturbing Kleis, she smacked Sappho's hand aside. Sappho looked at Alkestis like she'd been hit in the face. Alkestis spoke slowly and sternly. "There will be none of that, missy," she said. "I'm not one of your toys, nor do I want to be."

"All right," said Sappho. "I understand."

"No," said Alkestis, "I don't think you do. You know what your problem is, Sappho? You see every relationship you're in as somehow sexual in nature. I bet you've never had a friend. Just a friend. Am I right?"

Sappho thought of her playmates in Mytilene and started to protest, but then thought better of it. Alkestis would rip her argument to pieces. And anyway, had Larysa, Zosime, or Nastka really been her friends? Her mind strayed to what they had done to Thymaion, and she realized she had simply used those girls to get what she wanted. Sappho felt a burning shame creep into her soul. Was Alkestis right? Sappho didn't know. But it was possible.

"What do you think I should do?" she asked contritely.

"Don't concern yourself with being a lover right now," said Alkestis patiently. "Be a friend to me and a mother to Kleis for a while. I think you'll find things much less complicated and disappointing that way."

"Really?" Sappho asked doubtfully.

"Really," affirmed Alkestis. "Trust me, Sappho. I've been around a lot longer than you have."

"Thanks," Sappho murmured, depressed.

"You're welcome," said Alkestis. "Now, take this baby from me and give her some attention."

The next morning Sappho rose early and fed Kleis before the inn's patrons usually came to the common room for breakfast. Then she went about the motions of preparing the morning meal, mostly fruit and goat cheese. The sun had not yet risen and even Alkestis was still asleep. Sappho had passed a sleepless night and she was admittedly exhausted, but she wanted some solitude to consider what had happened between her and Diotrephes at the harbor the previous night. Sappho had been furious with him on the beach; it was true. But now what she felt was closer akin to profound regret. Diotrephes was a gentleman, and, as the saying goes, a scholar and he had simply wanted Sappho's friendship. And if Alkestis was right, a platonic friend was exactly what she needed. She did not stop to consider the fact that she had permanently discarded Thalia, her best friend in Mytilene, for exactly the same offense toward her as Diotrephes had inadvertently committed.

Such was the capricious nature of Sappho's heart.

She had even rehearsed a short speech she planned to deliver to Diotrephes when he showed up for his customary midday meal. *Diotrephes,* she would say, *I was really hurt by your rejection of me last night. But now I see that you only ever wanted to be my friend and kindred spirit. I accept you back in my life and on your terms. I'm sorry.*

The prospect of apologizing to Diotrephes galled Sappho bitterly, but she was determined to make things right. After all, hadn't she loved him up until last night? Surely that love had not gone away—at least not the *agapē* and the *philia*. And after Alkestis's rebuke, she had resolved to abandon *eros* for a spell.

When Alkestis arrived in the common room an hour later, she found Sappho singing to Kleis as she worked, the baby sitting in a basket on one of the tables. Alkestis was accustomed to whimsical behavior from Sappho—and this certainly qualified—and she merely raised an eyebrow and muttered, "You must have slept well."

"Oh, Alkestis," Sappho sang as she breezed about the room, "I've decided to take your advice to heart and leave romance in the past. No more dramatic trysts and secret affairs for me. I'm going to do just what you said I should do: be a mother and a friend."

Alkestis nodded. "Uh, huh," she said. "And Midas of Phrygia was wiser than Athena. Sappho, I know I told you you had a problem with your point of view, but people just don't change their natures that quickly."

"I'm surprised at you, Alkestis," said Sappho. "Why, in a few short months, I've transformed you from a jaded old woman into a cherished friend and aunt. If it worked with you, it can work for me."

"Perhaps," said Alkestis. "I see you've got breakfast well in hand. I think this jaded old woman will sit down with her niece and watch you work."

It wasn't long before the guests emerged from their rooms for breakfast. Sappho floated happily about the common room, making small talk with the regulars. Kleis gurgled contentedly in her basket, relishing the attention she was receiving from the guests.

At length, it was time for the noon meal and Diotrephes's customary arrival. Sappho stood by the exterior door to wait for him. It did not escape Alkestis's attention that she was neglecting her duties serving lunch in anticipation of accosting the learned chamberlain as soon as he entered.

But an hour passed, and Diotrephes had not appeared.

Then two hours were gone, and there was no sign of Sappho's friend.

By the third hour, it was clear he wasn't coming. Sappho began to panic. Had he been injured? Was he sick? Had that old charlatan Leotykhides enlisted the help of some neighborhood thugs and assaulted him? Sappho's mind was filled with images of all the dreadful possibilities her imagination could come up with.

Alkestis said nothing. It was obvious to her what had happened, but as she had told Sappho the other day, there were some things a woman had to learn for herself. And so she stood by the bar as the lunch crowd broke up, watching Sappho wait for the man who wasn't coming.

At half past the third hour, a boy about ten years old stepped into the common room, carrying a linen satchel over his shoulder. This struck Sappho as a little odd, as the usual patrons of The Battered Muse were significantly older. The boy cleared his throat and said, in a loud voice, "I'm looking for the lady Sappho! I have a message from the governor's chamberlain Diotrephes!"

Sappho immediately perked up and rushed over to the boy. "Diotrephes sent you?" she said in a rush. "Is he all right? Is he coming?"

"I don't know what's in this message, lady," stammered the boy. "The chamberlain told me only to give you this." And he offered the satchel to Sappho.

Alkestis drew near. "You might want to open that over there," she said to Sappho, indicating one of the tables. "Sitting down." She handed the boy a one-twelfth stater coin, and the boy nodded respectfully and dashed back out into the street.

Sappho sat down in a chair and stared at Diotrephes's package. Part of her knew what the chamberlain's message would be, and so she hesitated to take the next step.

But Alkestis had no such reservations. "Open it, girl," she said firmly. "Get it over with."

Sappho reached into the bag with a trembling hand and felt something dry and rough. She grasped the foreign object and withdrew it. It was a sheaf of papyrus. Sappho stared. There must have been enough for a hundred scrolls there.

But that wasn't all. Also in the bag were a clay bottle of ink and three sharp reed pens. Diotrephes had granted her request. Sappho turned the bundle of papyrus over in her hands and saw that there was already writing on one of the sheets. She undid the leather lace binding the bundle together, took the top page, and read.

My dear Sappho,

Here are the writing materials you asked for. I hope they will be sufficient for a while. When you run out, there is a merchant who has a shop, near where I chased away the beggar, where you can purchase more. I have given a great deal of thought to what you said on the beach, and I feel I have mistreated you. Therefore, I must sadly deprive myself of your company forever. I hope you understand. I will cherish the memory of you and of our times together for the rest of my life.

Keep singing, my nightingale.

Your friend always,

Diotrephes

Sappho put a hand to her brow and broke down. She wept openly, in front of Alkestis and the inn's two remaining patrons. Diotrephes had called her his nightingale.

Sappho's mother had used that word, too. It was an especially poignant compliment, as the Greek word for *nightingale*, *aēdōn*, also meant *songstress*. Sappho's talent was considerable and admired by many, though she reflected that everything she touched seemed to turn into offal.

Alkestis rested her hand gently on Sappho's shoulder. Sappho flinched in surprise at her friend's touch. Alkestis could move very quietly; Sappho hadn't even heard her approach. She looked up at the older woman standing over her and saw that Alkestis was not smiling.

"It was for the best, Sappho," Alkestis said. "It would never have worked the way you wanted it to. Not after what you did last night. You'd have pursued him anyway and gotten your heart broken by him a second time. You know it's true."

Sappho wiped her eyes. "I know," she said. "But I don't have to like it."

"Certainly you don't," agreed Alkestis. "It is a gift of the gods that none of us has to like being miserable. Imagine what a wretched life that would make for."

Sappho reached up and took Alkestis's hand in hers.

"What are you going to do now?" Alkestis asked.

"I think," Sappho said firmly, "I'm going to write a new song."

But Sappho did not write a new song that day. Nor the next. She found herself in the midst of a deep depression such as she had never known. She didn't even have the energy to copy down the songs she had already written with the materials Diotrephes had sent her. Once again, Sappho felt cursed. Perhaps Alkestis was correct. Perhaps her point of view regarding friendship was the problem. She certainly could not argue against the frustrating notion that all of her friendships up to this point, with the exception of Alkestis herself, had involved sex.

But Sappho had difficulty seeing this as a negative. Aside from her late uncle's unwanted ministrations, Sappho liked sex. How could something so pleasurable be so harmful? Of course, Agathon had gotten a great deal of pleasure from Sappho over the years, and Sappho would be the first to call that kind of attention harmful. Had Agathon ruined *eros* forever for her? She was not sure. But what he had done to her still brought out feelings of revulsion and shame whenever she thought about it, even all these years later.

Larysa, Nastka and Zosime had been Sappho's friends, but she had used them to get to Thymaion. Thalia had been her friend, but Sappho had spoiled that friendship by turning it into something Thalia could not live with. Palabos had been nothing more than a plaything, and not a very satisfying one at that. And getting involved with Kekonimenos in the first place had been a dreadful mistake. He had used Sappho as cynically as Sappho had Palabos and discarded her without a second thought.

And then there was Diotrephes. Gentle, chivalrous, scholarly, clever Diotrephes. A man who truly loved Sappho as she was, but who could not share *eros* with her because of his blameless physical limitations.

Sappho could only conclude that she had exceedingly bad luck. Three days after Diotrephes had sent her the papyrus and ink, Sappho resolved to leave romance in the dust for a while. Maybe then she could get her head in the right space so that she could have a healthy relationship with Alkestis and anyone else who came along. *Eros*, Sappho reasoned, was too damned inconvenient. Forsaking it for a while would bring much-needed relief, or so she hoped.

It would be a while before her capacity for having a new platonic friendship was tested.

Baby Kleis was loved by the patrons of The Battered Muse as if she were a daughter to all of them. As Sappho was their celebrity, Kleis had become their mascot. They poured affection upon the child, and Sappho was grateful. If Kleis would not be claimed by her father, or by Sappho's own father, then being claimed by the citizens of Ortygia would have to do. Kleis, by all accounts, was a happy baby, and seemingly relished the attention lavished upon her by the inn's guests.

Sappho threw herself into the role of mother, and with Alkestis's help, Kleis matured quickly. By the time Kleis was three and a half years old, she was speaking in polysyllabic words and imitating Sappho's singing. Kleis sang in nonsense words, not directly copying her mother's songs, but she had a sense for music and what was pleasing to the ear. Sappho could not have been more proud.

Sappho herself was also happier than she could remember. Plainly, simply happy. Without *eros* to cloud her judgment or betray her heart, Sappho had become the carefree, liberated spirit she had been in the early days of Thalia's friendship—only without the pain of being in love. She had never had any concrete idea that life could be this good.

Then, one day, her world was upended yet again.

Sappho was cleaning up in the common room after the noontime meal when something she had never heard before caught her ears. It was a man, and he was singing. He was singing her name.

With violet garlands in her hair
At Sappho's smile I need must stare
I cannot tell her how I die
Denying love, such is a lie

Sappho stood dumbstruck at what she was hearing, completely unaware that everyone was staring at her. Alkestis watched her from across the room, smiling her wry smile. Kleis had stopped babbling as she sat listening in her chair. The voice was clear and pure, that of a trained singer, and she did not recognize it. The song continued for what seemed like an age and Sappho's jaw fell slack. Finally, after lavishing every praise upon her that Sappho doubted she deserved, the song ceased. And a moment later an athletic man in his twenties, with curly brown hair and a reddish beard, entered the common room from the street. He was carrying a traveling bag, and to Sappho's great delight, a lyre in the style of Lesbos, much like her own.

Sappho found herself flustered and unable to speak, but the young man was undeterred as he strode boldly up to her and smiled warmly. "At last," he said. "I have traveled league upon league from my home to find that which was in my own garden for so many years. You are the lady Sappho, formerly of Lesbos, are you not?"

Sappho found all she could do was give a polite snort of laughter. Then, worrying that she might have offended the singer, found her voice at last. "You are correct, sir," she said, "but I fear you have me at a disadvantage."

The young man smiled even more broadly and affected a short bow. "Alkaios," he said, "of Mytilene. You are a difficult woman to find, Sappho."

"You're from Mytilene?" Sappho gushed. "I used to live there!"

"I know," said Alkaios. "I searched for you everywhere when I learned from an acquaintance who knows your father that you were a budding songstress. I was told you had moved here years ago, and though I'm afraid I suffer from dreadful seasickness, I was determined to seek you out. If your music is aught as fair as your face, I have not traveled in vain."

Sappho actually blushed. Alkaios's manner of speaking was formal and as florid as his song. Sappho could not help but smile.

Old Naukles, sitting across the room, spoke up. "Aye, young man, she's the real thing, all right. But you'll have to fight us for her!"

Everyone in the common room laughed, including Sappho and Alkaios.

"Seriously," said Alkaios, grinning and dropping his elaborate facade, "it is good to meet you at last. A young man named Aphelos spoke most highly of you."

Sappho's smile faltered, but it didn't disappear outright. It was impossible not to smile in Alkaios's presence. "Aphelos?" she said. "Why, I haven't thought about him in years."

"Well, he remembers you," said Alkaios. "He told me to tell you he is sorry things didn't work out. And don't worry. He didn't tell me anything else. Shall we sit?"

Sappho glanced up at Alkestis, but her friend gave a dismissive wave. Lunch was over; Sappho was free to take a break. "Of course," she said, and they took one of the empty tables.

"I'm actually quite surprised Aphelos had anything nice to say about me," said Sappho. "We were betrothed, you see. And he decided to break it off."

"You don't owe me an explanation," said Alkaios casually. "What I don't understand is how we never met, living so close together for so many years."

"Well, I'm not one to boast," said Sappho, "but I'm better known here in Ortygia than I was in Mytilene."

"What is the proverb about people being without honor in their own land?" Alkaios mused.

"I hesitate to ask," Sappho began, "but have you spoken to my father?"

Alkaios gave her a quizzical look. "Yes," he said simply.

"Is he well?" Sappho asked.

"Quite well, I believe," said Alkaios.

"Does he ever speak of me?" Sappho said.

"He's actually the one who introduced me to your poetry and told me where to find you," said Alkaios. "He misses you, Sappho."

Sappho gave an involuntary scoff before she could stop herself. "I would think he's still glad to be rid of me," she said.

"Well, he wouldn't throw you a party if you returned to him," said Alkaios seriously. "But he says the house is too empty these days. Why, if I may ask, did you leave Lesbos? Skamandronymous wouldn't tell me."

"I acquired a daughter," said Sappho without an ounce of shame, "but not a husband."

"Ah," Alkaios nodded, "I see. Well, such is life. Things happen, and you'll receive no judgment from me."

"Thank you," said Sappho. Eager to change the subject, she ventured, "How long have you been a musician?"

"Ten years," said Alkaios. "You?"

"Eleven," said Sappho. "I was given a lyre for my ninth birthday. I still have it, in fact."

"Really?" Alkaios said with a raised eyebrow. "I'd love to hear you play it. That is why I'm here, after all."

"I think that can be arranged," said Sappho.

Alkaios stared at her, smiling.

"Oh, you mean now?" Sappho said.

"Of course," said Alkaios, still smiling.

Sappho called out to Alkestis, "Alkestis, can I—"

"How many times do I have to tell you you're not a slave?" Alkestis said, throwing up her hands, exasperated. "Go. Get your lyre and play for him."

Alkaios settled into a chair at one of the empty tables, while Sappho dashed cheerfully off to her room to fetch her lyre. She picked up the instrument and turned to go back to the common room. Then, frowning, she paused, standing beside her bed. Alkaios seemed nice enough. And he was definitely a kindred spirit. Sappho wondered if—

No, she told herself. *Don't go there.* She was not going to ruin this by entertaining the idea of taking Alkaios as a lover. If it happened that way, he would have to initiate the relationship, and maybe not even then would she consider it. Sappho was determined to show Alkestis she could have a healthy platonic friendship with a handsome and talented man. She was *not* going to ruin this.

Sappho held her lyre close to her bosom and slowed her breathing, her heart fluttering maddeningly inside her chest. Was she ready for this?

Of course I am, she told herself. And she left her bedroom and returned to the common room.

Alkaios was still sitting at the empty table. While Sappho was in her bedroom, Alkestis had served him some beer, and he sat sipping it, smiling as he saw Sappho enter the room. "Ah," he said. "It's very much like my own. What are you going to play for me?"

"One of my new ones," said Sappho as she sat down at the table with her admirer.

"Brilliant," said Alkaios. "Go ahead."

Sappho gave her lyre's strings an experimental strum. They were horribly off-pitch. Blushing again—she could not help herself in Alkaios's presence—she quickly tuned the lyre from memory, then plucked an arpeggio—it sounded much better now—then began to pluck out the notes to the song she had selected.

Sappho sang:

The bridegroom's luck is with him now
His prayers answered, yes, and how
The girl he prayed for comes

The bride herself doth show her face
Full of beauty, full of grace
Aphrodite blesses her

Sappho sang the full seven verses of the song, then gave a flourish of chords, smiling as she showed off her talent a bit. Alkaios did not seem to fault her for her pride. On the contrary, he grinned broadly and applauded when she had finished and placed her hands in her lap.

"Bravo!" he said. "I admit, you are better than I. Are all of your songs about love?"

"Well, no," said Sappho complacently. "But most of them. Are all your songs about me?"

"Clever girl," said Alkaios. "My songs are about a variety of subjects, including love, politics, and general debauchery. If you'll forgive me, I'll play one of the more frivolous ones for you now."

"I'd be delighted," said Sappho eagerly.

"Very well," said Alkaios. He lifted his hands to his lyre's strings and plucked out a few instrumental chords, before lifting his voice in song:

Why wait for the light when we can drink?
The sun is fading, time I think
Serve the largest cups of wine
Bacchus brings us drink divine
Wine shall make our troubles flee
Mixed with water, yet strongly
Fill the cup right to the brim
Another follows, cheering him

Alkaios went on for another eight verses before ending the song and smiling at Sappho, who was looking at him with something akin to admiration. "What do you think," he said, "from one artist to another?"

"I think it's marvelous," said Sappho enthusiastically. "It's so good to meet someone with such talent."

"I feel the same way," said Alkaios. He looked at Sappho curiously. "So," he said, "where do we go from here?"

"Have you ever been to a library?" Sappho asked.

Alkaios was thrilled with the library when Sappho took him there the next day. Like Sappho, he found the tablet of Gelgames utterly fascinating. Sappho herself was relieved not to run into Diotrephes while they were there. She knew he went there often. She was not worried that she'd have to speak to him. She had nothing to say to the man. But she did not want him to think she had acquired a lover. Nothing could be further from the truth, she told herself.

But was that really how she felt?

Yes! she thought violently. She would entertain no other notion.

Alkaios took a room in The Battered Muse and became a regular for all three meals of the day. Sappho remained a little anxious that such close proximity to such an ardent admirer and fellow artist would lead to an unwanted—*was it?*—romantic entanglement. But Alkaios had made no moves in that direction, and after a week, Sappho's apprehension faded and she simply enjoyed the convenient fact that she now had an artistic partner who was happy to give her a break from entertaining the inn's patrons by playing his own music for them. Sappho felt for the first time in years that her life was finally settling into some much-needed order and harmony.

Alkestis had noticed Sappho's not moving in on Alkaios for a sexual relationship, and indeed her conversations with the young songstress revealed no such motive either. Sappho's employer was relatively impressed. But she would reserve judgment about the budding friendship for a few more weeks. It had been her experience that anything is possible in human interaction. After all, hadn't Euagoras duped Alkestis's father into marrying her off to the abusive lout?

As for that arrangement, Alkestis found it difficult to blame her father, who had passed away shortly after the wedding, before Euagoras had begun beating her. Arranged marriages were the way things were done in that time and place. It had never occurred to Alkestis that she should wait for true love before taking the vows. She trusted and accepted her father's authority in the matter. It wasn't until Sappho came along that she considered the fact that she might have been cheated out of happiness by the whims of societal norms. Though she was surrounded by friends and acquaintances, Alkestis felt strangely alone.

And so Sappho and Alkaios took turns playing their songs for The Battered Muse's patrons, and Alkestis was bringing in greater profits than ever. A few weeks into Alkaios's stay at the inn, he and Sappho started playing each other's songs, and the patrons began to ask for a duet. After some discussion, Sappho and Alkaios agreed to play and sing Sappho's *Hymn to Aphrodite*, the first song Sappho had ever performed for the guests, together.

It took a few days for the two poets to work out who would sing what, and how to modify the chords so that they would not be playing the same notes, while still providing some sense of harmony. After the fourth day of planning, they decided they were ready.

The performance could not have been more well-received. Playing along with Alkaios, Sappho reflected, felt perfectly natural, as if she had been waiting her entire life to discover this singular collaboration. Sappho had never known her brothers—it was understood Skamandronymous had three sons by a woman to whom he had been married before Sappho's mother. But aside from their names—Eurygios, Kharaxos, and Larikhos—Sappho knew almost nothing about them. When Skamandronymous married Kleis and fathered Sappho, the three young men faded out of the picture. Sappho never knew if this was because her father did not approve of them, or if perhaps they felt Skamandronymous had betrayed their mother's memory by remarrying. Anything was possible, Sappho supposed. She did not think about it much.

But, the point, she figured, was that Alkaios was becoming like a brother to her now. It was a relationship she discovered she needed, after having lacked it for so many years. And she was grateful to the gods for sending this poet of Mytilene across the sea to inject himself into her lonely life. Alkestis was a good friend, but one needs more than one friend, Sappho was beginning to realize. And Diotrephes would not be returning to her in that regard.

After their duet, Sappho and Alkaios played together often—sometimes performing Sappho's songs, sometimes Alkaios's. It was a partnership that brought joy to both poets as well as to their audience. It would be about a century before a poet named Thespis would become the first stage actor in the modern sense, and Greek drama was basically in its infancy. So, The Battered Muse was essentially the only venue in Ortygia for the performance of lyric poetry. It did not occur to Sappho to be proud of this. It was just the way things were. She, of course, could not know that millennia later poets and musicians would perform in bars and coffee houses in much the same way. She and Alkaios had effectively invented dinner theater.

Since her coming to Ortygia, Sappho's birthday had not been officially observed. She didn't really think about it much, the last few years in her father's house having felt rather less than celebratory. But as the new moon of the fourth lunar cycle of her twenty-first year approached, she felt a pang of regret. How misguided she had been years ago, how much the fool. Perhaps her father had been right to send her away. He had been so wrong about Agathon, but it was true that his lovely, talented daughter had played the harlot shamelessly. If she hadn't been spurned by Thalia, she would never have sought out Palabos; she would have married Aphelos and might never even have met Kekonimenos. How cruel hindsight was, she reflected. She could see clearly all the mistakes she had made, and at the same time knew she was utterly powerless to effect any meaningful changes. No, The Battered Muse and Ortygia at large were her home now. Alkestis and Alkaios were her friends. And she had her lovely daughter Kleis. But Sappho was, at the moment, dissatisfied.

There was no denying it. After four years in exile, Sappho wanted her birthday to be noticed.

Alkestis was not one for ceremony, but Sappho wanted to talk to *someone* about what was bothering her. The obvious person was Alkaios. And three days before the new moon, she sat down beside him in the common room after supper and sighed heavily.

Alkaios smiled his winning smile and put a hand on Sappho's as it rested on the table. "Something is vexing my friend," he said. "Being a man, I'm not much of a noticer. But I can see that much, at least."

Sappho gave a tired smile she guessed looked more like a haggard rictus, though it was easy to smile when Alkaios did. It was also easy to tell the truth, no matter how bitter. "You know me well," she said. "I'm sorry I've been depressed lately. The fact is, I've got a birthday coming up, and it's reminded me of the mistakes I've made."

Alkaios nodded in understanding. "Mistakes are universal to the human condition," he said. "I've made some whoppers in my time. Do you want to talk about it?"

Sappho hesitated. She *had* wanted to talk about it. She had wanted it very much. But now that she sat in the dimly lit common room, empty of patrons, as she held her friend's hand, she wasn't sure. "I don't know," she said truthfully. "I would do things differently if I could. Certainly, I would. But all my choices, all my mistakes, and dreadful decisions have brought me to this time and place in my life. And I'm actually quite comfortable here. I like who I am, Alkaios. Perhaps my regrets no longer matter. Am I making any sense?"

Alkaios nodded sagely. "Actually," he said, "you're making perfect sense. Can I tell you a story? I promise I won't boast."

Sappho laughed. If anyone deserved to boast, it was Alkaios. He was brilliant. But all she said was, "Yes."

"When I was a boy," Alkaios began, "about fourteen years old, my father was my hero. He was the wisest, strongest, most upright man I knew. Everything I did, I did to please him. Father was a farmer or rather a landowner; he had a vineyard in Lesbos that your father frequented, actually, and was also one of the oligarchs of Mytilene. It really is remarkable that we never met while we were both there. Anyway, Father wanted me to take over the vineyard when I came of age, and I fully intended to do it. There was no question I would follow his wishes. Then, one evening, a vagrant showed up at our front door, asking for a place to rest for the night. My father, being a kindly man, gave his consent and put the man up in one of the spare rooms, telling the house slaves to cater to his every need. The man was grateful, but he was also quite ill. Sometime during that night, he died in his sleep. Father was quite upset that a man had passed away in his home, under his care, and he paid for the vagrant's funeral. Being tied up with the burial arrangements, Father told me to go through the man's things and give whatever was useful to the poor."

"That was kind of him," Sappho agreed.

"Well," Alkaios continued, "the vagrant didn't have many possessions. Only a purse containing about three staters of gold, a walking staff, a lyre, and some odd pieces of papyrus. I didn't know much about music in those days, so I set the lyre aside and focused my attention on the documents. It turned out the man was from Cyprus. His name was Oribasios, and he was a traveling musician."

"That's remarkable," said Sappho.

"Remarkable to me at the time that anyone could make a living playing music all over the world," Alkaios agreed. "It was at that moment that I turned my attention to the lyre. It had six strings and it was made of apricot wood. And it was in exceedingly poor shape. But I was curious and I asked my father if I could keep it. Father didn't understand why I wanted the thing, but he gave his consent, and I started learning to play it. After about six months, I knew that I wanted to dedicate my life to music and poetry. But I needed to study under people who knew what they were doing, and I needed a proper instrument. Father was furious when I told him of my wishes. He had been counting on my taking over his vineyard, you see. But Mother came to my defense and said I should do whatever made me happiest. They had a dreadful row over the whole thing one night."

"But he changed his mind, right?" Sappho said. "I mean, clearly, he changed his mind. You're here, after all."

"Well," said Alkaios ruefully, "he wasn't happy, to be sure. Fortunately, I had a younger brother, Sinon, to whom my father agreed to leave the vineyard. As for me, I was made a laborer in the field, and my father gave me a stater a day to tend the grapes. And I was allowed to spend the money any way I wished, including on my music. So after a few months, I bought the lyre I carry now. And after a few years, I moved out of my father's house and began to study music from the masters of Mytilene."

"I never knew there *were* any masters in Mytilene," said Sappho wistfully. "Father never told me. I had no formal training at all."

"Well," observed Alkaios wryly, "you *were* a girl."

Sappho started to protest and then realized Alkaios was right. As proud as Skamandronymous had been of his daughter's talent, it would have been highly irregular to educate her formally.

"Anyway," Alkaios concluded, "to finish a story that I have made too long, I renounced my inheritance of a large tract of land and a considerable sum of money, and traded it for my music. And while I regret defying my father, as you have your regrets, I have always considered the sacrifice worth it. I am very happy now, Sappho."

"So what you're saying is—" Sappho began.

"What I'm saying, Sappho," said Alkaios, squeezing her hand, "is regret only serves to make us feel bad about our choices. It's an emotion that isn't worth entertaining."

"I agree," Sappho said quietly.

"Now," said Alkaios, "what can I do to make you happy?"

"Throw me a birthday party," said Sappho earnestly. "Something utterly extravagant and indulgent."

Alkaios nodded, smiling with his eyes. "As you wish," he said.

Alkaios informed Sappho he would need exactly one week to prepare for Sappho's party. Sappho was delighted that he was taking so much time to plan something which must be, given the week he requested, lavish indeed; however, she also was mildly irritated that this would place her first birthday celebration in years three days after the new moon. Sappho realized she was being unreasonably selfish for this attitude, and promised herself she would not let it show to Alkaios—or to Alkestis, for that matter, for Alkestis would surely have a hand in the planning, Sappho reasoned.

Sappho found the wait galling. She would work her shift in the inn's common room, as usual, but Alkaios and Alkestis would not speak to her much. Sappho figured they did not wish to risk divulging any details of the birthday party inadvertently. But the strangest part was Alkaios's treatment of Kleis. He had always loved the child, although he had never paid her any special attention before. But now, after the noon meal was cleared, he would take her off into the city, giving only a cryptic answer when Sappho asked where on earth they were going. Sappho's maternal instinct—while learned rather than innate—was strong, and it took an admonition from Alkestis to prevent her from demanding to be told what was going on.

"All good things to those who wait," Alkestis said calmly.

And so Sappho waited.

But waiting, she soon discovered, was agony. Not nearly as bad as being in love, but bad enough. As popular as she was with the patrons of The Battered Muse, Sappho hadn't had a fuss made over her—just because—in years. She was both enthusiastic and on edge. *What would it be like?* She found herself growing impatient.

Each day before her requested celebration, Sappho would rise early to help prepare breakfast as she always did. Alkestis remained infuriatingly closed-mouthed about the whole affair; indeed, she didn't even engage Sappho in her usual banter. Sappho felt ignored, but she told herself this behavior was attributable only to Alkestis's role in planning Sappho's party, and that the silent treatment would end after the week Sappho had granted to Alkaios to prepare had elapsed. Sappho was excited about the coming event, and she let it show. But she secretly longed for things to return to normal.

On the seventh day, Sappho slept late on purpose. She wanted to make a grand entrance into the common room, and a small, passive-aggressive part of her wanted to punish her friends for making her wait so long for her celebration. She got out from under the blankets about half an hour later than usual by her reckoning, noticing uncomfortably that Kleis was not on her mattress on the floor beside her bed. Sappho frowned. Kleis never got up before her mother. Sappho figured Kleis had risen at her normal time and gone on to breakfast. She would have to speak to the child about wandering off alone, although Sappho knew no one Kleis was liable to encounter in The Battered Muse was likely to harm her.

Sappho put on a clean peplos and stepped out into the hallway that led to the common room. Oddly, she could not make out the sounds of the morning meal being prepared. She could not hear anything, in fact. Had she misjudged how late it was in the morning? Was she early after all? Had she missed breakfast altogether? Sappho walked quietly down the hall.

Sappho stepped into the common room. The fire was burning in the fireplace as usual, but the oil lamps were not lit. The fire threw flickering shadows across the room. Sappho paused in the doorway, puzzled. What was going on? Nervously, she called out.

"Hello?"

"*Synkhairōmen se!*" cried a dozen people, including Alkestis, Alkaios, and Kleis, as they leaped into view from behind the bar. Sappho jumped, startled. She had not expected her birthday celebration to be a surprise party. She found herself grinning like the proverbial fool as her friends, her daughter, and the handful of regulars present crowded around her.

"Happy birthday, Sappho," said Alkestis, planting a kiss on Sappho's cheek.

"Good surprise?" Alkaios asked, smiling his usual smile.

"Not bad," Sappho allowed. "I was beginning to think everyone was still asleep."

"That was what we were aiming for," said Alkaios complacently.

"You should have seen your face," said Alkestis, chuckling.

"Happy birthday, Mama," piped little Kleis.

"So," said Sappho, looking around, "what now?"

"Breakfast," said Alkestis, "which you don't have to fix."

"Then, some entertainment worthy of a poet," Alkaios continued. "I think you'll be pleased."

"All right," said Sappho, suddenly flustered. "Where do I sit?"

"Right here," said Alkaios, indicating a table in the middle of the room.

He pulled out a chair and Sappho sat. Suddenly, Naukles was there with a tray of fruit and cheese. "For our favorite artist," he said gallantly and set the tray on the table before Sappho.

Sappho found herself overcome with emotion. After four years of working for Alkestis, serving men like Naukles day after day, having people like them care enough about her to indulge her like this was overwhelming. This was truly where she belonged, Sappho thought. She was among friends here. Friends who neither wanted to bed her, nor appeal to her vanity. For the first time, she understood what Alkestis had wanted her to understand about the value of platonic relationships. Discovering this truth after a lifetime of ignorance made that lifetime of ignorance entirely worth suffering. Sappho felt finally fulfilled.

Breakfast was delicious, made all the better because, as Alkestis observed, Sappho didn't have to prepare or serve it. There was goat cheese—the kind Sappho loved—as well as grapes, berries, oranges, and pomegranate seeds. And plenty of juice to wash it down. Alkestis had even toasted some flatbread to go along with it. Sappho ate until she was full, and Naukles carried away the tray.

As soon as Sappho had swallowed the last bit of cheese, Alkaios bowed deeply before her and said with dramatic flair, "And now, the music."

And without warning, little Kleis stepped forward, holding Alkaios's lyre. The child sat on a chair and glanced up at Alkaios. He nodded, and then Kleis raised her tiny hands to the strings and began to play a familiar tune. By the time she started singing, Sappho knew what she was going to hear, and she was not embarrassed by the tears that welled up in her eyes as she listened.

Aphrodite, be my guide
Eros loved me
But he lied

His arrow struck me in the heart
And here I am all

Torn apart

Kleis had just enough time to set the lyre down before Sappho jumped up from her chair and took her in her arms, weeping. Kleis hugged her mother back, and then said, "Did you like that, Mama?"

"Like it?" Sappho gasped. "I loved it. It was beautiful!" Sappho looked up at Alkaios as he stood over her and said, "No girl under the sun has such a gift as this, not for all the ages."

Alkaios just smiled and nodded.

That evening, after the patrons had gone to bed, Sappho sat with Alkaios and Alkestis in the common room, drinking beer. Sappho was thoroughly exhausted and entirely satisfied with the day's events. She could not remember having had such an enjoyable birthday, even if it was three days late—something she no longer held against her friends. It must have taken Alkaios the entire week to teach little Kleis to play and sing her mother's song, and Sappho decided wholeheartedly that it had been worth the wait.

Alkaios took a long sip of beer. "So, how old are you, then, anyway, Sappho?" he asked.

"Young man," said Alkestis feigning sternness, "that's a very rude question."

Sappho grinned. "It's all right, Alkestis," she said. "I'm twenty-one."

"And it was insensitive of me to overlook your birthdays up until now," said Alkestis. "I hope you'll forgive me. I've never been good at the niceties."

"Well," said Alkaios slyly, "the niceties happen to be an area in which I excel." He reached into a knapsack that had been hanging unnoticed on the back of his chair, and withdrew a length of polished pine wood about half a cubit long, with six holes drilled into it in a line. "Sappho," he said, "this is for you. Happy birthday and thank you for being my friend."

Sappho accepted the proffered object, which was clearly a musical instrument of some sort. She smiled nervously. "I don't know if I'll be able to play this," she said. "I tried an aulos once when I was little and it was too hard for me."

"That is a shepherd's flute," Alkaios explained. "It's much easier to play than an aulos because it doesn't rely on a reed to produce the sound. Go on, try it."

Sappho raised the mouthpiece tentatively to her lips and blew. The flute's sound was high and sweet without being piercing and required very little effort to produce. Sappho was delighted. "Thank you, Alkaios," she said. "I'm happy you're my friend as well."

The following day, Sappho threw herself wholeheartedly into learning the basics of her new shepherd's flute. She found it to be no harder to play than her lyre, and the notes were arranged just as intuitively. After a few minutes, she was playing scales, and within a few hours, she had mastered most of the accidentals. It wasn't long before Alkaios suggested they play a duet, with Sappho accompanying him on the flute as he played his lyre. They started with a few of Sappho's earlier pieces, before moving on to more complex ones. Sappho had written purely instrumental pieces before, of course, but now she was discovering the artistic merits of replacing the lyrics of her poems with simple notes. The music, she was beginning to realize, was as beautiful by itself as the words.

Alkestis was more than delighted. If Sappho alone had drawn customers to The Battered Muse, the duo from Lesbos made Alkestis's inn a musical Mecca twelve hundred years before Mecca itself became more than just another desert backwater to the world at large. Alkaios played and sang. Sappho joined him, sometimes on her lyre, sometimes on the flute, playing old songs and new ones. With Alkaios to inspire her, Sappho was writing songs like never before, and young Kleis was proving to be a fine apprentice to them both. By the time she was four years old, she was perfectly comfortable playing both lyre and flute, if not precisely a virtuoso, and occasionally performed in the inn's common room to the great admiration of all present. Sappho herself was truly happy.

That happiness lasted nearly a year before it was broken.

Sappho and Alkaios had forged an unshakable bond of friendship by the time little Kleis turned five. They performed in the common room at least four times a week, and Alkestis had started paying Alkaios as an employee of the inn. He and Sappho each received a stater a day for their music and other help, and Alkaios appeared content to live in Ortygia forever. Sappho loved Alkaios, plainly and simply, and Kleis seemed to look at the man like a surrogate uncle. Sappho reflected that her own uncle had been no friend to her, but Alkaios was nothing like Agathon. The four of them, Alkestis included, were essentially a family now, and Sappho relished the knowledge that she had found a healthy set of friendships at last.

One day, shortly after Kleis's birthday, Sappho and Alkaios were resting in the common room after a performance at the noontime meal. Sappho had just played a new song for the first time and was feeling euphoric. Alkaios seemed to have picked up on this, because, eventually, he said, "We should celebrate."

Sappho looked at him, bemused. "Celebrate what?" she asked.

"Well, us, of course," said Alkaios. "We are an unstoppable artistic force in this city now. What shall we do to recognize that fact?"

A thought of Diotrephes came to Sappho, unbidden. The ghost of a frown crossed her face before she had another, more welcome thought. "I have an idea," she said. "Let's go to the harbor tonight and watch the stars."

"That sounds marvelous," said Alkaios.

They set out for the waterfront at dusk, planning to spend at least a few hours stargazing. Despite his being unarmed, Sappho felt as at ease walking Ortygia at night with Alkaios as she had with Diotrephes. And she further reflected that, as celebrities, she and Alkaios were probably perfectly safe from violent criminals. They might get robbed, but not killed. The city would never forgive one who harmed these two musicians.

An hour after they had embarked, Sappho and Alkaios arrived at the harbor. The moon was waning and shown dimly on the creaking hulks of the docked ships on the quay. The stars and planets were clearly visible, along with the brilliant band of light, the Milky Way, which stretched across the sky like an arm embracing the firmament. The two friends kicked off their sandals, passed the quay, and lay down on the sand with their feet pointed toward the gentle surf. Sappho felt ready to burst with happiness.

"Have you ever done this before?" Alkaios asked softly.

"Once," said Sappho, frowning again at the memory. "A long time ago. It didn't go well."

"What went wrong?" Alkaios asked.

"Nothing, really," said Sappho, embarrassed. "I misread my companion's intentions. These things happen."

"Ah, yes," said Alkaios. "I understand."

A few moments passed in silence.

"Kleis thinks highly of you," said Sappho at length.

"She's a good kid," said Alkaios. "You've raised her well. She's lovely and talented. Just like you. She'll make a fine wife someday."

"Someday," Sappho agreed.

"Has anyone ever taught you the constellations?" Alkaios asked.

"The what?" Sappho responded, curious.

"The constellations," Alkaios repeated. "Groups of stars that make pictures. The gods honor men and animals by putting images of them in the sky."

"Really?" Sappho asked, delighted. "Show me."

Alkaios pointed directly overhead. "Well," he said, "that's the Crab. See the bright star and the three branching off from it?"

Sappho giggled. "That doesn't look like a crab," she said. "It's just a few stars."

Alkaios smiled in the dark. "Well, how about that one in the west?" he said, pointing. "The three stars in a row with the two that make a diagonal line? That's the hunter, Orion. The three stars are his belt and the line between the two form his baldric."

Sappho squinted and suddenly realized what Alkaios was talking about. "Oh," she said, "I see it now. Show me more."

Alkaios pointed again. "Those are the Twins, Kastor, and Polydeukes," he said, tracing with his index finger. "See the stars that look like two stick figures lying on their sides?"

Sappho saw them and was delighted. "I never knew," she said. "What's that one?" she said.

"Which one?" Alkaios asked.

Sappho pointed. "That one there," she said. "The bright one."

"Oh," said Alkaios, "that's the evening star. Except when you see it right before sunrise. Then it's called the morning star. It's one of the wanderers."

"What's a wanderer?" Sappho asked.

"They're special stars that don't move like the others," Alkaios explained. "They take a different path across the sky as the rest of the stars move predictably around the earth. Some people think they aren't even stars at all."

"What else would they be?" Sappho wondered aloud.

"Nobody knows," said Alkaios. "Nobody I've talked to, at any rate."

"You're such a wise man," said Sappho in contentment.

Alkaios laughed. "Not a bit of it," he said. "Haven't you heard all poets are fools?"

Sappho glanced at Alkaios and affected a mock scowl. "Are you calling me a fool?" she said.

"All of them but you," Alkaios chuckled. "All of them but you."

Neither one spoke for a while before Alkaios finally said, "What do you want out of life, Sappho?"

"I don't know," Sappho shrugged. "I've got pretty much all I want right now."

"And how do you feel about us?" Alkaios ventured quietly.

Something came to Sappho's mind, unbidden. Something was wrong. "What do you mean?" she asked.

Alkaios rolled to his side on the sand, facing Sappho in the darkness. "I mean," he said, "how do you feel about me?"

A knot had formed in Sappho's stomach. She willed herself to remain calm. "What should I say?" she asked. "You're my friend. Just like Alkestis."

Alkaios swallowed heavily before he spoke. "What would you say if I told you I wanted more than that?"

"More?" Sappho echoed, her mouth suddenly dry.

"More than a friend just like Alkestis," Alkaios clarified.

"I don't know what you mean," Sappho lied, feeling ill.

"Sappho," Alkaios said seriously, "I've never been good at this sort of thing, so I'll just say it plainly."

"No," said Sappho, "don't say anything, Alkaios."

"But I must," Alkaios said, the passion building in his voice. "Sappho, I love you. I love you and I want you to marry me. Would you, please?"

Sappho could feel his want in the air as she weighed what she would say next. "Alkaios," she said at last, "I can't."

"Don't you love me?" Alkaios asked.

"Of course I do," said Sappho quickly. "That's not it at all. It's just that…" Sappho fished in her heart for the right words. "I've never had a successful romance with anyone," she said. "And before Alkestis and you, I'd never had a successful friendship either. I can't marry you, Alkaios. It would mean I had failed at both again."

"But I want to make you happy," said Alkaios.

"Then, don't ask this of me," said Sappho plaintively. "Because it is a gift I cannot give."

"I—I don't know what to say," said Alkaios helplessly. "I had worked it out all perfectly in my mind."

"It's perfect the way it is," said Sappho. "Please, let's not ruin this."

"But how could things be ruined?" Alkaios said. "How can love ruin anything?"

"Trust me," said Sappho bitterly. "It can. I've seen it happen too many times."

"But why should it happen this time?" Alkaios said. "Why can't this time be different?"

"I don't know," said Sappho in desperation. "But it's a risk I'm not willing to take."

"And that's your last word?" Alkaios ventured. "I cannot prevail upon you to change your mind?"

"No," said Sappho, hearing the finality in her own voice. "And please don't ask me again."

"All right," said Alkaios. "I see. Very well."

"But we're still friends, Alkaios," said Sappho. "Right?"

"Friends always," Alkaios agreed.

But something in his tone told Sappho he was hiding something. "Alkaios?" she said.

"Don't," said Alkaios. "Don't spoil the moment."

They lay like that for a long time.

They walked back to the inn in silence, having spent another hour at the waterfront after their peculiar argument, and went to bed, also without speaking. Sappho lay awake for half the night, pondering her conversation with Alkaios about what he wanted that she couldn't give, and kept coming to the same conclusion that she had made the only choice she could. She dreaded the morning when she would have to face him at breakfast, and wondered if he would tell Alkestis what had happened between them before she could do it herself.

Dawn came and Sappho rose, the crusts of a couple of hours' sleep in the corners of her eyes. She put on her undergarments and a clean peplos, combed her hair, and stepped cautiously out of her room into the hall. She appeared to be the first one up in the inn.

Sappho crept down the hallway and entered the common room. Alkaios was already there, but there were no lamps burning and the fire had not been lit. It was just Alkaios, sitting at one of the tables with his back to her. As Sappho quietly approached, she noticed the traveling bag hanging on his chair back, and his staff leaning up against the table beside him, upon which rested his lyre. Sappho cleared her throat.

Alkaios turned his head slowly to face Sappho. He stared at her for a moment, then sighed and rose from his chair.

"Good morning," he said.

"Good morning," echoed Sappho. "I'm sorry, but are you going somewhere?"

"Yes, I am," said Alkaios simply. "I can't stay here anymore, that is, unless you leave."

"Why should I leave?" Sappho wondered aloud. "This is my home."

"I know," said Alkaios. "That's why I have to go. The only way this could be my home too would be if it were *our* home. Understand?"

"No," said Sappho. "I thought we decided last night we were friends forever."

"Well," said Alkaios, "what is said beautifully under the starlight seems awfully plain and tiresome under the morning sun. I can't be your friend, Sappho."

"And I can't be your lover," said Sappho. "Just, please, stay. You're needed here. You can feel differently about me eventually. And you'll find true love again. I know it."

Alkaios rose, took up his bag, his lyre, and his staff, and walked to the exterior door. "No," he said, "I really don't think I will." He opened the door. "And I hope you don't either."

And then he was gone.

Sappho managed to hold her emotions at bay as she lit the fire and began to prepare breakfast. When Alkestis arrived in the common room, the morning meal was ready to be served, and Sappho was standing at the bar, drinking a tepid cup of tea. Alkestis immediately knew Sappho was in a bad mood because her morning drink of choice was pomegranate juice. The tea leaves had been brought to The Battered Muse two years ago by a trader from the land beyond Persia and were kept only for special occasions. If Sappho had dipped into the stash on an ordinary day, something was amiss. And it just so happened that Alkestis knew exactly what it was.

"Alkaios is gone," she said as the overnight guests began to emerge from their rooms.

Sappho looked at Alkestis. "How did you—" she began.

"He came to me last night," Alkestis explained. "We had a long talk. You broke his heart, Sappho."

Sappho felt herself getting angry. "But what about—"

"And I'm very proud of you," Alkestis continued calmly. "You've passed the test."

"Alkestis," said Sappho, taken aback, "what on earth are you talking about?"

"You've finally managed to have a long-term relationship that didn't get physical," said Alkestis, "even when the perfect opportunity to stray presented itself. I officially pronounce you cured. Now, finish your tea and play us some music."

So, Sappho played. But she found no joy in it. Nearly every song she had ever written had been sung by Alkaios or the two of them together at some point over the last year, and each note, each chord, each word reminded her of him. She went through some of her instrumental pieces, avoiding the ones she had written about love, which was rather like avoiding the sun at midday. For she had loved Alkaios, hadn't she? And now he was gone. Her fingers plucked out a familiar tune.

Aphrodite, be my guide
Eros loved me—

Sappho cried out in anguish and dropped the lyre on the clay floor. She rose from her chair and put her palms to her forehead, breathing rapidly. She was vaguely aware of Kleis moving toward her and Alkestis taking the girl by the shoulders, saying, "Don't. She's got to do this herself."

Sappho dashed out of the common room and down the hall to the bedrooms. She flung herself through the door to her room and onto the mattress of her bed. Alkaios was gone. Her friend was gone. And she would never see him again.

She wanted to follow him, to run all the way to the harbor and find him before he boarded some merchant ship or bireme bound for Lesbos. She envisioned herself calling to him from the planks of the quay. He would hear her from inside his cabin and come on deck to answer. Then he would jump from the deck of the boat onto the quay and take her in his arms, never to leave again.

For that was what she had lost, wasn't it? She had learned what it was like to have a platonic friendship, yes. But then a handsome, kind, and talented young man had professed his love for her and had asked her to marry him. And what had she done—she who had wished for love all her life? She had rebuffed him. She had turned him down. And now that she could see this clearly—see what it was she had lost—she could not for the life of her understand why.

That was the question she could not answer. Why had she said no? She thought of Alkestis, who had challenged her to avoid romance. Surely it was her fault.

No, Sappho thought. That wasn't fair. All Alkestis had ever wanted for her was a friendship she considered *healthy*. But who was Alkestis to decide what was healthy for her? Sappho thought about her father. He had tried to impress upon her a healthy friendship with Thalia. But Thalia had turned out to be the love of Sappho's life. If only—

Sappho moaned in frustration. This was all too complicated. Thinking about it made Sappho's headache. One thing was certain, however. She could not go back into the common room this morning. In fact, she could not imagine being happy playing her music ever again. She thrust her face into her pillow.

"Mama?"

Sappho rolled over in the bed. Kleis was standing in the doorway, holding her mother's lyre. "What is it, Kleis?" Sappho grunted.

"You left this, Mama," said Kleis, indicating the lyre.

"Set it on the floor and leave me alone," Sappho muttered.

"Mama?"

"I said, go away!" Sappho shouted furiously. And she rolled over, her back to the door, so that she did not see Kleis linger in the doorway for a moment, before setting the lyre on the floor and retreating from the room.

Exhausted and with no tears remaining, Sappho sank into sleep.

It was after lunch when Sappho finally emerged from her bedroom and came back into the common room. Alkestis was sitting at one of the empty tables, talking to Kleis. She looked up when Sappho entered the room. "Go on," she said to Kleis. "Go play. Your mother and I have to talk."

Kleis glanced balefully at her mother before running past her to the inner rooms. Sappho approached Alkestis's table and sat down.

"I imagine you're angry with me," said Alkestis softly. "I don't blame you."

"Alkaios and I could have been happy," said Sappho. "I'm angry, but I'm not angry at you."

"Everything I did and said was to protect you," said Alkestis.

"I know," said Sappho. "I needed to be a mother, not a wife."

"Exactly," said Alkestis, "and—"

"None of this would have happened if it weren't for Kleis," Sappho continued. "This is her fault."

Alkestis looked sternly at Sappho. "Don't blame her," she said. "That isn't fair."

"Isn't it?" Sappho retorted. "I don't really care."

Sappho did her best to ignore Kleis over the coming weeks. Alkestis effectively took over the girl's care, dodging her questions when she asked why her mother was giving her the silent treatment. It wasn't that Alkestis thought Kleis shouldn't know her mother's motivation for this uncharacteristic behavior. Rather, Alkestis hoped Sappho's mood would abate quickly so that she would not have to explain anything to her adopted niece. But Kleis was a precocious child and Sappho's silence hurt her deeply. In one day, she had lost both Alkaios and her mother. And Alkestis had no idea how long this unfair treatment of Kleis would continue. At this point, she could only hope and pray.

About two months after Sappho stopped speaking to her daughter, Kleis came to Alkestis in the common room while Sappho was at the market, buying ink. She had borne the anguish of her mother's mistreatment of her for too long, and would no longer accept Alkestis's circuitous answers.

"Auntie Alkestis," she began while Alkestis was cleaning the tables after the noon meal, "why did Alkaios go away?"

Alkestis sighed and put down her rag. "Kleis," she said, "Alkaios wanted to be your papa, and your mama said no. That's why he went away. He got his feelings hurt." Kleis considered this for a moment before speaking.

"It hurts my feelings when Mama won't talk to me," she said.

Alkestis smiled in spite of herself. The girl was perceptive. "Yes, I know," she said. "You see, after Alkaios went away, your mother changed her mind about him. But he was already gone, so there was nothing to do about it. Now she's angry with herself and angry with the world."

"How can she be angry with the world?" Kleis wondered. "The world didn't do anything to her."

"That's true," said Alkestis. "But certain people did. I'll explain it a bit more when you're older. Let's just say your mother is damaged goods. And she doesn't always blame the right people."

"I think she blames me," said Kleis softly.

"And you're absolutely right about that," said Alkestis. "But listen to me when I tell you, she's wrong. You haven't done anything to be ashamed of."

Kleis nodded slowly, then looked up. "Okay," she said, "then I'll try not to be sad."

"Good girl," said Alkestis. "Now, help me finish cleaning."

When Sappho returned from the market, she went straight to her bedroom, ignoring both Kleis and Alkestis as she breezed through the common room. Alkestis, having had enough of Sappho's attitude, followed her. She opened the door to Sappho's room and entered without knocking. Sappho was sitting on her bed, reading, and looked up at Alkestis, annoyed.

"Alkestis," said Sappho, "whatever it is, I'm not in the mood."

Alkestis slammed the door furiously. Sappho stared. "I guess my mood doesn't matter to you, then, does it?" she said petulantly.

"No, Sappho," said Alkestis, "not today."

Sappho set aside her papyrus. "Very well, then," she said. "What's so important all of a sudden?"

"How dare you ask that question!" Alkestis said, doing her best to keep her volume low and her temper in check. "You are being a selfish brat and I'm not going to stand for it anymore."

"Me? Selfish?" Sappho said. "I don't know what you mean."

"Oh, yes, you do, missy," said Alkestis. "You know exactly what I mean."

Sappho stared neutrally at Alkestis, daring her to continue. Alkestis sighed. "May I sit with you?" she asked, suddenly weary.

"Suit yourself," Sappho shrugged.

Alkestis sat beside Sappho on the bed and looked her in the eye, causing Sappho to avert her gaze. "Look at me, Sappho," she said. And when Sappho did not, Alkestis took her by the jaw and firmly turned Sappho's head toward her.

"What do you want, Alkestis?" Sappho asked, affecting great irritation.

"Well, first of all," Alkestis began, "I insist that you speak to Kleis. She doesn't understand why her mother is treating her this way."

"She can go to the crows for all I care," said Sappho defiantly.

And that was when Alkestis slapped her quite hard. Sappho's face registered indignation, but Alkestis said, "Don't pretend you don't know what that was for. You had that coming. Kleis is your daughter, and whatever mistake you feel you made with Alkaios has nothing to do with her. Do I make myself clear?"

"Alkestis, I—"

"I said," repeated Alkestis, "do I make myself clear?"

"I suppose," said Sappho sulkily, rubbing her cheek with her palm. "Anything else?"

"Yes, as a matter of fact," said Alkestis. "You can stop being so damn sullen. It's affecting your work, and I won't have that."

Sappho smirked and looked at the floor. "I understand," she whispered.

"What's that?" Alkestis said. "Speak up."

"I said, I understand," said Sappho a bit louder than necessary.

"Good," said Alkestis. "And it starts now." She rose from the bed and offered Sappho her hand. "Let's go. Your daughter needs you."

Sappho took Alkestis's hand and allowed herself to be led back into the common room, where Kleis was poking the fire with a stick. Kleis looked up at them. "Mama?" she said. "Are you okay?"

"Yeah," said Sappho dully. Alkestis stepped lightly on Sappho's foot. "Yes," said Sappho. "In fact, I'm going to tell you a bedtime story tonight."

Little Kleis smiled.

That evening, Sappho tucked Kleis into her bed and knelt beside her. Kleis was still smiling from earlier in the day, happy to have her mother back. Sappho put her hand on Kleis's shoulder and smiled. "I promised you a bedtime story," she said, "so, here it goes."

"There once was a queen of Cyrene whose name was Lamia," Sappho began. "Now Lamia was beautiful and beloved by the people, but she had terribly poor judgment. She surrounded herself with a host of advisors to prevent herself from making serious errors as she governed the city-state. Are you with me so far?"

Kleis nodded.

Sappho continued, "Now, you know that Zeus loves beautiful women, yes? Of course, you do. Well, eventually, word of Lamia's beauty reached Zeus himself at the top of Mount Olympus. And Zeus decided he had to see Lamia for himself. Not wanting to destroy Lamia with his glory, he disguised himself as a prince of Arabia and went to Cyrene to meet her. Lamia was very much attracted to Zeus in his disguise and was flattered by his gifts of gold and spices, and she decided to take him as her consort. Zeus, of course, was quite happy with the arrangement."

"But, Mama," said Kleis, "isn't Zeus married?"

"Very much so," said Sappho. "Zeus had to use every trick he knew to conceal his affair with Lamia from his wife, the goddess Hera. It worked for a while and Lamia bore Zeus three sons whom Lamia loved more than life itself. But of course, men are stupid, and Hera eventually discovered Zeus was being unfaithful to her with a mortal."

"What did Hera do, Mama?" Kleis asked.

"Well, she was very angry, of course," said Sappho. "And so she decided to punish Lamia in the harshest way she knew how. She sent a cobra, a venomous serpent of the Libyan desert, to bite Lamia's sons. And just like that, all three of them died horribly painful deaths."

"But, why didn't Hera punish Zeus, Mama?" Kleis asked. "It was his fault, too."

"That's true," said Sappho. "But it's a man's world, Kleis. You'll do well to remember that."

Again, Kleis nodded. "What happened next?"

"Well, as you can imagine," said Sappho, "Lamia was very sad. She was so sad she completely lost her mind. And she decided to get revenge on the world."

"But the world hadn't hurt her," Kleis protested, echoing her words to Alkestis about Sappho herself earlier. "Why didn't she try to fight Hera instead? Or Zeus? He started it, anyway."

"You don't get revenge on a god," said Sappho darkly. "Shall I continue?"

"Yes, please," said Kleis.

"So she decided to get revenge on the world," said Sappho, "as I've already told you. And so she began to steal the children of her faithful subjects in the middle of the night. And she ate them."

Kleis's eyes widened. "She *ate* them?"

"Yes," said Sappho. "She ate them and drank their blood and made jewelry from their bones. As you can imagine, she was no longer fit to rule a city-state, so Zeus transformed her into a hideous creature, part human, part serpent. And he appointed her to stalk the children of the world at night."

"She's out there now?" Kleis said uneasily.

"Right now," confirmed Sappho. "She comes for all the bad children of the world and kills them in their beds and drinks their blood." Sappho placed her hand on Kleis's chest, as Agathon had done to her, years ago. "And so, Kleis, you must be a good girl to escape Lamia and her hunger. You must respect your elders, especially your mother, and never speak ill of them—or else Lamia will most certainly come for you, too. Do you understand what I'm saying?"

Sappho could feel the girl trembling against her bare hand. "I understand, Mama," Kleis said meekly.

"Good," said Sappho shortly, removing her hand and rising. "Now, go to sleep."

"Mama?" Kleis said suddenly as Sappho started to douse the oil lamp. "Can you leave the light on?"

"No, I can't," said Sappho. "And remember, only bad children complain about the dark."

Sappho snuffed out the lamp's light and exited the room, closing the door behind her, and leaving her daughter alone in the blackness.

The next morning, at breakfast, Alkestis noticed Kleis wasn't as cheerful as usual. In fact, the girl looked positively haggard, her hair hanging in strings and her eyes bloodshot. Alkestis asked her if she had had trouble sleeping, and Kleis merely nodded and ate her breakfast. She was about to press the matter, but Sappho interrupted her by saying, "Why don't you let me handle lunch today, Alkestis? And you can take Kleis to the governor's menagerie. She's never been before. It would be a nice treat for her and you deserve a break."

Alkestis regarded her with suspicion. Sappho was certainly not lazy—far from it—but she had never offered to take on a meal shift all on her own before. Perhaps her attitude was taking a positive turn.

Little Kleis had no concerns. "What's a magerie, Mama?" she asked.

"Men-a-ger-ie," Sappho pronounced slowly. "It's a very special place, Kleis. The governor has collected animals from all over the world for the people to see, and the menagerie is where they live."

"What kind of animals, Mama?" Kleis asked.

"Well," said Sappho, "when I went, they had a camel and a lion and an elephant all the way from Nubia."

"An elephant?" Kleis said, astonished. "How big was it?"

"Like this," said Sappho. And she stretched out her arms.

Kleis laughed and threw her arms around her mother. Sappho tensed at first and then returned the embrace. It was the first time in weeks she had hugged her daughter and she found herself suddenly full of emotion. How she loved this little girl. How could she have been so cruel as to ignore her and threaten her with scary stories? Sappho looked up at Alkestis as she held Kleis, and realized she was near tears. Sappho mouthed a silent, "I'm sorry." Alkestis smiled slightly and nodded.

Sappho held Kleis a moment longer and then released her. She wanted to apologize, to explain to her that everything had been a mistake. To tell Kleis she didn't blame her for what had happened with Alkaios. But in the instant Sappho let go of her, Kleis bounded toward the door to the street. Sappho stood and straightened her peplos self-consciously.

"Whoa, there, young lady," said Alkestis, taking Kleis by the shoulder. "Don't leave your auntie behind. We're going together."

Kleis beamed. "Yes," she said. "We're going to see an elephant!"

Alkestis smiled at Sappho. "We'll stop at the market on the way back and get you some of that goat cheese you like," she said.

"Thank you, Alkestis," said Sappho, taking her by the hand. She took a step toward Kleis, fully intending to give her a kiss on the cheek, but Kleis was already out the door. "Good luck keeping her on a short leash," said Sappho. There would be time enough for kisses later. She and Kleis had a lifetime ahead of them together.

"Right," said Alkestis. "We'll see you later."

And they were out the door.

Sappho had her hands full seeing to the noon meal crowd on her own. But the patrons were all known to her, and she reflected that Alkestis had done this many times herself before hiring Sappho to help out. Sappho was not sorry she had offered. The guests were kind to her, realizing she was overwhelmed, and kept their requests to a minimum. After two hours, a grateful Sappho found herself wiping down the last of the empty tables, relieved that lunch was over and that she could have a bit of a rest at last.

After cleaning up a little, Sappho poured herself a cup of the Egyptian beer—she knew Alkestis would not mind—and sat down to rest. Her thoughts strayed, unbidden, to Alkaios and what might have been and she sighed to herself. Had she really made the right decision concerning his proposal? She supposed she would never know. But the decision was made and there was nothing to be done about it. Perhaps it really was for the better. After all, they were both artists, and the artist's temperament was fickle at best. They might have been happy, yes, but it very well could have ended badly. Again, she thought, she would never know. All she could do at this point was go on with life as it was, be a mother, a friend, and, of course, a poet. She made a promise to herself then and there to be happy, always. She had Alkestis and she had Kleis. She needed nothing more.

Alkestis returned with Kleis three hours after lunch, bringing goat cheese and almonds, a favorite of Kleis's, from the market. Kleis was full of excitement about the menagerie and could not sit still. Giving Alkestis a tired smile, Sappho told her daughter to go play outside in the street until sundown. The happy little girl bounded out the door.

Alkestis helped herself to the beer and sat down with Sappho. "I don't know where she gets her energy," she said. "We walked all over the city and she's not the least bit tired. I, on the other hand, am exhausted. Was I ever that energetic? I can't even remember."

Sappho smiled. "I've decided not to mourn Alkaios's departure anymore," she said to Alkestis. "What's done is done, and I'm not going to blame anyone from here on out. I'm going back to being just Sappho. Kleis needs her mother."

"I'm pleased to hear it," said Alkestis, sipping her beer. "No offense, but you've been an insufferable bitch for weeks."

"No offense taken in the least," said Sappho. "I needed a good kick in the ass, I think."

"That you did," Alkestis agreed.

They sat in silence for a moment, then Sappho opened her mouth to speak again but was suddenly interrupted by a commotion outside in the street. There was a scream followed by the panicked neighing of horses and a great deal of shouting from both men and women.

"Now, what could that all be about?" Alkestis said.

Sappho felt a stab of fear. "Kleis," she said, rising from her chair and spilling her beer in the process.

"By Zeus," said Alkestis, and she followed Sappho quickly out of the inn.

A small crowd had gathered in the middle of the street. A chariot drawn by two dappled horses was parked haphazardly beside the circle of onlookers. The chariot driver, a very short, lanky man with graying hair and the purple chlamys of a nobleman had dismounted his vehicle and was attempting to get through to what the crowd was gathered around. His face was unfashionably clean-shaven. On his left hip, he wore a large Thessalian *kopis*, with a blade more than a cubit long. The great knife looked ridiculous hanging from its baldric on his exceedingly diminutive frame.

"See here," he said, frustrated. "Let me through, dammit."

Sappho and Alkestis rushed into the crowd themselves. "Out of the way, everyone," said Alkestis. "Here, let us see."

Sappho pushed through the circle of people and stared in shock at what they were gathered around. Kleis lay in a crumpled heap in the dust of the street. A line of blood trickled from her mouth. Nothing else seemed to be wrong with her, and Sappho had a moment of hope that she was merely injured. But Kleis didn't move when Sappho touched her shoulder and hung limply in Sappho's arms when she gathered her to her breast.

Alkestis and the chariot driver managed to get through the crowd a moment later. Alkestis took one look at Sappho holding the lifeless Kleis and swore. "Ah, Sappho," she said.

"No!" Sappho moaned. "Not my Kleis! Not my little sparrow!"

"She was your daughter?" asked the chariot driver.

"She was the breath in my lungs," said Sappho.

Alkestis turned to the chariot driver in fury. "And you!" she said. "What do you think you're doing? Racing through the streets like Zeus after a virgin! Don't you know there are innocents like her about?"

"I didn't even see her there," said the chariot driver in a rather high-pitched voice. "One moment I was driving in an empty street and the next the child was under my wheel." He glanced at the sky as if seeking divine counsel. Then he knelt beside Sappho and put his hand on her shoulder. "I have no words to express my sorrow, miss," he said. "I will of course compensate you however I can."

"Compensate?" Alkestis sputtered. "Compensate her? Are you so rich you can snatch this poor thing's only child back from the Elysian Fields? What a deep purse you must have!"

The chariot driver stood up and straightened his chlamys. "Of course, I can't do that, madam," he said. "I'm not a god. I know I couldn't make this right with the girl's own weight in gold. Where is your husband?" he asked Sappho.

"He wasn't my husband," said Sappho softly.

"I see," said the chariot driver. "And what is your name?"

"Sappho," Sappho whispered.

"Well," said the chariot driver, "what I must do seems clear. You will come to my house and live as my wife. I am old and have no heir. And I can give you another child."

"I don't want another child," Sappho sobbed. "I want my Kleis!"

"Sappho," Alkestis said, "nothing can bring her back. Perhaps you should—"

"Don't you dare patronize me, Alkestis," said Sappho quickly. "Not now. Not after all these years as my friend."

"Just who are you, anyway?" Alkestis asked the chariot driver.

"My name is Megasthenes," he said.

"That name means nothing to me," spat Alkestis.

"My nephew Erasistraus is chief advisor to the governor of Syracuse," Megasthenes explained.

Sappho wiped her eyes and chuckled darkly. "I suppose I should count myself lucky such a noble gentleman as yourself would be the one to kill my daughter," she said.

"I would not wish such luck on anyone," said Megasthenes. "But you would be comfortable in my home. I would be good to you. You'd never work another day in your life if you didn't want to."

Sappho looked at the ground.

"Well, speak up, girl," said Megasthenes in irritation. "Will you be my wife or won't you?"

"How could I possibly love you?" Sappho said.

"I don't expect you to," said Megasthenes. "But you need this union as much as I do. Please, give your consent."

"Sappho?" Alkestis said.

"Light my daughter's pyre with your finest oil and bury her ashes in a bed of roses," said Sappho dully, "and I shall be yours."

"It will be done as you say, everything," said Megasthenes. "I swear it."

"Sappho," said Alkestis, "you don't have to do this."

"Yes, I do," said Sappho. "Goodbye, Alkestis." Then, to Megasthenes, she said, "Take me home, my husband."

Sappho pushed her way back out of the crowd and mounted the chariot. Megasthenes nodded curtly and picked up Kleis's body before getting on board himself. The chariot was not meant to hold so many passengers, but Sappho ignored the cramped feeling. She didn't think she would ever feel anything pleasant again.

Megasthenes whistled to the horses and turned the chariot around, then cracked his whip and drove back the way he had come, opposite the harbor.

Part Three
Syracuse 604 BCE

ἐμπειρία τέχνην ἐποίησεν

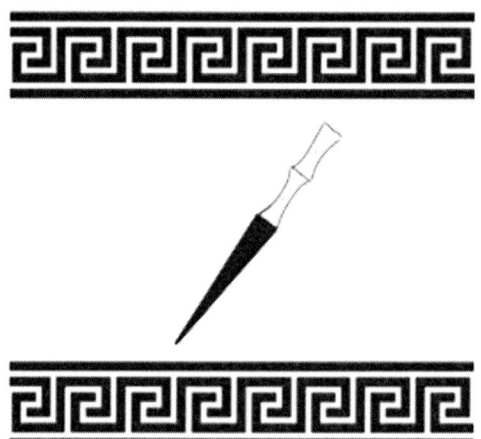

Megasthenes lived in Syracuse proper, across the water from Ortygia on the mainland. Sappho watched numbly as the chariot was driven onto the ferry and carried across to the massive island of Sicily. She barely noticed her surroundings at all until they reached Megasthenes's house, which was slightly smaller than the one Sappho had grown up in in Mytilene. Megasthenes drew the chariot up to the front door of the house and dismounted with Kleis's body.

Sappho followed him up to the front door, which Megasthenes was unsuccessfully attempting to open while burdened with Sappho's daughter. Finally, Sappho said, "Here," and she opened the door herself.

Megasthenes led Sappho into the atrium, looking around. "Aphronos! Exanthia!" he called out. "I have to apologize for my slaves," he said to Sappho uncomfortably. "They can be a bit idle."

"It's all right," said Sappho, not really caring. "You only have two slaves?"

"Well," said Megasthenes, a little defensively, "there's not much to do. Up until now, it's just been me living here."

"I see," said Sappho neutrally.

A moment passed in silence as they waited, neither knowing what to say. Then a young man in his twenties with brown hair and beard, followed by a girl in her late teens. The girl's skin was dark and lovely and she had long, black hair pulled back in a braid. Sappho was immediately struck by the girl's eyes. They were bright green and shown with an intensity that Sappho had to force herself to look away from.

Megasthenes was speaking. "Aphronos," he said, "take the chariot to the stable and unhook the horses and feed and water them. Exanthia, go fetch wood, oil—the good oil—and meet us in the garden. We're having a funeral."

The two slaves nodded wordlessly and obeyed.

"Aphronos and Exanthia are your slaves now, too," Megasthenes said to Sappho.

"I've never seen a black girl with green eyes before," Sappho said.

"What?" Megasthenes said as if startled. "Oh, yes. Well, Exanthia is from Cyrene in Libya. She tells me her mother is African. Her father is Greek. I suppose that is where the green eyes come from."

"Ah," said Sappho, pretending not to notice the twinge in her chest.

"And you'll have to get used to Aphronos," he said. "Poor boy fell off an ass in his youth and hit his head. He's a halfwit now, I fear. But they're both loyal. Don't know what I'd do without them."

"Right," said Sappho. "By the way, what should I call you? Megasthenes is a very formal name."

"Is it?" he said. "Well, I don't know, then. My mother used to call me Loudi."

"Loudi?" Sappho said. "You want me to call you Loudi? That sounds ridiculous."

"It is the name of a kind of flower that blooms only in the hills of Sicily," said Megasthenes testily. "But you don't have to—"

"Very well," Sappho interrupted. "Loudi it is."

"Well," said Megasthenes almost brightly, "the garden, then."

It was not until that moment that Sappho realized she had left her lyre and flute behind.

They proceeded to the garden. There was indeed a bed of roses—white ones. And a low stone altar to Apollo. They waited many minutes in awkward silence before Aphronos entered the garden with a large armful of kindling, followed by Exanthia, who was carrying a clay pitcher, presumably full of oil.

Aphronos arranged the wood on the altar. Megasthenes nodded to Exanthia, who poured a generous portion of the oil on the wood. Sappho took Kleis's body gently from Megasthenes and placed it on the pyre. Megasthenes opened his mouth to speak, but no one would ever know what he had been about to say, because Sappho immediately took one of the torches from the perimeter of the garden and set Kleis's pyre alight.

The oil caught quickly, and soon both the wood and Kleis's clothing were on fire. It wasn't long before the harsh, but sweet, aroma of crisped and burning flesh filled the garden. Sappho caught an inhalation of it and suddenly felt nauseous. She willed herself to ignore the feeling at first, but swiftly realized things were very much beyond her control. Her hand to her mouth, she rushed to the flowerbed—not the roses—and threw herself upon her knees before vomiting copiously onto the soil. She wiped her mouth with the back of her hand and rose, glancing at the pyre. Kleis's face was black and the skin was splitting open, revealing yellowish, bubbling fat beneath. Sappho had never seen anything so horrible.

She turned to Megasthenes and said weakly, "I need to lie down. This is too much."

"Of course," said Megasthenes fretfully. "Exanthia, take my wife to the guest room and tuck her in. In fact, from now on, I want you to see to her every need. You will obey her as you would me." To Sappho, as she left the garden with Exanthia, he said, "I will see you in the morning."

"Perhaps," nodded Sappho without looking at him. And she followed Exanthia out of the garden and into the interior of the house.

The guest room was situated right beside Megasthenes's own bedroom and was relatively small. But the bed looked comfortable and there was a window looking out onto the strait of water between Ortygia and Syracuse proper. Exanthia lit an oil lamp and placed it on the bedside table. "Is there anything else I can do for you, my lady?" Exanthia asked.

"Yes, actually," said Sappho. "You can talk to me for a while. Do you know what your name means?"

"Yes, my lady," said Exanthia. "It means *breaking out in blossoms*."

"Very good," acknowledged Sappho. "And how old are you?"

"Seventeen, I believe," said Exanthia. "I've never really known for certain."

"Really?" Sappho said. "What time of year were you born?"

"Midwinter," said Exanthia.

"Has your birthday ever been celebrated?" Sappho asked.

"Not that I can remember, my lady," said Exanthia. "I have been a slave since I was very young."

"Hmm," mused Sappho. "You're quite lovely," she said distantly.

"Thank you, my lady," said Exanthia uncomfortably.

"Especially your eyes," Sappho continued. "I like green eyes. I knew someone once…" Sappho's voice trailed off.

"My lady?" Exanthia said.

Sappho sat on the bed. "That is all," she said. "You may go."

"Yes, my lady," said Exanthia. And with a discreet nod, she left the room.

Sappho snuffed out the lamp and reclined on the mattress, but it was nearly dawn before she fell asleep.

The next morning Sappho awoke after only an hour or two of sleep. She was momentarily disoriented before remembering she was in Megasthenes's house, far away from her home at The Battered Muse, and Kleis had been dead for more than twelve hours. She wondered how on earth her life had been completely upended in so short a span of time, and briefly wished for the comfort of the hugging demon's presence, for at least that horror was predictable.

A few minutes after waking, she was disturbed by her new husband—*husband?*—knocking at the door, apparently to check on her. She pretended to be still asleep, and he eventually went away. After a decent interval, Sappho wiped the crust of fleeting sleep out of her eyes and rose, thirsty. Without bothering to fix her hair or put on her sandals, she emerged from the guest bedroom—her room, now, she supposed—and made her way, without knowing why, to the garden.

She had been hoping to find the garden empty, but the slave Aphronos was there, and he was diligently scraping the ashes—Kleis's ashes—off the stone altar to Apollo and into an urn. Suddenly furious—at precisely whom she did not care—she raised her voice and shouted, "What do you think you're doing?"

Aphronos jumped, badly startled, and nearly dropped the urn. Turning to her he said, meekly, "What?"

Half embarrassed, half insulted, Sappho quickly composed herself. "I am the mistress of the house now, boy," she said, "and you will treat me with respect. Now, what are you doing?"

Aphronos bowed his head. "Forgive me, my lady," he said. "I was gathering up the dead girl's ashes to bury them. Master said it was to be done as you asked."

Sappho straightened up self-consciously. "Yes," she said. "They are to go in the rose bed."

"Yes," said Aphronos, "I know. You're very pretty."

It was such a complete *non sequitur* that Sappho for a moment did not realize what the slave had said. And when she did, she found she had no words to express the loathing she felt for this poor addled boy at that moment. Aphronos had done nothing to offend her. Indeed, he was polite and deferential. But she realized she disliked him intensely for no discernible reason. At least, none she was aware of. "Thank you," she said archly. "Now, I would appreciate it if you kept your personal comments to yourself."

"Yes, my lady," said Aphronos.

Her throat now burning with thirst, Sappho turned to go in search of something to drink—she certainly was not going to ask this simpleton for help—when Aphronos suddenly spoke again.

"Lady," he said, "what is your name?"

Sappho tensed, feeling her anger settling right between her shoulder blades. Without looking at Aphronos, she said simply, "Sappho," and then went back into the house.

After a moment of wandering, she found herself in the dining room. Exanthia was there, clearing what appeared to be the remains of Megasthenes's breakfast. He had had goat cheese and fruit, a morning favorite of Sappho's. Now finding herself hungry as well as thirsty, she cleared her throat. The slave girl turned to face her and bowed her head. "Yes, my lady?" she said.

"Good morning," said Sappho awkwardly. "I should like some breakfast. Fruit and cheese. And pomegranate juice, if you have it. If not, anything will do. You may bring a tray to my bedroom. Thank you, that is all."

She turned to go, but Exanthia quickly set down Megasthenes's plate and shook her head.

"Oh?" Sappho said, trying to be as imperious as she had been with Aphronos. "Should I not go about as I please?"

"It isn't that, my lady," said Exanthia quickly. "It's just that the way to your room is through the other door." She pointed.

"Oh," said Sappho again. "Yes, well, just bring me that tray, then."

"Yes, my lady," said Exanthia.

And Sappho returned to the bedroom.

Sappho stayed in her room for the next four days, not speaking to anyone except Exanthia, who brought her meals and emptied her chamber pot. A couple of times Megasthenes came to the room, but she refused to acknowledge him. She knew he was frustrated with her, but she didn't care. He had killed her daughter—*the breath in her lungs*, she had called her. Kleis. She couldn't imagine ever being happy again.

On the fifth day, knowing she could not remain in seclusion forever, she rose at dawn and made her way to the dining room. She almost went to the garden first, but she could not bear the thought of seeing Kleis's roses just yet. Not now.

Megasthenes and Exanthia were in the dining room, the former having his breakfast served by the latter. Sappho cleared her throat weakly as she entered the room, and Megasthenes looked up at her. Exanthia averted her gaze.

"Ah," said Megasthenes, "there you are at last. Would you like some refreshment?"

"That depends," said Sappho sourly. "What do you have to drink in this house?"

"You want wine before breakfast?" Megasthenes asked, taken aback.

"I want wine *for* my breakfast," said Sappho. What she really wanted was to get drunk, such as she had never been before. Once, years ago, she had overindulged in Alkestis's beer, but that intoxication was nothing to what she wanted now.

"Very well," said Megasthenes, rising, his meal apparently finished. "I am going into town today, and I'm taking Aphronos with me. Exanthia will see to you while I am out." He motioned for Exanthia to join him in the doorway, where he said, "Prepare spiced wine for my wife," adding in a whisper, "Make the wine very weak, Exanthia."

The slave girl nodded and left the room to fetch Sappho's wine. Megasthenes put his hand on Sappho's shoulder. "I hope," he said, "that this will be a good beginning to your new life. I was wondering, what sort of wedding would you like?"

"Wedding?" Sappho echoed as she sat at the table. "I hadn't thought about it. None, I suppose."

"None?" Megasthenes said. "I was hoping we could have a nice ceremony in the garden to commemorate our happy union."

"I should be delighted to be married in the spot where my daughter was just incinerated," said Sappho sarcastically. "How utterly romantic of you, Loudi."

Megasthenes looked stricken. "I'm sorry," he said. "I wasn't thinking."

"No," said Sappho, "you weren't. I really don't care to have a wedding at all. If it pleases you, let us just be married by mutual agreement. That would suit me just fine."

"Well," said Megasthenes, "if you're certain…"

Sappho nodded without looking at him. Megasthenes bent to kiss her on the cheek, but Sappho dodged him. At a loss, Megasthenes straightened his chlamys, as he did whenever he was flustered. "I'll just be going now," he said. "I may be quite late."

"I won't wait up, then," said Sappho distantly.

"Don't," said Megasthenes, and he swept briskly out of the room.

Sappho leaned on the table in despair. How could she possibly spend the rest of her life with this man? It wasn't just that he had killed Kleis. He seemed to be a real dolt when it came to her emotions, a clumsy fool. And now she was stuck with him. If she were to survive, she would have to find someone else to cheer her. Someone like—

"My lady?"

Sappho turned to the doorway where Exanthia stood with a pitcher of wine and a bronze cup. "Exanthia," said Sappho, "bring me the wine."

Exanthia nodded and poured Sappho a full cup before setting both it and the pitcher on the table. Sappho drank the wine quickly and greedily but made a face afterward. "How much water did you put in this?" She asked the slave girl.

"I beg your pardon, my lady?" Exanthia said.

"This stuff's been diluted," said Sappho. "I know because I used to tend a bar. Does that shock you?"

"No, my lady," said Exanthia.

"No?" Sappho said. "Bring me another pitcher, and don't put anything in it this time."

"But, master—" Exanthia began.

"Master told you to obey me," said Sappho, "so, obey."

Exanthia nodded and went to fetch a fresh pitcher. In the few minutes, the slave girl was out of the room, Sappho drank the rest of the watered-down wine in the first pitcher. It was very good, she thought. Like the wine, her father imported to Lesbos. *Ah, Sappho*, she thought to herself, *how did we ever end up here?* Everything had been going so well in Mytilene until she met Thalia. *Certainly, this is her fault*, Sappho thought. But she could not blame Thalia. Not really. It seemed the fates had made a joke of her. There had to be some way out of this, but she couldn't think of a thing to do to improve her lot at this point. She was trapped for certain.

Exanthia returned presently with another pitcher. Sappho motioned for a refill of her cup, as countless patrons of The Battered Muse had to her for the last five years. Exanthia filled her cup and Sappho drank deeply and then sighed. "Now," she said, "that's better."

Exanthia bowed and started to leave, but Sappho stopped her with a word. "Stay," said Sappho. "Sit. Keep me company."

"Of course," said the slave girl, and she sat at the table with Sappho.

"Would you like some of the wine?" Sappho asked.

"I don't think it would be a very good idea," said Exanthia uncomfortably.

"Don't you?" Sappho asked. "Well, I do." She grasped the empty cup left from Megasthenes's breakfast and filled it with wine from the pitcher. She thrust the cup at Exanthia, who accepted it reluctantly and took a sip.

"For heaven's sake," said Sappho. "Don't drink so gingerly. Really *try* it." Exanthia took a large gulp and coughed.

Sappho laughed. "Never tried strong drink before?" she asked, amused.

"Never, my lady," said Exanthia.

"Well, sit a while, and let's get drunk together," said Sappho.

"Master—" said Exanthia.

"Is gone for the day," finished Sappho. "And I want you to help me relax. Drink up, Exanthia. That's an order from your new mistress."

Exanthia smiled slightly and took another drink. "It feels warm going down," she said.

"That's how you know it's working," said Sappho. "Come, let's have some fun."

Megasthenes returned at sundown. While Aphronos saw to the horses, he stood in the atrium and called for Exanthia. But after a couple of silent minutes, the slave girl did not appear. Megasthenes was irritated. Exanthia had never kept him waiting this long before. Angry, he strode into the house to find her.

He first went to the dining room, where he had left Sappho that morning. There was no one there, but there were five empty wine pitchers on the table, one of them lying on its side, a small puddle of wine on the table near its mouth. "Sappho?" he called in a raised voice. Something was wrong.

Megasthenes went straight to the guest room, now Sappho's bedroom, and found the door closed. He knocked. "Sappho, my dear?" he called.

Silence was his only answer. Megasthenes slowly opened the door. A single burning oil lamp illuminated a scene which shocked the master of the house. Sappho and Exanthia lay senseless upon Sappho's bed. Fearing they had been attacked by a burglar while he had been out, Megasthenes rushed to the side of the bed where Sappho lay. He put a hand on her forehead. "Sappho?" he said. "Are you all right?"

That was when he smelled her breath. It reeked of expensive wine and Megasthenes realized the truth. "Apollo's balls," he whispered. Frowning, he went to check on Exanthia. If she had dared do what he was guessing she had done—

He rolled the prone Exanthia over onto her back and was met by a hearty exhalation of alcohol from her inebriated lungs. Furious, he drew back his fist to strike the slave girl, but then reconsidered how he was going to handle this. Exanthia must be beaten—*oh, yes*, he thought. But it needed to wait until she was sober. He stood back up and walked out of the room, leaving all as he had found it, and closed the door behind him.

He met Aphronos on his way to the dining room, and said to him, "Exanthia is…indisposed. Prepare something for me to eat. Then I'm going to bed. Do not disturb my wife, Aphronos."

"Yes, master," said Aphronos, wondering what was going on. He went to fetch some bread.

Megasthenes continued to the dining room and sat down at the table. He picked up one of the cups sitting there. There was a bit of wine left in the bottom, and he tasted it. It was full strength. He slammed the cup back down on the table and swore.

Exanthia would surely pay.

Sappho awoke with an alcoholic belch in the early hours of the next morning. Her mouth tasted terribly sour and her throat burned for fresh water. She sat up and the headache hit her hard. She looked around and saw that

Exanthia was gone. Wanting a sip of anything but wine, Sappho rose in agony and exited her bedroom in the direction of the dining room.

She heard the voices of Megasthenes and Exanthia while she was still in the hallway outside the dining room. Thinking it unwise to interrupt, she stopped outside the doorway and listened.

Megasthenes was speaking. "I go to town for the day and what do I find when I return? My wife, drunk as a Trojan whore! You, too, as if the first weren't bad enough. I told you to dilute the wine!"

"I did dilute the wine, master," said Exanthia in distress. "But she knew it and she told me to keep bringing her more."

"And you obeyed her?" Megasthenes said.

"You told me to, master," wept Exanthia.

"But not when her orders contradict mine!" bellowed Megasthenes. "Bad girl. *Bad girl!*"

Sappho heard the sickening sound of Megasthenes's hand impacting Exanthia's face. Exanthia cried out in pain.

"If you ever disobey me again," said Megasthenes sternly, "I will sell you to the first Arab trader who comes along. Do you understand me?"

"Yes, master," wailed Exanthia.

Sappho heard footsteps approaching. She pressed herself against the wall. Exanthia emerged from the dining room in tears and ran past where Sappho was standing. She put a hand to her mouth, knowing this was all her fault. Then, Megasthenes followed Exanthia, stopping where Sappho stood. "Sappho," he said, "I am very disappointed."

"I know," said Sappho, wondering if he was going to hit her, too. "I behaved like a tart. It won't happen again."

"No," said Megasthenes, "it won't. I'm having Aphronos lock up the wine and hide the key. I'm going to my room now to read and I do not wish to be disturbed for the rest of the day. If you need anything, Exanthia is at your disposal."

"Yes, Loudi," breathed Sappho.

"Good," said Megasthenes, and he stormed off toward his bedroom.

Once Sappho was certain Megasthenes had secured himself alone in his room, she went looking for Exanthia. She was not certain where the slaves' quarters in Megasthenes's house were. In her father's house, she had only visited them on one occasion, and that had been to witness Irini's execution.

She pushed the memory aside and wandered into the hallways beyond the garden, allowing her fingertips to brush the blossoms of Kleis's roses as she passed through.

As she approached the bathrooms, she suddenly found herself face-to-face with Aphronos. She looked at him with disgust—his hands were dirty with horse manure—though she knew immediately she needed his help.

"Aphronos," she said, "I need you to tell me something."

"Anything, my lady," said Aphronos agreeably.

"I need to talk to Exanthia," she continued. "Do you know where she is?"

"I believe she is in her room," said Aphronos. "But I don't know for sure. I've been seeing to master's horses."

"Yes," said Sappho, "I know. I can smell them on you. Show me where Exanthia's room is."

"I can do that," said Aphronos uncomfortably, "but the slaves' quarters are not a fit place for the lady of the house to go."

"Fine," said Sappho, exasperated. "Then go find her yourself and tell her to meet me in the garden."

"Yes, my lady," said Aphronos, and he disappeared around a corner.

"And wash your hands!" Sappho shouted after him.

Exanthia came to the garden a few minutes later. Sappho knew Megasthenes had hit her, but she was still shocked to see the girl's blackened and bruised left cheek. Apparently, Megasthenes had used his fist and not an open palm. Exanthia appeared on the verge of tears, but she composed herself and said to Sappho, "What do you need, my lady?"

Without thinking of what was proper under these circumstances, Sappho went straight to Exanthia and put her arms around her. This was apparently too much for the slave girl because she began to weep bitterly into Sappho's shoulder. "I'm sorry," said Sappho. "This is all my fault. This would not have happened to you if it hadn't been for me."

"I disobeyed master," said Exanthia. "This is what I deserve."

"You were only obeying me," said Sappho. "And I never should have put you in that position. Here." Sappho took her mother's pearl ring off her finger and offered it to Exanthia.

Exanthia balked. "Oh, no, my lady," she said. "I couldn't."

"You can," said Sappho, "and you will. That bruise will last for days. We must do something to draw attention away from it." She took Exanthia's wrist firmly in her hand and slipped the copper band onto Exanthia's left index finger. "And anyway, it was only turning my finger green."

Tears poured from Exanthia's eyes and she nodded. "Thank you, my lady," she said.

"Now," said Sappho, "go to your room. I'll get Aphronos to help me if I need anything. I officially excuse you from duties for the rest of the day."

Exanthia boldly squeezed Sappho's hand in appreciation, then turned and left the garden in the direction of her chamber. Sappho stood alone in the garden for a moment and then returned to her own room to think.

Sappho met her husband in the dining room early the next morning as he was eating breakfast. Megasthenes looked up at her and smiled warmly as if the events of the other day had never occurred. "Sappho," he said, "you're looking well. That pleases me. Come, join me for breakfast."

"Thank you, Loudi," said Sappho graciously. She sat down beside him and helped herself to goat cheese and some grapes. "I must apologize again for my behavior. I—"

"Don't give it another thought," said Megasthenes. "It's all forgotten."

"Good," said Sappho, and she managed a smile.

Exanthia entered the dining room with a pitcher. She avoided Sappho's gaze as she refilled Megasthenes's cup with grape juice and poured a fresh one for Sappho. Megasthenes ignored Exanthia at first, and then suddenly seized the girl by the wrist, nearly making her drop the pitcher of juice. "Why are you wearing my wife's ring?" he demanded.

Sappho came immediately to Exanthia's defense. "She didn't steal it, Loudi," she said. "I gave it to her."

Megasthenes released Exanthia, who hurried out of the room. "You gave it to her?" he said. "What on earth for?"

Sappho wasn't certain how to answer, so she simply shrugged and said, "I did it because I wanted to."

"That is a very good reason," said Megasthenes with a smile. "From now on, you must do only what you want to do. I give you my permission. Just please stay away from the wine."

"That won't be difficult as you've had it locked up," said Sappho neutrally.

They ate in silence for a moment, before Sappho set down her cup.

"If I am to do as I please," she said, "I should like to go into Ortygia today."

"Really?" Megasthenes said. "Why?"

"Well," said Sappho, "after…what happened in the street that day, we left so quickly I forgot a few things at the inn."

"What things?" Megasthenes asked.

"I happen to be a musician, among other things," said Sappho, "and I would like to go back to the inn to fetch my instruments and a few scrolls of songs."

"A musician?" Megasthenes said, delighted. "What instruments do you play?"

"The lyre, mostly," said Sappho, "but I also have a shepherd's flute. I sing, too. And I write my own songs."

"You write?" Megasthenes said. "Just where do you come from, anyway?"

"I'm from Lesbos, originally," said Sappho.

"I was not aware that women were taught to write in Lesbos," said Megasthenes.

"Not women," Sappho allowed. "Just me. My father wished it."

"He must be a very strange man," said Megasthenes. "But I will not prevent you from pursuing any studies you wish to pursue. Just don't tell anyone."

"I promise I won't let word of it leave this house," said Sappho.

"This is acceptable," said Megasthenes. "Go and fetch your things. Take Aphronos with you. You may borrow two asses from the stable."

"Thank you," said Sappho, and she sipped her juice.

Aphronos saddled two of Megasthenes's three donkeys and he guided Sappho down the hill to where the ferry to Ortygia was launched. The ferry was on its way back from the capital, so they had to wait about half an hour. Aphronos was fretting, and while Sappho did not care that he appeared to be in distress, her crushing loneliness persuaded her to speak to him. "What's the matter?" she said.

"Just a bad memory, my lady," Aphronos answered uncomfortably. "I fell off my ass once, you see."

This statement was not as amusing in Greek as it might later be in English, so Sappho merely said, "I know. Megasthenes told me."

"I don't mind being foolish and slow," Aphronos continued. "Really, I don't. But it always bothers me to ride one now, you understand. Do you have bad memories, my lady?"

Sappho thought of Irini. "Yes," she said simply.

Aphronos had to guide Sappho through Ortygia's streets to The Battered Muse, as Sappho had only traveled the route between the inn and the ferry once, and as she was justifiably distracted then, she could not remember the way. Aphronos, on the other hand, had been this way many times before with Megasthenes, and although he had a reputation for being cognitively *off*, he was relatively familiar with the layout of the city. They had no trouble finding the inn.

It was time for lunch when they arrived, and Sappho ordered Aphronos to wait in the street while she went inside. Alkestis was busy with the guests and had her back to Sappho as Sappho stole up behind her and tapped her on the shoulder. "What is it?" Alkestis asked in irritation, then turned and faced her old friend. "Sappho!" she exclaimed in surprise and delight. "I wasn't expecting to see you back this soon. Did you change your mind?"

Sappho shook her head, suddenly too overcome with emotion to speak. Alkestis seemed to pick up on this, because she quickly said, "Would you like to sit down?"

Sappho nodded and allowed herself to be escorted to the only empty table. The common room was full of regulars who all knew Sappho well, but Alkestis signaled with a look that they should leave her alone. Alkestis fetched a cup of Egyptian beer and put it in Sappho's hand. "Drink this," she said. "It'll steady your nerves. We can talk after the crowd thins a bit."

Sappho gratefully sipped the warm beer, savoring its mild burn as it trickled down her throat. Without a thought for Aphronos standing outside, she waited patiently for the curious, but respectful, patrons to finish their lunch and, eventually leave the common room. When the last of them had gone, Alkestis joined Sappho at the table and sat down heavily. "I had forgotten what a chore that was to do on one's own," she sighed.

"I'm sorry," said Sappho softly. "I imagine it was terribly selfish of me to leave."

"No," said Alkestis. "I understand. You were born upper class. You were meant to live upper class. You couldn't work in an inn forever. We're square, Sappho. Entirely square."

"Thank you, Alkestis," said Sappho.

"I take it you've returned for your things, then?" Alkestis said shrewdly. "Your room is just the way you left it. I haven't had the heart to rent it out. Not just yet, anyway."

"Yes," said Sappho. "I don't feel like writing anything new. It's too soon after—You understand, I guess. But I need my music, Alkestis. I need to play and sing, even if I can no longer create. I miss it too much. It holds too many memories. It's a part of me. Oh," she sighed, "I can't really explain. I'm such a mess."

"You want my opinion?" Alkestis asked.

"All right," said Sappho, guarded.

"You're not allowing yourself to grieve," said Alkestis. "I admit, you may still be in shock. But you're going to have to mourn Kleis eventually. It's okay to cry, Sappho."

"I know," said Sappho.

"Do you?" Alkestis said. "I don't think so. You have a tendency to ignore your losses. Your governess. Your mother. You've avoided grieving for them for years. Just my opinion, of course."

"Well," said Sappho primly, "I will this time."

"I'll believe that when I see it," Alkestis said. "Let's get your things."

Sappho and Alkestis cleared out Sappho's room. In truth, there wasn't much for Sappho to retrieve. Aside from her lyre, her flute, and her songs on papyrus, there were a couple of changes of clothes and a spare pair of sandals. There were some clothes of Kleis's as well, but Sappho ignored those, and Alkestis let her. She had already said her piece.

Sappho did not linger in the inn after gathering her belongings, despite knowing Alkestis was quite concerned about her. She could tell Alkestis wanted to talk and probably had a great deal to say, but she wasn't interested and her body language said as much. Alkestis followed her to the door to the street to say goodbye and saw Aphronos standing there, holding the donkeys. "You didn't tell me you had an escort," Alkestis said.

"He's just a slave," said Sappho.

"He might be hungry," ventured Alkestis.

Aphronos opened his mouth to speak, but Sappho interrupted. "He's not," she said. "I shall try to visit you often, Alkestis."

"You do that," Alkestis frowned. "And try to be a little more in touch with your feelings."

"I will," said Sappho in a tone that indicated she was going to ignore this bit of advice. As Aphronos was helping her mount her donkey, she asked him, "Is there an armorer's forge nearby?"

"Yes, my lady," Aphronos answered.

"Then take me there at once," Sappho said. She leaned toward Alkestis, "I'll see you soon."

Alkestis nodded soberly and watched as Aphronos led Sappho away from the inn.

It took nearly an hour to reach the armorer's stall because Aphronos had only been there once and took them on several wrong turns. Sappho's patience was near the breaking point when they finally got there. The stall was like many merchants' establishments in the city, with a bench out front, a tent concealing an inner room, and an awning overhead. Smoke from the forge rose into the air and the armorer's apprentice could be heard hammering metal in the background. Sappho dismounted her donkey and instructed Aphronos to stand in the street. Then she walked up to the front bench and rapped her knuckles on its top.

After a moment, the armorer emerged from the tent. "My lady," he nodded. "What can I do for you?"

"My husband carries a *kopis* whenever he goes out," said Sappho. "It's much too big to be suitable and it makes him look like a common butcher. I would like to purchase something else for him instead. Some kind of *skiphos*, but small."

"You're not from around here," said the armorer. "It's pronounced *xiphos*, lady." *Xiphos*, or *skiphos* in the Aeolic dialect, was simply the Greek word for *sword*. In modern English terms, it refers to a particular style of sword with a double-edged, leaf-shaped blade, designed to be wielded with one hand. This weapon's design first appeared in the early Iron Age and was apparently never forged of bronze.

"I'm from Lesbos, if you must know," said Sappho. "And I need a blade, not your lip."

The armorer was clearly irritated by this, and judging Sappho to be a foreigner acting above her station, he might have said something harsh. But a sword was expensive, and if Sappho could pay—and she clearly believed she could, otherwise she would not be at his forge—then she must be upper class, by association, at least, if not by breeding. "Sorry, my lady," he said gruffly. "The *kopis* is a popular weapon for horsemen. Your husband rides a horse, does he?"

"No," said Sappho. "He drives a chariot."

"Probably why he favors a *kopis*, then," said the armorer. "It's better than a *xiphos* for striking from above. But if he's a small man…"

"Yes," said Sappho. "Short and thin."

"Then I can understand how that might look awkward," said the armorer.

"Yes," said Sappho.

"And I have just the thing," said the armorer. He went behind his bench and withdrew a broad, dagger-like weapon with a sharp iron blade about two spans long. The hilt was olive wood. He slid the blade into a wooden scabbard with bronze rings near the throat for hanging on a baldric.

"That?" Sappho laughed. "It looks like a toy!"

"This is as short as a *xiphos* gets, my lady," said the armorer. "Very subtle in appearance, but deadly in the right hands. It's quite popular as a sidearm among the hoplites of Sparta, so I'm told."

"Soldiers use these?" Sappho said doubtfully.

"Absolutely," said the armorer. "The *xiphos* is a last resort weapon for use in a phalanx after the spear is broken or discarded. And for a gentleman like yours, it would be effective for self-defense at close quarters without advertising itself too much, if you know what I mean."

"All right," said Sappho, "you've convinced me. How much?"

"Well, that's the bad news," said the armorer with a smile. "I can't let it go for anything less than four hundred."

Sappho frowned, admittedly shocked. Four hundred staters were well more than a year's wages for the average laborer. Sappho had only thirty-seven in her purse. "That's your final price?" she said, dismayed.

"Afraid so," said the armorer. "You don't have the money, do you?"

"Not with me," said Sappho. "But I can get it. Will you hold the *xiphos* for me for a couple of days?"

"Two days," said the armorer. "After that, you take your chances."

"Fine," said Sappho. "I'll be back." She turned back toward the street where Aphronos was standing with the donkeys. "I assume you can get us home without getting lost?" she said.

"I think so, my lady," said Aphronos.

"You inspire such confidence," said Sappho wearily. She glared sternly at Aphronos.

"What is it, my lady?" he asked.

"The ass?" Sappho said.

Aphronos stared.

"Help me get on?" Sappho said.

"Oh!" Aphronos exclaimed. "Of course, my lady." He dismounted his donkey.

Sappho rolled her eyes.

Megasthenes was not in when they got back to the house. While Aphronos took the two donkeys to their stable, Sappho went looking for Exanthia. She was not in the atrium, the dining room, or the garden. Sappho stood in the garden for a few minutes, transfixed by Kleis's roses. It had only been a few days since her little girl had died, and whatever reassurances she had given to Alkestis, Sappho had not allowed herself to fully come to terms with her loss. She had reached out her hand to touch one of the rose blossoms, when she heard the sound of trickling water coming from inside the house, in the area where the slaves' quarters were.

Curious, Sappho left Kleis's roses behind and followed in the direction of the sound. She was halfway down the hall when the trickling sound stopped. She paused in the hallway, unsure how to proceed, when a faint splash of water met her ears. Zeroing in on the sound, she made her way deeper into the house. Here she came across a wooden door that stood open. Glancing inside, she saw two simple beds. This was clearly where Exanthia and Aphronos slept. She passed by the door and went on.

Sappho eventually came to a doorway without a door and she stepped through it cautiously.

Exanthia was there in a smallish room with no furnishings, naked before Sappho, her back to her. She had taken the braid out of her long hair and was massaging ointment into the dampened tresses. Two pitchers of water and one empty one sat on the floor beside her. Sappho, both mildly embarrassed and greatly intrigued, realized she had caught Exanthia in the middle of bathing. She took in the view appreciatively, admiring Exanthia's smooth, light brown skin, her firm, round buttocks, her small feet, and delicately protruding shoulder blades. Here was perfection and beauty as she had rarely had the pleasure to see it. Sappho's lips parted and her breath caught in her chest where her heart throbbed strongly. She figured she should say something, but she found herself loath to interrupt Exanthia's bath, knowing this curiously arousing experience would then end. She also did not wish to humiliate Exanthia. But perhaps—

"My lady?"

Aphronos's voice made both Sappho and Exanthia jump in surprise. Exanthia let out a little yelp and turned to face Sappho, who found it difficult to tear her eyes away from the lovely slave girl; her breasts were full and perfect, her dripping pubic hair black and wild. She found it difficult to look away, but not impossible. She faced Aphronos.

"Aphronos!" she said, flustered and upset. "Don't sneak up on me like that!"

Aphronos cringed in distress. "Sorry, my lady," he said, "but, as I said, the slaves' quarters are not a fit place for the mistress of the house."

Exanthia's mouth was hanging open and she had instinctively placed her hands over her breasts. "Was there something you needed?" She asked Sappho.

Sappho quickly composed herself. "Yes," she said, "but you must finish up here first. Aphronos, take me to the dining room. I shall meet you there, Exanthia. No need to hurry."

And with that, she turned and marched out of the bathroom without waiting for Aphronos to escort her. Aphronos glanced at Exanthia, apparently unable to appreciate the awkwardness of the situation, before following Sappho out.

Sappho and Exanthia had each composed herself by the time Exanthia joined the waiting Sappho in the dining room. Sappho, badly wanting a drink, had contented herself with eating a few pomegranate seeds that had been left on the table from Megasthenes's breakfast; it was clear Exanthia had been neglecting her duties. Sappho didn't care. If Exanthia wished to bathe rather than clean up, what was that to Sappho? And furthermore, if she *hadn't* taken a bath, Sappho wouldn't have seen her—

No, Sappho thought. *Don't go there.*

The slave girl, newly washed, her hair hanging unbraided down her back, entered the dining room and stopped deferentially a few cubits away from Sappho and cast her gaze downward. "My lady?" she said.

"I need your help," Sappho said gently. She did not wish to torment the girl—far from it; she felt for some reason that she wanted Exanthia to be happy. "I need to know where your master keeps his money."

Exanthia's face clouded over. She was too polite to frown, but it was clear Sappho had asked a question she could not answer. "My lady," she said, "I'm afraid I don't know."

"You don't know," said Sappho, "or you won't tell me? You can tell me the truth. I won't be angry."

Exanthia screwed up her face as if in pain, then said, "There is a room in the back of the house that Aphronos and I are not allowed to enter. I don't know what's in there, but Master always goes there before he travels into the city."

"That may be what I need," said Sappho. "Show me this room at once."

"I—It is difficult, my lady," said Exanthia. "Master—"

"Is not home," finished Sappho. "Megasthenes told you to obey me, and when he isn't home, I am in charge of the house. I do not ask you to enter this room you speak of, but I insist you show me where it is."

"Very well, my lady," said Exanthia in a tone that said all was not very well indeed. "Come with me."

Exanthia led Sappho down a hall past the bedrooms that Sappho had not yet explored and they eventually came to a closed door. Sappho examined the door. "It's not locked?" she said, surprised.

"Master trusts us," Exanthia explained. "He knows we know what the punishment would be if we entered this room. He wouldn't beat us or sell us for this. He would kill us, my lady. And we both know it."

"Well," said Sappho, "he won't find out from me that you showed it to me." And she reached out her hand and pushed the door open. The room was small and had no windows. Sappho couldn't see a thing. "Get me a lamp," she said to an increasingly anxious Exanthia. The slave girl ran off and soon returned with a lighted oil lamp. Sappho took the lamp and carried it before her as she entered the room. What she saw took her breath away.

Inside the room was a table. On the table was an open box. And in the box rested the largest pile of gold she had ever seen. Sappho had learned a great deal about money working for Alkestis, and she estimated there must be five or six thousand staters of electrum here. She wondered if even her father had been this rich. It wasn't all hers, just for the taking, she realized. But she could easily help herself to four hundred staters without Megasthenes ever being any the wiser. She reached out her hand and seized a handful of coins. Yes, they were one-stater pieces, each a day's worth of work as she had been used to it.

Sappho turned to Exanthia. "Hold out the hem of your peplos," she said. "I'm going to fill it with gold."

Exanthia balked at this, but Sappho glared at her. "I'm not going to tell anyone," she said. "Come on, Exanthia."

But Exanthia obviously feared her master too greatly to help Sappho in this way, so Sappho sighed and said, "Very well. Go and fetch me a bag of some sort."

Exanthia dashed off gratefully and soon returned with a leather pouch big enough to hold several pomegranates. Knowing Megasthenes could return from town at any moment, Sappho counted out the sum of coins the armorer had requested, no more and no less, and put them in the bag. When the deed was done, she tied the bag's drawstring and closed the door.

"Thank you," she said to Exanthia. "Now, go clean up the dining room before Megasthenes gets home."

Exanthia looked extremely relieved to be done helping to rob her master, and she dashed off to carry out Sappho's instructions. Sappho herself went straight to her bedroom and placed the bag of electrum on the bed. There was a small cabinet with a drawer beside the bed where she presumed she was allowed to keep her belongings. She opened the drawer and threw her clothes and shepherd's flute into it, then placed the bag of coins under a clean peplos. She closed the drawer, her heart pounding with the thrill of having just gotten away with grand theft. Then she picked up her lyre and went straight to the garden to play music for a while.

Sappho was not certain whom she was playing for—Kleis, Alkaios, Thalia, her mother, Irini, Exanthia. In the end, it was probably for herself.

Megasthenes was in a good mood that night as he and Sappho sat in the dining room having dinner together, attended to by a fretful Exanthia. Sappho plied her new husband with questions. What was his business? Where did he go when he went into town nearly every day? Megasthenes dodged everyone, and Sappho gave up. She didn't really need to know anyway.

Megasthenes was amused when Sappho asked to borrow Aphronos and the donkeys again the next day. "What on earth could be so interesting about Ortygia that you must visit it again?" he asked. "Isn't my house grand enough for you?"

Sappho smiled demurely and answered, "I would think a present for my husband would merit my going into town twice in one week."

Megasthenes chuckled. "Well," he said, "I suppose I can allow it under those circumstances. Just don't make it a habit."

Sappho did not visit The Battered Muse when she returned to Ortygia the next morning to purchase Megasthenes's sword. This was a calculated move. Alkestis had strong opinions about Sappho's life, and Sappho did not feel up to hearing a lecture that day. Aphronos was as affable an escort as ever. He was polite and followed Sappho's every instruction, not speaking unless he was spoken to. Even so, Sappho felt her usual, peculiar disdain for him. She could not explain it. He simply rubbed her the wrong way, and not through his actions. His mere existence seemed to offend her. That was the way she felt and there was nothing to be done about it.

If the armorer was surprised to see Sappho again so soon, he did not show it. He merely counted the electrum coins and handed over the *xiphos*. Sappho was quite excited. The sword was really quite elegant, and would not look so out of place on Megasthenes's hip. It was *subtle* as the armorer had said, and Sappho thought it was perfect. Sappho thanked the armorer and then headed back to the house in Syracuse to wait for her husband to return from town.

And perhaps to see Exanthia.

Megasthenes was tired when he got home that evening. Sappho had instructed Exanthia to prepare a nice meal for them—lamb, bread, olives, and stuffed grape leaves. She felt a light pang of disappointment that she could not have Exanthia serve wine as well, Aphronos being in possession of the only key and Megasthenes having instructed him not to give it to her. But even without wine, dinner would be pleasant. And Sappho had purchased some sesame cakes at the market in Syracuse proper before returning home.

Sappho sat opposite Megasthenes as Exanthia served the lamb and flatbread. "So," she said, "how was your day on the town?"

"Fine," said Megasthenes through a mouthful of lamb. "I thought about you all day."

Sappho shuddered at this thought; this was the man who had killed her daughter. But she managed to say, respectfully, "Did you, Loudi?"

Megasthenes nodded. "I'm especially curious about this gift you said you were obtaining for me," he said. "Do I have to wait very long?"

Sappho smiled an artificial smile as she sipped a cup of unfermented grape juice. "Only until after dessert has been served."

"Good," said Megasthenes.

After the sesame cakes had been consumed—with particular gusto by Megasthenes—Sappho stole off to her room and collected the little *xiphos* for her husband. As she approached the dining room where he was waiting, she called out, "Close your eyes, Loudi!"

"Very well," answered Megasthenes. "They are closed."

Sappho entered with the *xiphos* behind her back. She returned to her seat across the table from Megasthenes and sat down again, placing the sword in her lap, just under the table. "All right," she said. "You can open them now."

Megasthenes opened his eyes. "And?" he prompted.

"Here," said Sappho as she lifted the sword into Megasthenes's view. His immediate expression was one of shock, followed by delight.

"Oh, Sappho," he said, "it's marvelous. May I hold it?"

Sappho nodded and passed the *xiphos* across the table to Megasthenes's outstretched hands. He slid the blade out of its scabbard and inspected the sharp iron edge. "Beautiful," he said. "Absolutely beautiful. Is this one of Tykhaios's blades?"

"It's from an armorer in Ortygia Aphronos showed me," Sappho answered. "I didn't ask his name."

Megasthenes admired the polished olive wood hilt and the scabbard with its bronze rings. "How ever did you afford this on a barmaid's wages?" he murmured.

Sappho had already decided how she would answer this question. "My father in Mytilene is a very successful businessman," she said. "When I came to Sicily, he sent me with a great deal of money." This was not precisely a lie, although the money Skamandronymous had sent with Sappho actually belonged to Simonides.

"Yes," said Megasthenes, unable to tear his eyes away from the sword. "This is very nice. Thank you, my dear. I am most pleased." He placed the weapon on the table between himself and Sappho. "I've been thinking of what else might please me, Sappho."

"Yes?" Sappho said, feigning interest.

"I should like it very much," said Megasthenes in a low voice Sappho figured was his attempt to sound seductive, "if you would share my bed tonight. After all, we have been married, by mutual agreement, for several days now. And we have yet to consummate the union."

Sappho had been dreading this, but a Greek man of those times had a legal right to insist upon sex with his wife—indeed to force it upon her—and Sappho knew he could make her life miserable if she did not acquiesce. Summoning her most winning smile and her huskiest voice, she said, "I've been looking forward to that, actually."

"Good," said Megasthenes. He wiped his mouth with his serviette and then raised his voice again. "Exanthia," he said, "Lady Sappho and I are going to bed and we do not wish to be disturbed. Clear the table and then do what pleases you. We'll want a late breakfast in the morning."

"Yes, master," Exanthia said with a deferential nod.

Sappho lay awake in Megasthenes's bed long after her husband had fallen asleep. The sex had been extremely disappointing. Worse, in fact, than what she had experienced with the smith's apprentice Palabos when she was a girl. Megasthenes had clearly never heard of foreplay, and after six quick thrusts, was finished and completely uninterested in prolonging the mood. It was worse than unfulfilling. Sappho felt as if she had been attacked, raped, by this man who was now her master forever.

She felt like crying. But Sappho was too headstrong to concede defeat at finding happiness. Perhaps she could take a lover. *Right*, she thought to herself. *He told me not to make going to town a habit.* It seemed she was stuck. She would have to concentrate even more on her music now, or risk going mad. For that was the eventuality that seemed most likely to Sappho. She was never meant to be caged. She racked her brain for what to do with herself.

And on top of everything, she thought, *he snores!*

Once again, it was a long time before she could fall asleep.

The next morning, Sappho was awakened well after dawn by Megasthenes's shaking of the bed as he got up. She moaned and turned on her side, and Megasthenes glanced at her.

"Sleep well?" he said, smiling.

"Quite," Sappho lied.

"Good," said Megasthenes as he rose and slipped on his chiton. "I was thinking," he continued, "the *xiphos* was an excellent wedding present. I know you didn't want a fancy marriage ceremony, but would you accept a gift from me as well?"

Sappho considered this. She hadn't thought about what she might want from Megasthenes in the way of material possessions. She honestly didn't feel she needed anything, but he was trying to be kind, she realized and would be very hurt if she didn't show some appreciation. So, she said the first thing that came to her mind.

"A new lyre, perhaps?" she said.

"A new one?" Megasthenes said, amused. "What's wrong with the one you have?"

And Sappho suddenly knew the answer to this question. Her old lyre was part of her old life. It had seen her through her experiences with Irini, her mother, Thalia, Diotrephes, Alkaios and little Kleis. It held too many memories for her. Sitting up in bed, Sappho said, "It's old and it's time to make a fresh start. I don't suppose you understand?"

"I understand completely, darling," said Megasthenes. He tied his sandal thongs and moved toward the door. "A lyre it is, then. I shall go into town and fetch it immediately."

"Spare no expense, Loudi," said Sappho as he left the room.

Megasthenes smiled at her and then walked away. "I won't," he called out to her from the hallway.

Sappho sat alone on the bed, wondering how she had gotten to this point. Little more than a week earlier she had been happy. She had friends, admirers, a daughter, and a life she had loved. Things would certainly be different now. Far different. Megasthenes was not a bad man; he certainly was not a heartless bastard like Kekonimenos had been, though she had hoped he might turn out to be at least half as good a lover. Certainly, things could be far worse.

There was something bothering Sappho, however. Megasthenes wanted an heir and expected Sappho to provide one for him. Try as she might, she could not entertain the idea of having another child. So, she pulled on her undergarments, retrieved her peplos from the bedroom floor, and slid into it.

After slipping on her sandals, she stepped out into the hallway and made her way to the dining room.

As she had anticipated, Exanthia was there, laying out a simple breakfast for her. Sappho sat down and started nervously peeling an orange. Surely Exanthia, as a woman, would understand the seriousness of the request she was about to make. The slave girl had been nothing but helpful and loyal to her so far, so Sappho decided to trust her again.

"Exanthia," said Sappho conversationally. "Now that I am married, there are a few things I need as a matter of course. Will you talk to me about it?"

"Of course, my lady," Exanthia answered.

"You see," Sappho continued, "I have decided I cannot afford to get pregnant. And I really don't have a practical, reliable way to prevent it. When I was younger, I used to use fennel, but seeing as how I had a daughter while I was using it, you'll understand my wanting something a bit more effective now. Do you know a method I could use? Something foolproof?"

"Nothing is foolproof, my lady," said Exanthia carefully. "But there are ways to reduce the risk. There is something called silphion, which is supposed to work better than fennel for that." Silphion, or laserwort, is a presumably extinct plant once popularly used for seasoning food and as a chemical abortifacient and contraceptive and was found almost exclusively in and around Cyrene. In fact, its great popularity in the ancient world is what is blamed for its extinction, and led to the coins later minted in Cyrene being stamped with an image of the plant. "We keep a supply of it in the house for master's meals. Shall I fetch you some?"

"How much do I need to take at a time in order for it to have the desired effect?" Sappho asked.

"I'm not really sure," Exanthia admitted. "I've never used it for that, myself. I've never needed it."

"Then I'm going to need a lot of it," said Sappho firmly. "I want you to saturate every meal with the stuff, understand? And I want to take some privately every day. Will you see to that? I'll be eternally grateful."

"Of course, my lady," said Exanthia.

Megasthenes found Sappho sitting in the garden, playing her flute, when he returned from town. He stood in the entryway for several minutes, listening to her music, before clearing his throat. Sappho stopped playing and looked up.

"You play beautifully, Sappho," he said appreciatively.

Sappho lowered the instrument. "Thank you," she said. "I actually haven't been playing very long. The flute was a gift from a friend about a year ago. I'm much better at the lyre."

Megasthenes smiled warmly. "Then," he said, "I can't wait to hear you play this one." And he reached behind the doorpost and produced an instrument so beautiful Sappho gasped in spite of herself.

The lyre was big—almost half again as tall as her old one. It had twelve gut strings, which was impressive, but what took Sappho's breath away was its wooden frame. The instrument was primarily constructed of the blackest ebony she had ever seen, polished to a mirror shine and inlaid with purple oyster shell. Its arms were not wood, but the twisted horns of some large animal. It was more than she could have hoped for. Sappho reached out her hands eagerly. "May I hold it?" she asked.

Megasthenes crossed the garden and placed the lyre in Sappho's hands, and she immediately inspected the instrument. The wood was as smooth as silk and she ran her hands over its surface. She tested the tuning pegs and found them satisfactorily tight. The sounding board, she saw, had been engraved with a little epigram in the Doric dialect of Syracuse, attributed to the legendary musician Orpheus, about music being the purest form of art. Finally, Sappho gave the strings an experimental strum. The strings produced a deep, sonorous, mellow sound which delighted Sappho. What music she would be able to create with this!

"You like it?" Megasthenes said in his excitement.

"Like it?" Sappho said breathlessly. "Oh, Loudi, I adore it."

"I picked it out myself," said Megasthenes proudly. "It's made of blackwood from the deepest, darkest reaches of Africa, far beyond the Nile where the *anthropophagoi* live."

"*Anthropophagoi*?" Sappho echoed, distracted by the lyre. "You mean they literally eat each other?"

"Well, yes," said Megasthenes uncomfortably.

"How silly of them," Sappho commented absently. "Loudi, this is the most extravagant piece of craftsmanship I've ever seen in my entire life. I didn't know such things existed. It must've cost a fortune!"

"A small fortune, yes," Megasthenes agreed. "Aren't you going to play something?"

"Would you like me to?" Sappho asked.

"Very much," said Megasthenes.

"All right," said Sappho. "I'll do my best. This lyre has four more strings than my old one, but the notes follow the same basic arrangement. It just has a greater range. Don't worry, Loudi," she said, seeing the expression on Megasthenes's face. "That's a good thing." She plucked a simple arpeggio, then sang:

There was a cup
With nectar filled
Which Hermes served with grace

The gods all drank
The bridegroom found
Good fortune cheered his face

Sappho had written this song years ago when she still believed a happy marriage was possible, and it was no accident that she chose to sing it for Megasthenes now. As she sang all eight verses, her new husband smiled even more broadly, and Sappho reflected that while she had lost most of her admirers when she left The Battered Muse, Megasthenes would be able to take their place, at least in a very small way.

That night, after Megasthenes had both listened to more of her music and had his way with her once more, Sappho resolved to begin writing again. She needed to create. If she did not, she would surely go mad.

Sappho found that she had plenty of inspiration for her music now that she was writing once more. She had Megasthenes provide her with wax tablets which, erasing being easy with them, were superior to papyrus and ink in the composing stage. Once a song was perfected to Sappho's satisfaction, she would make a permanent copy on the ingenious Egyptian precursor to paper.

But all artists need a muse, and Sappho discovered that hers was the slave girl Exanthia. The young woman was as lovely as any she had ever seen, and the fact that she was entirely beyond Sappho's reach made her all the more desirable. The literary trope of the forbidden fruit had a place in Greek culture at that time in the story of Demeter's daughter Persephone and Hades's cursed pomegranate seeds, and Sappho would have been intimately familiar with it. She ached with longing for Exanthia, and it showed in her poetry. Fortunately, Megasthenes was thick enough not to notice.

One afternoon, while Sappho was sitting composing in the garden on a rock she had come to think of as hers, there came a knock on the front door. Sappho did not even pause in her work at this; it was Aphronos's job to answer the door. But then there were voices coming from the atrium and Sappho put down her stylus and listened. She distinctly heard an unfamiliar adult male voice say her name.

Footsteps echoed on the tile floor and presently Aphronos entered the garden with a man in his late twenties whom Sappho did not know. "A man to see you, my lady," said Aphronos before retreating back into the house.

The young man was completely unknown to Sappho, but there was something about the shape of his face that Sappho found familiar. Irritated as she was that her work had been interrupted, Sappho did not wish to appear rude. "May I help you, sir?" she asked.

"You are the lady Sappho?" the young man said. "The poet from Mytilene in Lesbos?"

"The same," acknowledged Sappho. "I fear you have me at a disadvantage."

"I'm sorry," said the young man. "My name is Larikhos, and I'm your brother."

Sappho could not have been more surprised. She had never met, nor had she expected ever to meet, any of her brothers. And yet, here was one of them, who had evidently sought her out. Only one reason immediately occurred to Sappho, and she put her hand to her mouth. "It's about Papa, isn't it?" she said in sudden terror. "He's dead, isn't he?"

"No," said Larikhos. "No, nothing like that. I'm sorry if I alarmed you. That was not my intention. No, I'm here because our father wants you to come home."

Sappho was so surprised she let go of her lyre and it toppled over into the grass. "He what?" she stammered. "Why?"

"Did you think your becoming the most prominent musician in Ortygia would not come to his attention?" Larikhos said. "You're famous, Sappho. People all over the world know who you are."

"I'm stunned," admitted Sappho. "I mean, I knew Alkaios had heard of me, but he's a fellow artist. You're really serious about this?"

"Yes," Larikhos confirmed. "The archon of Mytilene would like you to be his personal lyrist, and our father wants you to come back to his house and live there once more. He regrets he could not come here himself to ask you in person, but his foot has been paining him and he was unable to make the journey."

"Amazing," said Sappho. "And has he forgiven me?" she asked. "I don't know if you're aware of the reason I left Lesbos in the first place. He said he was ashamed of me. On top of that, Alkaios said Papa wouldn't be overjoyed if I returned. You do know Alkaios, don't you?"

"Yes, of course," said Larikhos. "Everyone knows Alkaios. He's almost as famous as you. He's made a name for himself in the years since you left."

"This is all too much to take in," said Sappho. "I suppose you know I just got married?"

"Yes," said Larikhos. "The woman at the inn in the capital told me. That's how I knew where to find you."

"Then you know," said Sappho, "that I can't just pick up and leave. Syracuse is my home now."

"Father would be delighted for both you and your husband to move into his house in Mytilene and live with him, I'm sure," said Larikhos earnestly. "He's quite made up his mind about this."

"All right," said Sappho, "let me get this straight. Papa exiles me to Sicily because he's ashamed of me, but now that I'm a world-famous musician he wants me back? Am I hearing this correctly?"

"That's the general idea," said Larikhos soberly.

"Well," said Sappho angrily, "it's quite impossible."

"I beg your pardon?" Larikhos said, taken aback.

"My falling out with our father was as much his fault as mine," said Sappho. "There are things about him you don't know. Old things he did, or failed to do that—I'm sorry. I can't talk about this right now. Let's just say he is not forgiven and I'm not going to come crawling back to him just because he wants me to be a star in his crown!"

Larikhos looked stricken and Sappho felt a stab of shame. She hadn't meant to shout. It was just that she had finally put some emotional distance between her father and herself, and his reasons for wanting her to come home felt so incredibly petty to her that Sappho could not possibly entertain his request.

"I'm sorry," said Sappho, "but I cannot leave my husband and he would never agree to move to Lesbos. And it's quite too late for Papa to make amends. No, I cannot oblige him."

Larikhos looked Sappho in the eye. "That's your last word?" he said.

"Yes," said Sappho simply.

"Well," said Larikhos, "I must say I'm disappointed. So will Father be."

"I understand," said Sappho, "and I don't care. My life is far from perfect, but I'd rather live in my present circumstances than return to his house."

"What was your daughter's name?" Larikhos asked softly. "The woman at the inn didn't tell me."

"Her name was Kleis," said Sappho, "after my—"

"Your mother, yes," said Larikhos. "You wouldn't know this, but I actually met her once before you were born."

"She was wonderful," said Sappho ruefully. "The fates took her far too soon. Forgive me, but why have I never met you before now?"

"Well," said Larikhos, "after Mother died, Father sent the three of us, my brothers and me, I mean, to Athens to live with relatives. You see, Mother's death affected him greatly, and for a time he was sequestered in an *asklēpieion* quite beyond his wits. For a while, we feared he would never recover. But then he met your mother, who was at the *asklēpieion* visiting a relative, and she drew him out of his despair. Within a year they were married. That's where I met Kleis, in fact. Father invited the three of us to the wedding. Only I was able to attend."

"So that was why Papa refused to send Mama to the *asklēpieion* when she was sick," said Sappho softly. "He must've hated the place."

"I'm sure he did," agreed Larikhos.

"And you and Eurygios and Kharaxos have been living in Athens all this time?" Sappho marveled. "What have you been doing?"

"Well, Eurygios became a soldier," said Larikhos. "He's somewhere in Anatolia right now, I believe. Kharaxos went into politics. He works for the archon in Athens. And I'm a teacher."

"What do you teach?" Sappho asked.

"Mathematics," said Larikhos. "It's a fairly dull life, but I manage."

"And what about your inheritance?" Sappho asked. "Papa always told me my husband would inherit his business."

"His business, yes," confirmed Larikhos. "But not all his money. Father gave my brothers and me our share when he married your mother. It was all quite contrary to custom, but he insisted for your sake."

"Well, I'm sorry to have given you an answer you didn't want to hear, but I'm glad to have met you," said Sappho candidly. "Would you stay for dinner?"

"I'm afraid I can't," said Larikhos. "And I really am sorry. If I had my way, I'd like to get to know the sister I never had. But I have to get back to Ortygia, I'm afraid. I've secured passage back to Lesbos on a military trireme, and it sails from the harbor at first light. Father really rather thought convincing you to come home would take only a few minutes." Larikhos chuckled. "I suppose there's no accounting for a woman's behavior."

"Indeed not," agreed Sappho. "Allow me to see you out?"

"Of course," said Larikhos.

Sappho rose from her rock and escorted Larikhos through the house to the front door. Larikhos opened the door, and then turned to his sister. "Father does love you, you know. That never changed."

"I love him, too," said Sappho. "But it isn't enough. You can tell him I said that."

"Are you happy, Sappho?" Larikhos asked. "Father will want to know. And frankly, so do I."

"Is anyone really happy?" Sappho said wistfully.

"Yes," said Larikhos. "I do believe so."

"Must be nice," said Sappho. "Tell Papa I'm sometimes happy. Just sometimes."

"You won't reconsider?" Larikhos said.

"No," said Sappho. "Not now. Someday, maybe. But not now."

"Very well," said Larikhos. "I will respect your decision. I wish you all the best with your new husband. Goodbye, Sappho. And good luck." And he turned and walked down the hill that led to the water.

Sappho closed the door, leaned against it, and exhaled slowly. Her father wanted her back, but she would rather stay with Megasthenes than return home. The tragedy of this simple truth was overwhelming. She was unable to sing for the rest of the day.

Life in Megasthenes's house was comfortable but incredibly boring. Megasthenes went to town almost every day. Aphronos was clearly fond of Sappho, and eager always to talk to her, but he was really not much of a conversationalist, and despite his limited cognitive abilities, was often sent to the market to purchase food for their meals. And Sappho found interacting with Exanthia unbearably painful. Exanthia was so beautiful, so perfect in every way. But Sappho could not pluck this Libyan flower that bloomed. She had made that mistake with Thalia. And the gods only knew what Megasthenes's reaction would be if Sappho seduced his slave.

So Sappho contented herself with admiring Exanthia from afar, and it was heartbreaking at best. As with Thalia in her childhood, Sappho found Exanthia to be the inspiration for all her songs these days. Megasthenes listened on the rare occasions he was at home during the day. Surely, Aphronos could not appreciate the passion behind Sappho's music. And Sappho found Exanthia to be entirely unreadable. Sappho longed to tell Exanthia how she felt, even as she slept with Megasthenes night after night, but she could not think of a way to approach her that would not set Sappho herself up for disappointment.

But things could not go on like this forever. And so, one afternoon, a few months after Larikhos's visit, Sappho found herself sitting on her rock in the garden, composing while Exanthia listened.

Zeus's equal
That he is

Listening to your laughter
So it seems to me
Shaking in my
Chest, my heart
When I look at you, girl
And I cannot speak

My tongue fails
My flesh on fire
I am going blind, now
And I hear a hum

I feel chilled
My body quakes
I am green and new, now
Yet I may be dead

For although
The poorest man—

Sappho paused, seeking the right words to come next. She chewed the butt end of her wooden stylus, as was her habit of late when she needed to think. Finally, she looked up at Exanthia, who was listening intently from the other side of the garden.

"I'm stuck," Sappho admitted. "Where should I go from here?"

"I know not, my lady," said Exanthia. "I am no poet."

"Perhaps not," said Sappho. "But you are more important to my work than you know." Sappho hesitated. Did she dare? *Of course, she did*. And it was about time, too. "You see," she said, "this song is about you."

Exanthia appeared ready to cry. "I know," she said. "All your songs are about me these days. I have always known it."

"I wondered if you might," said Sappho seriously. "What are we going to do about it?"

"We can't do anything, my lady," said Exanthia. "You have a husband."

"I have a husband who lets me do whatever I want," said Sappho. "What I'm asking of you—what I feel for you is no crime. Please, Exanthia, tell me if you feel it too."

"It doesn't matter what I feel," said Exanthia. "Not as long as you share his bed."

"What about me?" Sappho said. "I need some passion in my life. You cannot imagine how tiresome it is to receive love from a man like mine. Sex without orgasm is the most colossal waste of time."

"My lady!" gasped Exanthia.

"Oh!" Sappho exclaimed angrily. "So, *now* I've shocked you? You know nothing about life or love, Exanthia. I don't know why I asked you what I did."

"My lady," Exanthia began, "I don't know if you—"

"I don't care," said Sappho quickly. "Be gone, blossom. You annoy me."

Exanthia ran sobbing from the garden. Sappho pushed over her lyre into the grass, put her face in her hands, and cried bitterly.

Sappho lay awake in her bed that night, thinking about the lot the fates had set for her, and wondering what she could have done to avoid ending up in the situation in which she now found herself. Where had she gone wrong? Try as she might, she could not accept that where she was now was the result of her own actions. Yes, perhaps Palabos had been a mistake, but Thalia had driven her to it. And she had misjudged Kekonimenos, but hadn't his treachery been worse than her intentional seduction of a married man? Sappho needed someone to blame, and she kept coming back to the same conclusion. This was Agathon's fault and his fault alone. Agathon had ruined her life.

Sappho was on the threshold of sleep when there came a pounding on the front door. *Never mind*, she told herself. Aphronos would answer it. And indeed, she heard the footsteps of the slave and the sound of the door opening and closing again. She had turned over in bed for more sleep when there came a shout from the atrium.

"My lady! My lady!" came Aphronos's voice. "Come quickly!"

Sappho groaned. Surely there was nothing so urgent at the front door that it required her immediate attention. But Aphronos kept shouting, so she threw off the blanket, lifted herself from the mattress, and got out of bed.

As she neared the atrium, she called out drowsily, "Aphronos, I swear by Olympus if this isn't a matter of life and death—"

What she found when she entered the atrium silenced her immediately. There were two men she didn't know standing inside the front door, and between them, they held up a limp Megasthenes, who appeared to have been knocked senseless. His eyes were open, but he was bleeding from his left ear and an abrasion over his eyebrow.

"What happened?" Sappho said breathlessly.

"You are the lady Sappho?" said one of the men.

"Yes," Sappho confirmed. "What has happened to my husband?"

"An accident, my lady," said the other man. "His chariot's axle broke. He was thrown, landed on his head."

Sappho immediately took charge. "Aphronos," she said, "go find Exanthia. Tell her to fetch oil and bandages. And bring me wine. I don't care if Master told you not to give it to me. This is an emergency. Understand?"

Aphronos stared at her and nodded.

"Well, don't stand gawking," said Sappho. "Follow my instructions. Now!"

Aphronos ran off. Sappho turned to the two Sicilians. "Thank you for bringing my husband home. Please, come with me. We must get him to his bed."

Sappho led the Sicilians to Megasthenes's bedchamber and had them lay him on his back upon the mattress. Sappho untied and removed Megasthenes's sandals and then bent over him. "Loudi?" she said. "Loudi, can you hear me?"

Megasthenes was completely unresponsive. Sappho turned to the two Sicilians. "What do I owe you for this service?" she asked them.

"Nothing, my lady," said the first of the two. "We'll just be on our way."

Sappho nodded. "Can you manage to see yourselves out?" she asked.

"Yes, my lady," said the first Sicilian. The two of them bowed and left the room. Aphronos appeared with a pitcher of wine and a bronze cup. Exanthia came right behind him with a cup of oil and a handful of linen strips. Sappho took the pitcher and poured a cupful of wine. The two slaves watched as she quickly drank the entire cup—"For my nerves," she explained—then poured more and dipped a handful of the linen in it, soaking the cloth. Sappho carefully cleaned the wound on Megasthenes's forehead with the wine-soaked cloth and then wiped away the blood that issued from his ear. "Oil, now," she said, and Exanthia handed it over. Sappho soaked two more strips of the linen in the oil and tied them around Megasthenes's head, covering both his ear and the cut above his eye. A line of spittle dripped from the corner of Megasthenes's mouth, and Sappho wiped it away with a final clean strip of the linen.

"There," said Sappho. "That's all we can do for now. Exanthia, I want you to sleep in here tonight in case he wakes up. Make a bed on the floor. Aphronos, as soon as the sun rises, go and fetch a doctor. Any doctor you can find. Understand? Now, I'm going to bed."

Aphronos and Exanthia nodded and watched as Sappho left the bedroom. They exchanged worried glances, then went to follow Sappho's instructions.

It is worth noting that, with all the excitement surrounding her fight with Exanthia and Megasthenes's injury, Sappho failed to notice her period was late.

Sappho slept late the next morning, and it was only when Aphronos shook her by the shoulder that she finally awoke. "What is it?" she groaned.

"My lady," said Aphronos fretfully, "I've brought the doctor."

Sappho nodded and rose. "Thank you," she said. "Take him to Master's bedroom. I must do something with my hair."

"Yes, my lady," said Aphronos, and he left the room.

After making herself passably presentable, Sappho went to Megasthenes's room to speak with the doctor. She found him leaning over her husband, listening to his heart. Sappho cleared her throat and the doctor looked up at her. "Ah," he said, "the lady Sappho, yes? My name is Bakenor. I have been your husband's personal physician for the last six years. Tell me, how did this happen?"

"I don't know the details," said Sappho, "but I was told he was thrown from his chariot and struck his head. He's been like this since."

Bakenor waved his index finger in front of Megasthenes's face, from left to right. Megasthenes followed the doctor's finger with his eyes but did not move his head.

"Fascinating," said Bakenor. "His heart is strong and he is fully conscious, but he can neither move nor speak."

"I experienced something similar when I was a child, doctor," said Sappho. "While I was trying to sleep, I couldn't move or speak. Will this be like that? Will he eventually wake and be able to respond to us?"

"Was your condition the result of a blow to the head?" the doctor asked.

"No," Sappho frowned. "It was part of an *ephialtēs* attack."

"Ah, I'm afraid those two experiences are not the least bit related," said Bakenor dismissively. "No, your husband has hurt himself badly and there is nothing to be done but wait. I will of course do some research to see if there is a treatment of which I am not currently aware, but you must prepare yourself for the worst. He may die in a few days, or stay in this state for years. Or he may recover. I really don't know."

"Very well," said Sappho calmly. "Thank you for coming, doctor."

"Of course, my lady," nodded Bakenor, and he left the room.

Exanthia entered with a bowl of broth. "My lady," she said, "the doctor says we must feed master. He must keep up his strength if he is to recover."

"Yes, of course," said Sappho, distracted. "By all means, feed him. He may indeed recover, and quickly." She moved toward the bedroom door.

"And if not?" Exanthia prompted.

Sappho paused in the doorway. "If not?" Sappho shrugged. "If not, winter."

That night, Sappho dined alone. Exanthia and Aphronos were looking after Megasthenes on Sappho's orders. Sappho had been wishing for a way out of her situation, and it appeared she had finally found it. Of course, there was a chance that Megasthenes would recover fully, but Sappho did not think it likely. The cut on his forehead was clearly not serious. But he had bled from his ear as well, and that meant an injury to his brain. Greek medicine of the time considered the heart the seat of thought and reason. The brain was not so well understood. But it was known that a blow to the head of sufficient force that did not kill could incapacitate a man. Apparently, Megasthenes had been hurt badly enough for this.

Presently, as Sappho was finishing her supper, Aphronos came into the dining room. "My lady?" he said.

Sappho looked up at him. "Yes?" she said.

"Exanthia told me to come check on you, lady," Aphronos said. "Do you require anything?"

"No," said Sappho. "I'm done eating. Just clear the table would you?" She rose from the table. "Then give Master some more broth. I'm going to go read for a while."

"My lady?" Aphronos said as she passed him on the way out the door. "Why do you never smile at me?"

Sappho stopped and glanced at him. "Why don't I smile at you?"

"You smile at Exanthia," said Aphronos, "but never at me. You have such a pretty smile. I just wish you would show it to me sometimes."

"Why ever should I smile at you?" Sappho asked.

"It would make me happy," said Aphronos.

"Happy?" Sappho said in incredulity. "You're a slave."

"Slaves have feelings," Aphronos said quietly. "Is Master going to be like me from now on?"

Sappho stared at Aphronos for a moment, inscrutable, and then said, "I really don't know."

And she left him standing there, alone in the dining room.

Midnight. Aphronos had gone to bed; he and Exanthia were looking after Megasthenes in shifts, alternating every few hours throughout the day. This night, Sappho could not sleep, and so went to Megasthenes's bedroom for some company. She found Exanthia sitting on a stool beside the bed, washing Megasthenes's face with a damp cloth.

Exanthia looked up. "Master is resting now," she said. Indeed, Megasthenes's eyes were closed and he was breathing peacefully.

"I had to see someone," said Sappho carefully. "I had to see you."

Exanthia looked frightened. "Don't say it, my lady," she begged.

"I want you to call me Sappho, Exanthia," Sappho said softly.

"That would not be proper," said Exanthia.

"You know how I feel about you," said Sappho as she drew nearer. "I've been very transparent. Only a fool would not have noticed. And you're not a fool." She knelt beside Exanthia's stool beside the bed.

Exanthia placed the cloth in a bowl of water that rested on the bedside table. She looked at Sappho. "No," she agreed. "I know how you feel."

"And?" Sappho prompted.

"And?" Exanthia echoed.

"And how do you feel?" Sappho said, completing the question. When Exanthia hesitated, Sappho said, "Exanthia, I must know."

"It is difficult to say," said Exanthia. "Master may hear."

"So what if he does?" Sappho said dismissively. "You know as well as I do he's not going to get any better, no matter what the doctor says. He's got the wit of a turnip now and forever. So, I ask you again. How do you feel about me?"

Exanthia brushed her hair out of her face. "You're the only person, besides Aphronos, of course, who's ever been kind to me," she said.

"Then let's be together," said Sappho. "We need each other. What could be wrong with that?"

"I wasn't meant to be happy in that way," said Exanthia with a catch in her voice. "I'm a slave."

Sappho drew nearer, putting her hand on Exanthia's cheek. "Everyone deserves to be happy," she whispered, realizing uncomfortably that she was essentially quoting Aphronos from earlier as she looked deep into Exanthia's lovely green eyes. A snippet of one of her new songs flitted through her mind:

You came
To me
And I was mad for you
You breathed on me
And quenched my thoughts
Of flame

And then she kissed her.

Sappho and Exanthia threw their arms around each other in their passion, as if each had been waiting a lifetime for the other. And perhaps they had. The kiss went on for many minutes before Sappho broke their embrace and smiled at Exanthia, caressing her face with her fingertips.

"We can have this," said Sappho firmly. "We were meant to have this. Now, turn around."

"What for?" Exanthia asked breathlessly.

"I'm going to braid your hair," said Sappho.

It was Sappho's happiest night in years.

Sappho and Exanthia's affair was hot and heavy, but very discreet. Though Sappho reflected that there was only Aphronos to catch them at their trysts, and she gave him absolutely no credit for being able to appreciate the nature of their new relationship. She would later realize she was very wrong. The doctor came and went two or three times a week over the next month, and the three able-bodied people remaining in the house took turns looking after Megasthenes.

Sappho was growing concerned, however. Her period was over a month late, but she did not allow herself to think about what that might mean. She knew menstruation was not an exact science with precise rules. But the fact remained, it had not come, and her cycles had always been fairly predictable.

She would deal with whatever was going on when she had to, she told herself.

Five weeks after Megasthenes was injured, Sappho was sitting on her rock in the garden, writing a new song on a wax tablet. Writing came so easily to her these days amidst the joy of having Exanthia at last, and she was almost finished with the latest poem.

Eros shook my heart

Blowing on me like a mountain breeze
Through the oak trees

As she sat, making notes, there came an insistent pounding on the front door. At first, Sappho ignored it completely, not even pausing in her work to look up. Aphronos would answer the door. But the pounding continued and Sappho remembered that Aphronos was at the market, purchasing groceries, and she had told Exanthia not to leave Megasthenes's side. And even though she considered Exanthia no longer a slave, but her equal, she knew Exanthia would be unable to disobey her instructions. Sappho huffed in annoyance and went to see who was knocking.

Sappho opened the door. Standing on the front step was a man Sappho had never seen before. He was dressed well in a clean, off-white chiton and a deep green chlamys with a bronze clasp. He was also, Sappho noticed, wearing a dagger on a braided leather belt. "Yes?" Sappho said. "May I help you?"

"I have business with Megasthenes," said the man in a Peloponnesian accent.

"Megasthenes is ill and not seeing visitors today," said Sappho quickly. "You'll have to come back some other time."

She started to close the door but the man put out his hand and stopped her. He smiled. "I know what's supposed to be wrong with your husband, woman," he said. "Let me see him, or I will make you sorry."

Sappho was incensed. "How dare you speak to me that way!" she said. "My husband is related to some very important people."

"I have pressing business with your husband," the man repeated. "Very important, pressing business. I mean to determine if he is truly ill or just hiding from me. Now, let me in. If he is indeed sick, I will leave and wait until he is well before I return. I am a patient man, madam. Now, please, let me in."

Sappho looked him in the eye. *Whatever*, she thought, and she opened the door all the way. "Come with me," she said. "I'll take you to him."

The strange man smiled and said, "Thank you." And he followed Sappho to Megasthenes's bedroom. Exanthia looked up at them when they entered and started to rise. Sappho stilled her with a quick gesture. The strange gentleman stood at the foot of Megasthenes's bed and stared for a moment. "How do I know he's not faking?" he said.

"Look," said Sappho angrily, "I don't know who you think you are, but my husband has been gravely injured. He's not going to snap out of it, and that's that. I am the mistress of the house and I am in charge of Megasthenes's affairs at present. Either tell me what business you have with him or go away."

"You're a bold one," said the gentleman with a smile. His hand fell to the hilt of his dagger. Sappho glanced at the bedside table. A bronze bowl of water and Megasthenes's *xiphos* rested there. "Very well. I shall deal with you instead. Megasthenes owes me money. He has owed me money for a very long time. I am here to collect."

Sappho's eyes narrowed. "And how do I know this is true?" she asked.

"You'll just have to trust me," said the gentleman.

"Not likely," said Sappho. "How much?"

"With the accumulated interest," said the gentleman, "two hundred thirty-four staters. But you've been rude, so let's make it an even two hundred and fifty."

"I'm not giving you any money," said Sappho evenly. "Now, turn around and leave this house and count yourself lucky I don't call for the provost marshal."

The man's smile broadened. "I didn't think you'd agree," he said, and he took a step toward her.

"Wait!" said Sappho, glancing at Exanthia. "I've changed my mind. Let me get you your money."

"Good decision," said the gentleman.

Sappho turned her back to the man and bent over the bedside table. Quick as a cat, she seized the water bowl and the hilt of the *xiphos* and spun back around. In the same movement as turning, she flung the bowl at the gentleman's face. The stranger had no time to react and the bowl hit him on the bridge of his nose, breaking it, by the sound. He staggered backward and tripped, falling on his backside on the floor. He put a hand to his injured nose and started to get up, but found the point of a sword very close to his throat, with Sappho's hand on the other end.

"Now," said Sappho, "you, sir, have worn out your welcome. What is your name, so I know whom the governor's magistrate may charge with extortion?"

"My name is Herodianos," he said. "And your husband really does owe me money."

"And precisely how did he come to be in your debt?" Sappho asked.

"Go to the crows," sneered Herodianos.

Sappho slashed at his face with the point of the *xiphos*. She had only been meaning to threaten the man, but her aim, in her inexperience, was off, and she cut him below the left eye.

"Are you insane, madam?" Herodianos sputtered.

"Probably," said Sappho, feeling a lot less confident than she hoped she sounded. "Now, answer my question, or I give you another scar."

"All right," said Herodianos, putting up his hand. "Megasthenes is a gambler. A dogfighter. You didn't know, I see. He's been betting against me for months and losing. I came to collect my winnings, that's all."

"Dog fighting?" Sappho said. "So, that's where he's been going off to?"

"Dog fighting is illegal in all of Ortygia and Syracuse," said Exanthia softly. Sappho jumped even at Exanthia's whispered statement, quite forgetting in the melee that she was even there.

"I think you should go," Sappho said to Herodianos firmly. "You're not getting a stater from me. If you go now and forget about this, I won't tell the authorities about your little hobby or about your attempt to shake me down. If not, I will cut off your nose right here and now."

"You're bluffing," said Herodianos with a quaver in his voice.

"Then call my bluff," said Sappho evenly.

Herodianos stared into Sappho's eyes and made his choice. He got to his feet. Blood dripped on the tile floor. "You're making a mistake," he said.

"Won't be the first time," said Sappho. "Now, get out!"

Herodianos turned and walked out of the room. Sappho waited until she heard the exterior door close behind him, then dropped Megasthenes's sword on the floor and collapsed. Exanthia was at her side in an instant with her arms around her. The two women held each other that way until Aphronos got home from the market.

Neither of them told him what had happened.

The doctor came to the house the next day, accompanied by a slave with a large jar of water in a wheelbarrow. "I have something that might help your husband," he said.

"Please," said Sappho, "come in."

"I shall require a full bathtub," said Bakenor. "And your husband himself, of course."

"Certainly," said Sappho. "Follow me."

She led Bakenor and his slave into the house. Passing Aphronos in the hall, Sappho asked him to bring both Megasthenes and several buckets of fresh water and meet them in the master bathroom. In fifteen minutes, Megasthenes was naked and had been settled into the bath.

"What, exactly, are you going to do?" Sappho asked the physician.

Bakenor indicated the jar his slave had wheeled in. "I have with me some thunderfish from the Nile," he said. "They have in them the power of Zeus's lightning. The Egyptians have been using them for centuries to treat minor aches and pains as well as the falling sickness. I think they are your husband's best chance for recovery."

Sappho glanced at the swishing tails of the two small electric catfish swimming about in the jar. "You really think this could work?" she said doubtfully.

"I know of nothing else that might," said Bakenor.

"Do it," said Sappho.

Bakenor took a reed net, carefully scooped the two fish out of their jar, and dropped them both into the tub with Megasthenes. Their effect was immediate. Megasthenes's body trembled and a high-pitched moan issued from between his loosely closed lips. Sappho and Aphronos both watched in horror until Aphronos could bear no more and ran from the room. Sappho waited perhaps half a minute more before turning to Bakenor.

"Doctor," she said, distraught, "stop this. Please, stop this."

Bakenor nodded. "Very well," he said. "If they were going to help, it would have happened by now." He scooped up the fish and deposited them back into their jar. Megasthenes relaxed and stopped moaning. "I'll be leaving now," said Bakenor.

"Wait!" said Sappho quickly as Bakenor's slave wheeled the fish out of the bathroom. "I have another matter to discuss with you, doctor."

"A medical matter?" Bakenor asked.

"Yes," said Sappho. "And it concerns me. You see," she said, keeping her voice low, "I may be pregnant. I'm not completely sure, but I think it's quite likely."

"Congratulations, then," said the doctor.

"No," said Sappho. "You don't understand. A pregnancy is unacceptable to me. I need you to help me ensure that the baby isn't born."

"I see," said Bakenor. "I'm afraid I cannot help you there."

"Surely, you know how to accomplish such a thing," Sappho said insistently.

"Of course I do," said Bakenor. "But it is my personal belief that terminating a pregnancy is against the will of the fates."

"But you're a doctor," Sappho pressed. "Aren't you going against the will of the fates every time you treat an illness?"

"I won't be drawn into a hypothetical debate with you," said Bakenor. "At any rate, I doubt such a procedure would be legal even if I were of a mind to help you. It is common knowledge that Megasthenes always wanted an heir. To end your pregnancy now would be to go against your husband's wishes, and that, my lady, is a crime."

"I cannot have this child, doctor," said Sappho.

"You have no choice," said Bakenor with finality. "We'll see ourselves out. Good day."

Sappho was so upset over the events of the day that even passionate lovemaking with Exanthia could not lift her spirits. Exanthia noticed and asked her about it as they lay in Sappho's bed together. Sappho took a deep breath and then told her what was bothering her.

"You're pregnant?" Exanthia said. "Why, this is marvelous. We can raise the baby together."

"I don't want this baby," said Sappho firmly. "Megasthenes killed my daughter. It would be an obscenity to bear him a child of his own. Exanthia, you must tell me, how do I get rid of it?"

"I don't know," said Exanthia in distress.

"You're telling me the truth?" Sappho said.

"Of course I am," said Exanthia.

"Then tomorrow I must go to town," said Sappho, "to see a friend. Let's get some sleep."

And Sappho extinguished the lamp.

Sappho took Aphronos into Ortygia with her the following day. She did not feel she particularly needed an escort, especially in broad daylight, but Sappho was a small woman, and she required help mounting a donkey. And as Exanthia could look after Megasthenes on her own, it made sense to have Aphronos accompany her. They rode the ferry in complete silence; Sappho had nothing to say to the addled slave. In fact, she thought, slavery itself was an issue that would require her attention when she returned to the house. It was Sappho's opinion that Megasthenes would never recover. She believed the doctor thought that too. That made her Aphronos and Exanthia's legal owner and she could do with them what she pleased. And at the moment, it pleased her to free Exanthia. With Megasthenes incapacitated, she and Exanthia could live together as lovers, beyond society's judgment. For the rest of the world, Sappho would be Megasthenes's wife. But for Sappho's purposes, Exanthia would be her spouse.

They could never make it official, of course. Same-sex affairs were far from illegal in Greek society at that time. In fact, many prominent men took boys as lovers, and despite Sappho's birthplace being the origin of the English word *lesbian*, she was not the first woman to seek love from another woman. No, the issue was that they could not marry officially under Greek law, and if Megasthenes eventually succumbed to his injuries and died, Sappho would most likely be expected to take another husband. And her second husband might not be so happy with his wife having a lover on the side, whatever the lover's sex was.

But Sappho could not think about that right now. The pressing concern was the baby she believed she was carrying, and how to get rid of it. There was only one person she knew and trusted who might be able to help her do this, and that was Alkestis.

The ferry docked at its quay on the island of Ortygia, and Sappho disembarked with Aphronos. As was the custom, she offered the ferryman a one-twelfth stater coin as a gratuity. She turned to go, and then turned back to the ferryman. "I'm sorry," she said. "You've given me a ride several times now, and yet I've never asked your name."

The ferryman smiled as he pocketed Sappho's lump of electrum. "You can call me Kharon," he said.

Sappho felt a sudden chill. "Kharon?" she said. "You're joking."

"Nope," said the ferryman. "That's my name."

"And I suppose the stretch of water we just crossed is the Strait of Styx?" Sappho said, attempting to sound humorous.

"Well, actually—" said Kharon the ferryman.

"Never mind," said Sappho firmly. "I don't want to know. Come, Aphronos." And they rode away from the dock and into the city.

This time Sappho had timed their arrival at The Battered Muse to coincide with the space between the noon and evening meals. Now that she no longer sang there every day, she was confident she and Alkestis would have some privacy. Leaving Aphronos in the street with the donkeys, she walked calmly into the inn.

The common room was empty. But the fire and several oil lamps were burning, so she figured Alkestis was around somewhere. She went to the bar and fetched a pitcher of beer and two cups, then sat down at the table nearest the fire and filled both cups.

Sappho was halfway through her first cup of beer when Alkestis entered from the bedrooms. Alkestis did not smile when she saw Sappho, but nodded, wiping her hands on a rag. "I see you found something to drink," she said.

Sappho beamed. "Come sit with me, Alkestis," she said. "Here, I've poured you a cup."

Alkestis sat wearily across from Sappho and took a grateful gulp. "Good of you to come by," she said. "I was beginning to think you had forgotten I existed."

"And I'm sorry about that, Alkestis," Sappho said. "It's just that I've been so very busy." And she told Alkestis about Megasthenes's injury and the visit by the gambler Herodianos.

"Zeus on stilts at the circus!" Alkestis exclaimed. "You *have* had a lot on your plate. I can't say I'm sorry about your husband. And did you really attack a man with a *xiphos*?"

"Yes," said Sappho. "And there's one more thing. I need a favor."

"Really?" Alkestis said. "Something you could not procure with your husband's money?"

Sappho suddenly burst into tears. "I think I'm pregnant," she wailed. "And I don't want to be."

Alkestis let her cry. After a few minutes she said, "And now you want me to help you out of this mess."

Sappho nodded. "Kleis was my daughter," said Sappho. "I cannot bear to have another child. Please tell me you know how to get rid of it, Alkestis. The doctor wouldn't help me."

"I see," said Alkestis. "Well, a lot of women swear by silphion for doing what you want done. It's easy enough to get your hands on."

"Yes, I know," said Sappho. "I was using silphion to prevent things like this from happening in the first place. I need something else. Something more reliable."

"All right," said Alkestis calmly. "There are other options. There is a man I know who can do it surgically. He uses a knife. But I don't recommend it."

"Why not?" Sappho asked, wiping her nose with the back of her hand.

"Because it's extremely painful and extremely dangerous," said Alkestis.

"I don't care," said Sappho miserably.

"Well, I bloody do," said Alkestis. "Women have died undergoing that procedure. Fortunately for you, there may be another way. How far along are you?"

"Less than two months," said Sappho. "Why?"

"There is a draft a woman can drink in the first twenty weeks or so that will cause an almost immediate miscarriage," said Alkestis softly. "It's pretty damn effective, if unpleasant."

Sappho felt a pang of hope. "And do you know how to make this draft?" she asked.

"I do," said Alkestis.

"And will you make it for me?" Sappho asked.

"If it were any other woman," said Alkestis, "I'd say no. But for you…"

"Oh, thank you, Alkestis," Sappho gushed. "I knew I could count on you. When can you have it ready?"

"Ten days," said Alkestis.

"Why so long?" Sappho asked.

"You have no idea what kind of experience you're so eager to rush into," observed Alkestis. "I'll need ten days to make it because it has to age a bit. And because it will take some time to acquire all the ingredients. Some of them are poisonous and illegal."

"Very well," said Sappho. "Ten days it is."

"Now," said Alkestis, "I think we should change the subject. Did you bring that boy who stares with you this time?"

"Who? Aphronos?" Sappho said. "Yes."

"Then do me a favor," said Alkestis. "First let me give him something to eat. Then sit and talk to me a while."

"Certainly," said Sappho. "I owe you that much at least."

Alkestis stood with a groan, then fetched a loaf of flatbread from behind the bar and took it to Aphronos in the street. She returned to the table and sat down. "Kill a king," opined Alkestis, "and you'll rightly be called a saint. But if you mistreat your slaves, redemption will never be yours. Remember that, Sappho."

"I will," said Sappho.

"So, what is your plan to deal with this Herodianos character?" Alkestis asked.

"What do you mean?" Sappho asked.

"You know he's not going to let this drop," Alkestis said patiently. "Two hundred and fifty staters is a lot of money. And you're just one woman with no able-bodied husband to protect you. He's going to come back and he won't be alone next time. Who knows what he'd do to you to collect Megasthenes's debt? And he'll be wanting revenge on you for the way you humiliated him, too. I imagine he'd rape you for starters, and then break your legs."

"What should I do?" Sappho wondered.

"I have an idea," said Alkestis. "But you won't like it. It might be time to ask for help from a friend close to the governor."

"You're not suggesting we contact Diotrephes?" Sappho said in disgust.

"That's exactly what I'm suggesting," said Alkestis firmly. "He's a good man. An important man. And he gives as much of a damn about you as I do."

"All right," said Sappho sullenly. "You can ask him for help on my behalf. I can't think of anything better."

"That's showing some sense," said Alkestis. "Now, I think there's something else you'd like to tell me."

"Is there?" Sappho wondered, confused.

"It was all over your face when I walked into the room," said Alkestis. "And I've seen it before. You're in love. Don't deny it. Tell me, is it going well?"

Sappho beamed. "I never could fool you, Alkestis," she said. "And, yes, it's going very well."

Alkestis took Sappho's hand. "That's all I want to know," she said. "I'm happy for you, Sappho. That's the truth."

It seemed to Sappho that the clitoris was the most sublimely beautiful creation of the gods. Kekonimenos had known it. Exanthia knew it. In a twisted way, Sappho supposed Agathon had known it, too.

That night, in the throes of passion in Sappho's bed with Exanthia, Sappho reflected on her good fortune. When her father had exiled her to Sicily all those years ago, she had counted her life finished. Now she knew her father had been right: she had had a fresh start in a new country. And even though she had experienced loss—Diotrephes, Alkaios, and Kleis, of course—she was now living her life as she pleased, free from major obligations and her husband's clumsy advances, and she had two real friends in Exanthia and Alkestis. Yes, despite certain tragic circumstances that she still had not come to terms with, Sappho felt lucky and content.

After love, Sappho lay breathless beside her new *agapē*, fulfilled as she had not been in years. Exanthia, despite her inexperience, was rather talented with her fingers, and receiving that kind of attention from someone Sappho truly loved and implicitly trusted was exquisite beyond measure.

Exanthia sighed beside Sappho.

"Yes?" Sappho whispered.

"The first day you came to master's house," Exanthia began, "you spoke of someone you knew once. Someone with green eyes. Who was it?"

Sappho tensed slightly, then relaxed again before speaking. "Her name was Thalia," she said. "We were children together. She was my first love."

"As you are mine," said Exanthia. "Did she make you feel beautiful?"

"At first," Sappho said. "But then she betrayed me. I don't like to think about it."

"You make me feel beautiful, Sappho," said Exanthia.

Sappho turned to her. "I believe that's the first time you've addressed me by my name," she said.

"Does that please you?" Exanthia asked.

"More than I can say," Sappho said. "Listen, Megasthenes is never going to get any better. I am in charge of the household now. We can still pretend you are my slave, if you wish, but to me you will always be free. From now on, we are equals in this house. Even Aphronos must obey you."

"It will be difficult to get used to," admitted Exanthia.

"I'll be there to help you," said Sappho. "As long as we're together, everything will be different. Everything will be fine."

"I like the sound of that," breathed Exanthia. "Free… I like the sound of that rather a lot."

"I think we're both free now," said Sappho. "For the first time in both our lives."

"So," said Exanthia, "what shall we do with this freedom?"

"Live, Exanthia," said Sappho resolutely. "Live like each day is our last."

A knock came at the door in the late morning, four days later. Sappho, as usual, was sitting on her rock in the garden, attempting to write a new song. Exanthia was at the market, but Aphronos was in, so Sappho allowed him to see who was calling. She was concentrating so hard on this new song, a song about the brothers she had never known, that she didn't even notice who had stepped into the garden until he spoke to her.

"Hello, Sappho," came the familiar voice.

Sappho jumped in surprise, knowing now who it was who had addressed her. Without looking up, she answered, "Diotrephes," she said, "I didn't expect to see you again."

"I figured as much," said Diotrephes. "Alkestis told me about your problem, with your permission, she said, in fact."

"Yes," said Sappho neutrally. "I told her she could contact you."

"Sappho," said Diotrephes plainly, "I'm sorry about how things went between us. I never meant to hurt or mislead you."

"It's forgotten," said Sappho quickly. "I assume you have another reason for intruding other than to make an unnecessary apology."

"Yes," said Diotrephes. "I was able to speak with this Herodianos who called on you the other day. He's a local oligarch I've met two or three times before. He claims to be a respectable gentleman, but his behavior makes that assertion impossible to accept. I confronted him about Megasthenes and this debt supposedly owed him. He was rather brazen about it, in fact."

"What did you say to him?" Sappho asked.

"I told him," said Diotrephes, "that if he didn't leave you alone I would expose his dog fighting activities to the public. That might compromise his position in local government as the current governor despises the sport."

"So, that's it?" Sappho said.

"Not quite," said Diotrephes. "Herodianos was rather put out about being strong-armed that way, and he asked me what would happen if he didn't agree to my terms."

"And what did you tell him?" Sappho asked.

Diotrephes grinned. "Let's just say I assured him I would see to it that he would be quite qualified to look after the governor's harem himself if he ever came near you again," he said.

Sappho smiled in spite of herself. "That was clever," she said.

"I thought so," said Diotrephes. "Anyway, I don't think you have to worry about Herodianos anymore."

"Thank you," said Sappho. "I wasn't sure you'd help me. The last time I saw you I told you I hated you."

"I remember," said Diotrephes.

"So," said Sappho, "why did you help me?"

Diotrephes took a deep breath. "It has long been my belief," he said, "that we humans would do well to treat each other the way we wish to be treated and not the way others treat us. I don't mean to sound self-righteous, but there it is. I think if we all followed that philosophy, the world would be such a wonderful place. What do you think, Sappho?"

"I think people should get what they deserve," said Sappho.

"You've been hurt badly before," said Diotrephes, "haven't you?"

Sappho willed the tears away. Diotrephes was just so *nice*. "Yes," she said simply. "But I don't wish to discuss it. Or anything else at the moment."

"Not with me, you mean," said Diotrephes.

"No," said Sappho, "not with you."

"May I make an observation?" Diotrephes asked.

"Oh, why not?" Sappho said.

"I think you're a very proud person, Sappho," said Diotrephes. "And I think that pride keeps you from admitting that you make mistakes just like the rest of us. You're content to play the victim because it's all you know. It feels safe to you. And you will never have a healthy relationship with anyone because of it. In fact, I don't think you'd recognize *healthy* if it bit you on the leg."

Sappho's anger was simmering just beneath the surface. "That's what you think, is it?" she said, clenching her teeth.

"Yes," said Diotrephes, "it is."

"Well," said Sappho tersely, "you're quite wrong. I happen to be in a perfectly healthy relationship at this very moment, thank you very much."

"I honestly hope that's true, Sappho," said Diotrephes. "And with that, I believe I have taken up enough of your time. Thank you for speaking with me. I'll see myself out." Diotrephes turned to go and then faced Sappho. "I hope to hear you sing again someday. You're really quite good, you know. It is another one of my firmly held beliefs that even a broken person can be so very beautiful."

That afternoon, Sappho went to Megasthenes's bedchamber. Exanthia was attending to him, feeding him broth from a cup. All Megasthenes was capable of doing these days was stare and swallow. Exanthia looked up when Sappho entered. "Leave us alone a moment, Exanthia," she said.

"Are you all right, Sappho?" Exanthia asked.

"Perfectly," Sappho assured her. "I just want to talk to my husband."

Exanthia set the cup of broth on the bedside table and rose from the stool she was sitting on. "I'm not sure he can hear you," she said.

"Oh, he'll hear me," said Sappho. "He'll hear every word."

"All right," said Exanthia. "I'll be in the garden." And she left the room.

Sappho sat down on the stool beside the bed. There was a bowl of water with a wet linen rag on the bedside table. Sappho wrung the excess water from the rag and began to dab at Megasthenes's forehead as she spoke.

"Well, Loudi," she said, "you've really done it now. I have to say, I thought it was a nice turn of fate that the vehicle you killed my Kleis with ended up being what turned you into something akin to a houseplant. Nice touch, indeed. Anyway, now that I am in charge of the house, there are a couple of things you need to know."

"First, I have freed Exanthia," Sappho continued. "That shouldn't surprise you. You knew I liked her. But there's more. I have taken her as my lover, and she is infinitely more exciting than you ever were. She can do things with her hands that…Well, I find myself quite satisfied every night these days. She's a great improvement over you, Loudi. That's not an exaggeration."

"Does that bother you, Loudi, dear?" Sappho said as she wiped Megasthenes's cheeks. "Well, if that didn't, this will. I'm with child. Your long-awaited heir is now growing inside my belly. There's just one problem. I don't ever want to be a mother again. So, this is what's going to happen. I'm going to get rid of the baby, Loudi. The details are already being worked out. You took my daughter, so I am going to make sure your line dies with you. And there's absolutely nothing you can do about it. Fitting, wouldn't you agree? I would go so far as to call it *poetic*."

"Anyway," Sappho concluded, "I hope you live a good long time yet. I hope you live long enough to fully appreciate both what you have done to me and what I am doing to you."

Sappho placed the rag back in the bowl, stood, and walked toward the door. "Rest well, Loudi," she said with a smile. "I'll send Aphronos to serve you your dinner later, while Exanthia and I are making passionate love."

Sappho blew Megasthenes a kiss, then turned her back on him and left the room.

Sappho went back to The Battered Muse at the end of Alkestis's requested ten days. As usual, she took Aphronos with her, and, as usual, she left him standing in the street with the donkeys. The noon meal was breaking up, and when Sappho walked into the common room, Alkestis met her at the door.

"Have your boy tie the asses outside and come in here for a spot of lunch," she said.

"Aphronos doesn't require anything," Sappho said dismissively.

"Have you had your lunch?" Alkestis asked pointedly.

"Well, no," Sappho admitted.

"Then he eats, too," said Alkestis firmly. "Call him in here. At once."

Sappho scoffed petulantly but obeyed her friend. Alkestis sat the three of them down at a table and brought out a tray of meat, bread, and turnips, as well as three cups of Egyptian beer. "Tuck in," she said.

Sappho glared at Aphronos as he ate, choosing to blame him for sharing a table with her, rather than blaming Alkestis, who had insisted upon it. She still hated the young slave but would have been at a loss to explain why if asked. He was polite, obedient, and compassionate, as well as one of Sappho's most ardent admirers. And he really wasn't as cognitively challenged as Megasthenes had told Sappho. There was no reason for her to dislike him so much. She simply did.

Alkestis, infuriatingly to Sappho, actively engaged Aphronos in conversation. She asked him where he was from, how long he had worked for Megasthenes, even his favorite color. And Sappho's patience began to wear rather thin. Aphronos had apparently never tasted beer, and actually spat his first sip back into his cup. Sappho fumed, but Alkestis responded with good-natured laughter.

"It's a bit bitter at first, I know," she said. "The more you drink, the more you get used to it. In fact," she said with a conspiratorial smile, "if you drink enough of it, the taste becomes completely irrelevant."

"I don't understand," Aphronos admitted.

"That's all right," said Alkestis kindly. "I doubt your mistress would stand for me getting you drunk."

Aphronos laughed at this, but Sappho silenced him with a look, and said, "Not at all, Alkestis. Some things are better left just to the imagination."

As they finished lunch, Alkestis turned serious. "I guess we'd best turn the discussion to other matters," she said to Sappho. "This is not a social visit."

"No," agreed Sappho.

"I have the concoction ready," said Alkestis uncomfortably. "But we have to wait until after dark to use it."

"Aphronos," said Sappho sternly, "go wait outside."

"It's hours till sunset," Alkestis pointed out. "What do you expect him to do?"

Sappho reached into her purse and withdrew two one-stater coins, irked at having to give Aphronos any money at all, let alone two days' worth of an honest man's work. "Go to the market for the rest of the afternoon," she told the slave. "Buy whatever you want for yourself. Just don't get used to such indulgences."

Aphronos accepted the coins with wide eyes. He stood, thanked Alkestis for lunch, and exited to the street.

"So, why do we have to wait for dark?" Sappho asked.

"I don't want us to be interrupted," said Alkestis. "That could be quite awkward."

"We're not doing anything against the law, are we?" Sappho asked.

"No, no, no," said Alkestis quickly. "No, not at all. This is done all the time. You know how it is. The rich get abortions. The poor leave their unwanted children in the fields for the dogs. No, this is quite legal. It's just you will most likely react badly to the draft. Probably very badly."

"I thought you said this stuff was safe," said Sappho nervously.

"I said it was safer than using a knife," Alkestis clarified. "But it's far from pleasant."

"How do you know?" Sappho asked.

"Because I've drunk the cursed stuff myself," said Alkestis sharply. "You really think I was going to bear my lout of a husband a child or two after the way he treated me? No, ma'am. Wasn't going to happen. Pretending to be infertile was my best revenge against him."

"What should I expect this to be like, Alkestis?" Sappho asked. "What is it going to do to me?"

"Well, first off," said Alkestis, "it tastes like shit. And that's the pleasant part. You'll most likely vomit and lose control of your bladder and bowels.

And there will be visions. Violent, disturbing visions. You may meet all sorts of monsters or even gods before it's over."

"I can cope with anything," said Sappho, feigning nonchalant confidence.

"We shall see, missy," said Alkestis. "We shall see. Now, go and rest. You'll need your strength. You can take my room. Then, if you wouldn't mind, help me with dinner? After everyone's gone to bed, we'll get this done."

Sappho squeezed Alkestis's hand. "Thank you, Alkestis. I know I've said it before, but you're my best friend."

"And that's the only reason I'm doing this," said Alkestis. "Now, go lie down."

After supper was served and cleared, and the common room had emptied of patrons for the night, Alkestis directed Sappho to sit in a chair beside the fireplace. Sappho watched as Alkestis placed a large, bronze pot in front of her—"For accidents," Alkestis said—and sprinkled sawdust all over the clay floor around the pot. Then Alkestis set another chair in front of Sappho and sat down with a small, clay cup and a large linen towel. "This is going to be messy," Alkestis said in answer to Sappho's questioning glance.

Alkestis looked Sappho in the eye. "Are you ready for this?" she asked. "'Cause I'm not convinced. In fact, it's my opinion you have no idea what you're getting yourself into."

Sappho reached for the cup. "Is that it?" She asked.

"That's it," Alkestis confirmed.

"Then, give it to me," said Sappho firmly.

Alkestis passed Sappho the cup. Sappho looked down at its contents. The entire draft measured less than a *tetarton*—about half of a modern baker's measuring cup. "That's it?" Sappho said. "There's hardly anything there."

"It's strong stuff," said Alkestis. "Much more than that would probably kill you."

"Well, then," said Sappho, and she threw back her head and swallowed the entire draft. She made a face at the strong, rather muddy taste of Alkestis's medicine, and then passed the cup back to Alkestis.

The two women sat staring at each other for about a minute before Sappho said, "Well, Alkestis, that was rather anticlimactic. Are you sure you got the recipe right?"

"Just give it a moment," said Alkestis grimly.

That was when the pain hit, sharp and clear, in Sappho's abdomen. "Alkestis!" she tried to say, but what came out was a stream of vomit that only partly hit the bronze pot on the floor in front of her. Sappho gasped as she recovered from this antiperistaltic spasm and clutched her midsection with both hands. "Alkestis," she croaked.

"This is perfectly normal," Alkestis said calmly.

"But, it hurts!" Sappho cried.

"Of course, it hurts, you silly girl," said Alkestis. "But there's nothing to be done about it now. Hang on and be brave."

"But…but…" Sappho gasped.

And Sappho lost consciousness.

She found herself in her bed in her own room in her father's house in Mytilene. The pain in her abdomen was even sharper now, though she could not remember where she had been just moments earlier. She found that she was drenched with sweat and she saw that there were others in the room. Her father was there, and her mother. The priest of Artemis from the agora stood beside her parents. And Irini was bent over Sappho, her hands between Sappho's akimbo thighs.

"It won't be long now," said Irini to the others. "She's bearing down."

Sappho suddenly realized she was giving birth.

Sappho's mother gave Sappho an encouraging smile. "Push hard, darling," she said. "It's almost over."

Sappho gritted her teeth as the contractions hit in waves. "This isn't real," she groaned. "This isn't real."

"Of course it's real," said the priest of Artemis. "The goddess's vengeance is swift."

"Oh, for Zeus's sake, just have the cursed child, Sappho," said her father.

"What do you think I'm doing?" Sappho screamed. She pushed with the next contraction as hard as she could.

"There she is," said Irini gently. The baby started to cry and Irini cleaned it off with a linen towel, before swaddling it and placing it into Sappho's arms. "It's a girl."

"It's a bastard, is what it is," said Skamandronymous.

"*Agapē!*" Sappho's mother admonished. "It's our granddaughter!"

"Good, Skamandronymous is right," said the priest of Artemis. "The child is an affront to the goddess of chastity. It must not be allowed to live."

"No!" said Sappho protectively. "She is mine! And her name is Kleis."

"Oh, Sappho," said her mother, sounding touched.

Sappho looked down at the baby in her arms and her jaw dropped open in shock. The baby's face was a ruin of corruption. Withered flesh clove to the baby's skull and wriggling white maggots poured from its eyes, nose, and mouth. Sappho shut her eyes and wailed.

Sappho opened her eyes and sat up. She was sitting in a vast field of wild Greek peonies that stretched to the horizon in every direction. The sky was a brilliant cobalt blue and there was not a cloud in sight. The sun was high overhead, but Sappho found its light neither blinding nor hot. She breathed in the sweet fragrance of the scarlet flowers which surrounded her. "Irini?" she said. "What is this place?"

"Mama?" another voice came from behind her.

Sappho stood and turned around. There, before her, lovely as ever, was five-year-old Kleis. The girl was dressed in a simple blue peplos and her hair fell in braids. "Hello, Mama," she said.

"Kleis!" cried Sappho, and she knelt, throwing her arms around her daughter. "They said you were dead."

"Oh," said Kleis sweetly, "but I am dead, Mama. Don't you know where you are?"

Sappho felt suddenly cold. She knew indeed. "The Elysian Fields," she whispered.

"I've been waiting for you, Mama," said Kleis, burying her face in Sappho's hair.

"Kleis," Sappho said, "it's really you, isn't it?"

"Of course, Mama," said Kleis.

Sappho released her daughter and smiled, all the pain now forgotten. She reached down and picked a peony. Ever so gently, she tucked the flower into Kleis's hair behind her left ear. "Don't ever leave me again," she said.

"Mama?" Kleis said.

"Yes, darling?" Sappho said.

"Why did you let me die?" Kleis asked.

The sun was suddenly darkened by a stray cloud. "What?" Sappho said.

"Why did you let me die?" Kleis repeated. "Why did you let me die in the street and then share the bed of the man who killed me?"

"Kleis," Sappho began, "darling, I—"

There was a crack of thunder.

"You were a bad girl, Mama," said Kleis in a low, guttural voice. "Artemis is very angry with you."

"Kleis?" Sappho gasped.

There was a sharp twang and the bronze point of the head of an arrow punched through the front of Kleis's throat. Dark blood showered Sappho's face.

"No!" cried Sappho in despair. "Not again!"

Kleis fell forward, dead into Sappho's arms. Sappho looked up at the figure standing before her. It was a young woman—younger than Sappho—fiercely beautiful with narrow hips and a small bosom. Her hair was golden brown and her eyes a sharp, wild blue. She wore a plain, masculine-looking chiton of a color Sappho could not name, and held a heavy recurve bow in her left hand. Slung over her shoulder was a quiver of arrows identical to the one that had just felled Kleis. A great stag with hide and antlers of silver stepped up beside her. The woman's gaze seemed to penetrate into Sappho's soul.

"You killed my child!" Sappho cried. "Who are you?"

"You know who I am, mortal," said the woman.

"Artemis," breathed Sappho in quiet terror.

"Whom were you expecting, girl?" Artemis asked sternly. "Eros? You believe he would be kinder to you than I? You do not know him quite as well as you think."

"Please have mercy!" Sappho cried. "You've taken my daughter. I've been punished enough!"

"I will decide when you've been punished enough, pitiful child," said Artemis archly. "I will not bear the insult of your wanton promiscuity any longer. You are a shameless harlot. You know it to be true."

"What are you going to do to me?" Sappho asked.

"To you?" said Artemis. "Nothing. But I will take everything you hold dear in this shadow that passes for your life."

"My father," breathed Sappho. "Please, not my father."

Artemis smiled. "How do you know I haven't killed him already?" she said.

Sappho seized the hem of the goddess's chiton. "Take me, lady," she begged. "I am your willing victim. I offer myself as a sacrifice to appease you and atone for my sins."

"You don't know what you ask," said Artemis coldly.

"Yes, I do," said Sappho. "Please."

"Very well, then," said the blue-eyed vision. She calmly nocked an arrow to her bowstring, drew, and released.

Sappho had plenty of time to see the arrow speeding toward her face before it struck her between the eyes and she fell into screaming darkness.

"Sappho. Sappho!"

A voice was breaking through the blackness in which Sappho was swimming. She looked upward at a point of light somewhere above her. Feeling wearier than she had ever felt in her life, Sappho lifted her leaden right hand and reached for the light. Someone took her hand and pulled. The light grew and moved from overhead to just beyond Sappho's right shoulder. And then she knew what the light was.

It was a fire, burning as it always did in the stone fireplace of the common room of The Battered Muse. Her arm was stretched out in front of her and she saw Alkestis sitting on her chair opposite Sappho. A large bronze pot sat between them. A low groan escaped Sappho's lips.

"Welcome back," said Alkestis with a smile.

"Thank Zeus," Sappho breathed. "That…That was awful."

"I said it would be," said Alkestis. "What did you see?"

"I saw my parents," said Sappho, her head still spinning. "And Kleis. And Artemis. She said she was going to take away everything I held dear. Alkestis, could that possibly come true?"

"I wouldn't put much stock in anything you saw," said Alkestis. "I told you it could be disturbing."

"Did it?" Sappho breathed. "Did it work?"

"It did," said Alkestis gravely.

"What…What was it?" Sappho asked.

"It was a boy," said Alkestis.

"Loudi would have been pleased," said Sappho, her strength returning. "May I see him?"

"Are you sure you want to?" Alkestis asked.

"Yes," said Sappho. "After all, there's a part of me in him."

"Very well," said Alkestis. She reached down to the floor beside her chair where a small bundle wrapped in linen lay. "Here he is," said Alkestis as she unwrapped the bundle.

Sappho stared at the tiny fetus. She remembered thinking when Kleis had been cremated that she had never seen anything so horrible. But here, now, Sappho thought what she was seeing matched that, and yet at the same time she honestly, truly did not care a whit for the bit of dead *something* that Alkestis was holding for her to see. "Get rid of it," she said.

Without a word, Alkestis drew the linen back over the fetus and placed the whole bundle in the fire. Sappho ignored the now-familiar smell of burning flesh. But there was another smell, one Sappho had just noticed for the first time. She looked down at her clothes. "I've soiled myself," said Sappho neutrally.

"I told you that might happen, too," said Alkestis. "Let's get you cleaned up. We'll have to burn your clothes; there will be no cleaning them. You can have some of mine for your trip back tomorrow morning."

"But I want to leave now," Sappho protested.

"Absolutely not," said Alkestis firmly. "You may feel all right, but you're in no condition to travel."

"Thank you," said Sappho earnestly. "You have no idea how grateful I am for this."

"I'd rather you didn't thank me, Sappho," said Alkestis. "I'm not sure I did you any favors. You're most likely barren now."

"I don't care," said Sappho almost blithely. "I told you I didn't want another child. That hasn't changed and it never will."

"So be it, then," said Alkestis grimly as she rose to her feet. "Go and take a very long bath. I'll bring you something clean to wear."

Alkestis reached out her hand and Sappho took it and stood.

Sappho slept harder and more soundly than she ever had before that night. And when she woke, she was not surprised to see through the window of her room in the inn that the sun was relatively high in the sky; she must also have slept later than usual. Sappho sat up in bed and winced at the headache that suddenly greeted her. She reached for the clean clothes Alkestis had set out for her. She pulled on the *perizōma*, ignoring the pain in her abdomen, and tied the *strophion* around her breasts. The peplos was a bit large for her and was a shade of pink that she didn't really care for, but she put it on gratefully. Finally, she tied on her sandals; in addition to the *strophion* they were the only articles of clothing that had survived the experience of the previous night. Sappho stood and made her way to the common room.

Sappho thought that she had never felt, could never feel, more miserable than she had upon getting up. But when she entered the common room she saw something that made everything worse. Aphronos was sitting at one of the tables, having a late breakfast, and talking animatedly with the other guests. Naukles was there, laughing at a joke Aphronos had presumably just told to the company. Sappho watched as Aphronos ate a piece of cheese, smiling with the others. It was probably the best he had been treated in his entire life, and Sappho felt burning anger at the idea.

Alkestis stood behind the bar and Sappho approached her dizzily. Sappho knew her face was screwed up in a scowl, and Alkestis returned her gaze neutrally. Sappho reached the bar and leaned heavily against it. "What is he doing in here?" Sappho asked more weakly than she had intended.

"He's having a bit of breakfast and enjoying himself," said Alkestis.

"He's a slave," said Sappho. "He's not supposed to enjoy himself."

"Really?" Alkestis said with a raised eyebrow. "I thought I told you even slaves should be treated well. And, anyway, your Aphronos says you have freed Megasthenes's female slave and taken her as your new paramour."

Sappho's rage was barely containable. But all she said was, "Whatever."

"Headache?" Alkestis asked.

"How'd you know?" Sappho said.

"I told you," said Alkestis, "I've taken the stuff too. Here." Alkestis poured a cup of beer. "I know it's still morning, but drink this." She also produced a small piece of rough wood. "And chew this," she said.

"What is it?" Sappho asked.

"Willow bark," said Alkestis. "It's bitter, but it'll fix your head."

"Thanks," said Sappho gratefully.

"Hungry?" Alkestis asked.

"Yes," Sappho said. "I can't imagine how, but I am."

"That's a good sign," said Alkestis. "Go sit down—don't worry, you don't have to sit with *him*—and I'll bring you something to eat."

Sappho sat and had breakfast with the other patrons. Even though none of them had any idea why Sappho was back in their midst, or what she had gone through the previous night, they welcomed her as if she had never left them. They also sensed she was not in top form; none of them asked her for a song. They just chatted with her and wished her well. Sappho began to feel a bit of happiness again. Even looking at Aphronos and the smile on his face did not dampen this feeling.

Sappho and Aphronos left for the house around noon. The patrons of The Battered Muse had stayed later than usual after breakfast just to talk to Sappho. They complimented her and asked no questions. For that, Sappho was grateful.

Sappho didn't utter a word as she and Aphronos rode their donkeys back to Syracuse proper. She gave Kharon the ferryman a generous tip, but she didn't speak to him. When they reached Megasthenes's house—*my house now*, Sappho thought—

Exanthia answered Aphronos's knock. Exanthia took one look at Sappho's haggard expression and her face registered shock. "Are you all right?" she asked.

"Perfectly," said Sappho confidently, and she promptly vomited on the front step and fell forward into Exanthia's arms.

"Clean that up, Aphronos," said Exanthia. "I'm taking Lady Sappho to her bed."

"Bed," Sappho echoed. "That sounds good."

Sappho slept for the rest of the day and through that night. The next morning she rose early, feeling better than she had since moving into Megasthenes's house. The effects of Alkestis's draft seemed to have worn off completely. She got up, got dressed, and made her way to the dining room with a spring in her step.

Exanthia and Aphronos were both in the dining room when Sappho entered. They looked up at her, concerned. Sappho noticed their expressions and said, "No need to worry. I'm quite all right."

"Thank heaven," said Exanthia. "Did you get…what you went for?"

"Yes," said Sappho as she sat at the table. She reached out her hand and took a piece of cheese. "Everything is going to be just fine." She looked at Aphronos and said, "Leave us." Aphronos turned to go when Sappho spoke again. "And if you ever tell my business to strangers again, I'll make you sorry you were ever born. Do you understand?"

Aphronos nodded, "Yes, lady." And he left the room.

Exanthia sat opposite Sappho. "What did he tell to whom?" She asked.

"It doesn't matter," said Sappho. "What matters is we're both free now, you and I. We can live the way we like and no one can say anything."

"I'm glad for that," said Exanthia. "What are you going to do today?"

"I'm going to sing," said Sappho. "I'm going to sing for you."

Sappho played her music for Exanthia for the rest of the day, and Aphronos kept his distance, just as Sappho wished. Sappho played and sang until her fingers ached and her voice failed her. Exanthia listened happily until Sappho finally set down her lyre and said, "That's it. I'm spent."

"That was beautiful," said Exanthia. "I never get tired of your music."

"Bed?" Sappho said hopefully.

"Yes," Exanthia agreed.

Sappho led Exanthia to the bedroom they now shared, feeling free enough to sprout wings and fly. The two women undressed each other and fell upon the mattress in a tangle of arms and legs. They kissed passionately and soon Sappho found herself sighing as Exanthia pleasured her in the way Sappho liked most. Just before she reached orgasm, she sighed, enraptured, "I love you, Thalia."

Exanthia tensed and ceased her attention. She lifted her head and looked up at Sappho in shocked silence.

Sappho immediately realized her error. The excitement drained from her loins. She hadn't thought of Thalia in a while. Why had she said her name now? Surely she wasn't still in love with the little girl who had spurned her advances when they were children? Horrified and embarrassed with herself for speaking a name from the past, and frustrated that climax had been denied her here and now, Sappho quickly said, "I don't know where that came from. Keep doing what you were doing."

"No," said Exanthia. "My name is *not* Thalia. Thalia is the name of the girl you told me about. The one with the green eyes. Are you in love with her? Have you been thinking about her all the time you've been with me?"

Sappho stared dumbly at Exanthia.

"Answer me, Sappho," Exanthia insisted. "Do you think about her when we're together?"

"No!" said Sappho honestly. "I don't know why I said that. Come, let's continue."

"I'm not in the mood," said Exanthia.

"Oh, don't be like this," said Sappho, annoyed. "You should be grateful to me for freeing you from your servitude."

"I wish you never had," said Exanthia. "I was happy as a slave. Now, I'm little more than a penny whore!" She got out of bed and started getting dressed.

Sappho sat up in the bed. "Exanthia, don't do this," she said. "Let's talk about this."

"Talking won't help it," said Exanthia miserably. "You need to do some thinking. You need to think for a very long time."

Exanthia left the room and Sappho, unfulfilled and ashamed and confused, flopped face-first into her pillow and groaned in frustration.

Sappho woke the next morning, and for a moment she did not recall what had happened the night before. Then the memory came back and she sat up. Everything was going to be fine, she told herself. It had been a simple slip of the tongue and it meant nothing at all. Exanthia could not blame her for it. Sappho would not allow her to blame her for it. Everything had been Exanthia's fault, in fact, Sappho thought. She had been unreasonable. Sappho would talk to her and make her see reason. *Yes*, she thought, *that's the answer.*

Sappho went to the dining room. It was empty, but breakfast had been laid out. Sappho calmly ate a small meal of fruit, cheese and bread, and then decided she was going to play her lyre for a while before confronting the presumably sulking Exanthia. She made her way to the garden, intending to sit on her rock and perhaps even compose a new song. What she found when she reached the garden made her gasp in fury.

Her lyre lay on its side in the grass beside her rock. Every one of its strings had been cut. *This behavior is unacceptable*, she thought. She balled up her fists and screamed out loud, "*Aphronos!*"

The young slave came quickly. "What is it, my lady?" he asked.

"Look at my lyre and tell me you didn't do this," said Sappho venomously.

Aphronos's eyes widened. "No, my lady," he said. "I didn't."

"I thought not," said Sappho. "It wouldn't occur to you to do something like this. Where is Exanthia?"

"I don't know," said Aphronos. "I haven't seen her this morning. But she spent the night in the slaves' quarters."

"Then, come with me," said Sappho. She was going to sort this out. She was going to sort this out right now.

The door to the slaves' bedroom was closed. It was heavy oak with iron bands. Sappho reached out to open it, but it would not budge. She threw her weight against it but with no effect. She gave Aphronos a questioning look.

"I don't know, my lady," he said. "The door has no lock."

"Exanthia!" Sappho shouted, pounding on the door. "Stop acting this way! Open this door at once! *At once!*"

There was no reply and the door remained closed. Sappho turned to Aphronos. "Break it down," she said.

Aphronos nodded. He got a running start and rammed the door with his shoulder as hard as his frame would allow. There was a scraping sound and the door opened a few finger widths.

"Again," Sappho ordered.

Aphronos threw himself against the door once more and the door opened wide enough for Sappho to see what had been blocking it. A wooden dresser, the only piece of furniture in the slaves' bedroom besides the beds, had been pushed up against the door to prevent its opening.

"Move it," said Sappho.

Aphronos leaned against the door and pushed with all his might and the door came open wide enough to allow them both to enter. There was no light in the room at all. "Bring me a lamp," Sappho said to Aphronos, who nodded and dashed off, returning a moment later with the requested light. Sappho took it from him and, holding it high, stepped into the bedroom. What she saw in the light of the yellow oil flame took her breath away.

Exanthia lay on her back on top of the covers of one of the beds. Her hands and arms hung over the edge of the bed, and Sappho could see in the lamplight that they were covered in dark, glistening blood. Lying on the floor beside the bed was something that shone in the light. Sappho stared numbly at this object, wondering what it was.

Aphronos's reaction was immediate. He burst into tears and ran to Exanthia's side. "Exanthia!" he cried in dismay. "Exanthia, wake up! Don't do this to us!"

Sappho bent to examine the shiny object on the floor. It was a bronze razor—the one Megasthenes used to shave with. It finally dawned on Sappho what had happened. Exanthia would not come back as Aphronos had begged her. She had cut her own wrists deliberately.

Sappho dropped the clay oil lamp, which shattered on the floor and started a small fire. Sappho ignored the blaze and ran from the slaves' quarters. She ran all the way to the garden, where she knelt beside Kleis's roses and began dry-heaving.

No, no, no, no, no, she thought to herself. This could not be happening. She fell on her side and wept openly. She cried until a shadow fell over her and she heard Aphronos speak her name. "Sappho, lady," he said gently.

Sappho sat up and looked up at him. His face was stained with tears and he held his hands behind his back.

"How dare you use my given name," Sappho croaked.

Aphronos ignored her. "What did you do to Exanthia?" he asked.

"What?" Sappho said.

"What did you do to Exanthia," Aphronos asked, "that was so bad she hurt herself, my lady?"

Sappho could not imagine how any of this was her fault. "I didn't do anything to her," she said. "Exanthia was a foolish girl."

"No," Aphronos insisted boldly. "You did something to her. I know it."

Sappho felt the old anger rising again. "Are you accusing me of—" she began, then, "Never mind. You couldn't possibly understand."

"That's what everyone says," said Aphronos sadly. "Poor Aphronos who fell and hit his head. He doesn't understand. He's a halfwit and he couldn't possibly understand!"

This last bit he shouted louder than Sappho had ever heard him shout and she responded in fury. "All right!" she screamed, leaping to her feet. "I'll explain it to you! I loved Exanthia! I loved her more than anyone else in this world aside from my only daughter! She was the light of my life. Do you understand that?"

Aphronos nodded. "I understand," he said softly. "I understand very well, my lady. You didn't love her at all. She was just a toy to you. Just the same as I'm just a fool to you. You sing about love and beauty but you really don't know what those words mean. You do not love. You cannot love. You can't see love even when it's standing right in front of you."

"How dare you speak to me in this way!" Sappho fumed in Aphronos's face, spraying him with spittle. "Who do you think you are, slave? What is this love that's standing right in front of me? It cannot be your poor master. Tell me about this love that's staring me in the face, because I've longed for it all my life, Aphronos! To love, to be loved. Simply, plainly, faithfully, and forever. Tell me!"

"It's me, lady," said Aphronos simply. "I love you."

Sappho was having difficulty taking this all in. "What?" she gasped. "You? You're mad! You presume to lecture me about love when you're just a...just a—"

"A feeble-minded slave?" Aphronos finished dryly.

"I don't love you, Aphronos," said Sappho in a leaden tone.

"I know," said Aphronos. "But you could. You could if you tried. You said yourself it's what you've always wanted. Here I am, Sappho, the answer to that wish. That's all I want to be."

"Fuck off, Aphronos," Sappho said savagely. "You disgust me."

Aphronos nodded and brought his hands out from behind his back. He was holding Megasthenes's *xiphos*. "Then I think it would be best for you to kill me now," he said.

"I'm not going to kill you, you idiot," said Sappho, exasperated.

"But, I want you to," Aphronos insisted. "Go ahead." He pressed the hilt of the sword into Sappho's hands. "It won't hurt. You've already broken my heart as much as it can be broken."

"I'm not going to kill you, Aphronos," repeated Sappho.

"Yes, you are," said the slave.

"You're trying to manipulate me," said Sappho. "It won't work. You're a fool."

"Yes, I am," said Aphronos. "I am a fool." And he pushed Sappho hard.

"Don't you lay your hands on me!" shouted Sappho in anger.

"What will you do?" Aphronos said, pushing her again. "Kill me?"

"I don't love you," Sappho repeated.

"I'm the one you've always hoped for," said Aphronos calmly. "You're a coward." He pushed her again.

"Don't you push me!" Sappho screamed.

"That's it, isn't it?" Aphronos shouted, matching Sappho's volume. "You're afraid! You're afraid to take love when it's right in front of you! You coward!"

Sappho snatched the *xiphos* out of Aphronos's grip, not really realizing what she was doing. "I'm not a coward!" she shouted.

"Then, prove it!" said Aphronos, shoving her again, hard.

"Here, then!" Sappho screamed. And she thrust the blade deep into Aphronos's chest. She had done it without thinking and now that she saw the blood pouring rapidly from the wound onto Aphronos's chiton, she felt sick and dizzy. Aphronos coughed up more blood and fell on his backside in the grass.

"I was right," Aphronos gasped, blood bubbling in his mouth. "You're afraid of love, afraid to be loved." He fell on his back. The blood gurgled in his throat as he spoke his last words, "Don't ever forget what I could have given you." And he was still.

Sappho stared at the horror of her own making, lying there in the grass of the garden. The blood was bright red and it was everywhere. Sappho began to hyperventilate, her gasping breaths soon turning to sobs. She ran from the garden, through the atrium, out the front door, and into the drive. Feeling despair like no other, she gave one long, wild scream.

Megasthenes was lying senseless in his bed when Sappho entered about an hour later. She looked at him for a long time before speaking.

"So, it's just the two of us now, Loudi," she said. "Just the way I imagine you like it. But don't worry. Someone will remember us, I know it. Even in another age."

Sappho sat beside Megasthenes on the bed and started to wash his forehead with the damp rag on the bedside table. Softly and gently, she began to sing a lullaby, a wordless tune from her childhood with Irini, swearing to herself she would never love again.

In the end, it would not be true.

Author's Note

Little is known about the historical Sappho, who has been called *The Poetess* and *The Tenth Muse* by Ancient Greek scholars and philosophers. I have here given her a story that is almost entirely fictional. With the exception of the first, which is my pitiful creation, all poems herein attributed to Sappho and her contemporary Alkaios of Mytilene are adapted, not translated, from the original Aeolic Greek using various modern English translations as well as my own knowledge of this magnificent language as guides. I hope Sappho will forgive my presumptuousness in making these base recreations of her work. I have done my best to avoid anachronisms, though I may have missed one or two, particularly by affording women a higher status in Greek society than they would have had historically.

Sappho eventually left Sicily and continued her quest for true love, ultimately taking her own life in the effort. Only fragments of her writings, and none of her music, have survived to the present day—a loss the magnitude of which cannot be properly measured.

ἡ ἀφροδίσια ἄνευ ὀργασμοῦ μάταιος ἐστίν χρόνος, καὶ ἡ κλείτωρ θέσφατος καὶ καλὸς ἐστὶ τᾶν θεᾶν δημιουργία.
—Ψάπφω